Jenni Fletcher was born in the north of Scotland and now lives in Yorkshire, with her husband and two children. She wanted to be a writer as a child, but got distracted by reading instead, finally getting past her first paragraph thirty years later. She's had more jobs than she can remember, but has finally found one she loves. She can be contacted on Twitter @JenniAuthor or via her Facebook Author page.

AN UNCONVENTIONAL COUNTESS

Jenni Fletcher

MILLS & BOON

First Published in Great Britain 2020
by Mills & Boon, an imprint of HarperCollins*Publishers*
1 London Bridge Street, London, SE1 9GF

© 2020 Jenni Fletcher

ISBN: 978-0-263-27287-1

MIX
Paper from
responsible sources
FSC® C007454

This book is produced from independently certified FSC™ paper
to ensure responsible forest management.
For more information visit www.harpercollins.co.uk/green.

Printed and bound in Spain
by CPI, Barcelona

For my biscuit-loving grandmothers

Historical Note

I grew up with a collector of Nelson memorabilia, so I knew it was only a matter of time before I wrote a story with a naval hero that referenced the Battle of Trafalgar.

This altercation, on the twenty-first of October 1805, proved to be one of the defining events of modern European history. The defeat of the combined French and Spanish forces by the English fleet, under the command of Vice Admiral Horatio Nelson, ensured that Wellington's soldiers were kept supplied with provisions throughout the remainder of the Napoleonic Wars and established British naval supremacy for the next hundred years—up until the start of World War I.

The ship referred to in this story, the *HMS Colossus*, really did take part in the battle. I've tried to keep the details as accurate as possible, although the actual commander was a Captain James Morris. Fighting in the very midst of the action, the *Colossus* suffered the highest casualty figures of the British fleet and sustained so much damage that it had to be towed to Gibraltar for repairs before returning to England.

I've used it as a tribute to William Wheldale, a sailor who was press-ganged from my home town of Hull in the north of England in 1803 and died aged just twenty in the battle. The details are taken from David Wheldon and Richard Turner's book *Family Connections*.

The first part of the story is set in Bath for my grandmother, who lived there for most of her life. As a teenager I stayed at her house with my sister for several weeks every summer, mainly reading Jane Austen novels. She didn't like history, but she took me to the costume museum, which I loved, and she never made a meal with fewer than three kinds of dessert, for which I will always have the greatest affection and respect.

Finally, the Water Gardens in the second half of the story were inspired by those at Studley Royal in North Yorkshire, completed in 1767 and declared a World Heritage Site in 1986. It's one of my favourite places to visit and the scene of many happy picnics. Obviously with biscuits.

Chapter One

Bath—March 1806

'"**B**elles of Bath, purveyors of the finest quality confectionery."' Captain Samuel Delaney read out the words painted on a wooden sign beside a smart yellow-and-white-striped awning, then turned to confront his companion. 'It's a *biscuit* shop.'

'Not just any biscuit shop.' The Honourable Ralph Hoxley tapped a finger against the side of his nose. 'The finest biscuit shop in the whole of England.'

'The finest…?' Samuel threw a quick look around, assuring himself that nobody else was in sight before shoving his fist none too gently into the other man's shoulder. 'Ralph, we may not be in the first flush of youth any more, but I draw the line at tea and biscuits in the middle of the afternoon.'

'Ow!' His companion rubbed his arm gingerly. 'I say, that's no reason to attack me. The biscuits are delicious, actually, but that's not why we're here.'

'Then why are we?'

'You'll see in a minute. Now, stop complaining and come on.'

Samuel looked about him, inwardly debating whether or not to simply turn around and leave. Swainswick Crescent was less Palladian in style than most of the streets in the fashionable shopping district, though it was built in the same distinctive honey-coloured stone and had a somewhat charming aspect. It was also only a five-minute walk from the house his grandparents had rented on the Circus, but on the other hand he was bored and his curiosity was piqued. Heaving a sigh, he waited until a carriage had rolled past before crossing the street, amused to note that his companion kept just out of arm's reach until they arrived at the shop windows.

'There!' Ralph pointed through the glass triumphantly. 'Now look and tell me if she isn't the most extraordinary creature you've ever seen.'

She? Samuel rolled his eyes. He might have guessed his wayward friend would only display this much enthusiasm over a woman, yet another unsuitable paramour most likely, but since he was already there… He threw a cursory look inside and then looked again, surprised to find that, for once, Ralph was right. Usually their tastes in relation to the opposite sex were a world apart, but this time *extraordinary* was exactly the right word.

The woman standing behind the shop counter was of medium stature, slender but not too slender, with a shapely figure and a mass of dark corkscrew curls barely contained in an unruly knot on the top of her head. They gave her an attractively dishevelled aspect, as if she'd just rolled out of bed, an effect exacerbated by the presence of a frilly white apron that put him in mind of a chemise. Unfortunately she was looking downwards, her features obscured by shadow as she tied a ribbon around a barrel-shaped tin, but what he could see of her face was square-shaped and extremely pretty. He couldn't tell the colour of her eyes, but he would have hazarded a guess that they were the same coffee shade as her hair. He felt a strong urge to find out. Succeeded by an even stronger urge to shove Ralph off the pavement for seeing her first…

'Isn't she the most delectable morsel you've ever seen?' If he wasn't mistaken, Ralph actually licked his lips.

'Not bad.' Samuel stepped away from the window and folded his arms. Unlike his companion, he had absolutely no intention of drooling over a woman in public, no matter how drool-worthy she might be. 'Although it still doesn't explain why you've dragged me halfway across the city. Much as I enjoy admiring your conquests, obviously.'

'She's not one of my conquests, not yet, and she never will be without your help.'

'Really?' He quirked an eyebrow, surprised and somewhat heartened by the news. If Ralph hadn't yet managed to seduce her, then that meant... *No.* He stopped the thought in its tracks. His life was complicated enough these days without any romantic entanglements, even if she was the prettiest, most intriguing looking woman he'd set eyes on since arriving back in England four months ago. Longer than that, even. He couldn't remember ever feeling such an instant attraction to someone. 'You don't usually have problems talking to the opposite sex on your own.'

'I don't.' Ralph sniffed with irritation. 'Only I need you to distract the other one.'

'What other one?'

'The termagant who runs the place. She's over...' His companion pressed his nose up against the glass and then started indignantly. 'Wait, that *is* the other one! *She's* the termagant!'

'Her?' Samuel unfolded his arms and took another, more eager look. The coffee-haired woman didn't look much like a virago, not enough to justify the tone of disgust in his friend's voice anyway, though he had to admit there was a certain brisk, no-nonsense efficiency to her manner as she walked around the shop, serving one customer before moving on to the next. She looked self-assured and capable, qualities he personally found to be virtues rather than faults in a woman. Damned if they didn't make her even more attractive.

He let his gaze follow her while she worked. The wall behind the counter was essentially made up of just shelves, stacked with different shapes and sizes of tin and a few trays of loose biscuits. Both they and the counter were made of dark wood, oak or beech maybe, though any suggestion of gloominess was dispelled by the shafts of yellow sunlight streaming in through large, south-facing front windows. The whole place had a cosy, inviting ambience and he *was* feeling quite peckish. A biscuit at that moment sounded like a quite excellent idea.

'I'm talking about the blonde!' Ralph shot him an exasperated look.

'What blonde?'

'There!'

As if on cue a small head popped up above the counter, its owner having presumably been searching for something underneath, in a manner that put Samuel in mind of a Punch and Judy show.

'*She's* the one I brought you to see. My golden nymph.' Ralph sounded as if he were drooling again. 'Her eyes are almost as pale as yours.'

'I trust that's where the comparison ends.' Samuel threw him a sardonic look. 'Much as I like water, I doubt I'd make a very good nymph.'

'Isn't she delectable, though?'

Samuel narrowed his eyes, regarding the 'nymph' critically as she passed a small cloth bundle across to an elderly gentleman customer. She was undeniably attractive, though surely not a day above eighteen, with delicate elfin features, a minuscule waist and glossy hair swept up into an elegant chignon. Everything about her was sleek and shiny, in striking contrast to her messy-looking companion, though he found his gaze drawn inexorably back to the messiness.

'Well?' Ralph prodded him. 'What do you think?'

'About the nymph? She looks young.'

'Not that young. Eighteen.'

'Which you know because…?'

'Because I asked her the last time I was here.'

Ralph pinched his lips together. 'Before the termagant told me it was none of my business and chased me away.'

'You must have made quite an impression.'

'Harumph. You'd think she was the girl's mother the way she hovers around her. As if I'm only after one thing!'

'Aren't you?'

'And now you sound like her father!' Ralph looked affronted. 'Can't a man enjoy a little casual flirtation?'

'That would depend. Specifically on whether it's the kind of casual flirtation you enjoyed with your mother's lady's maid last month?'

'*Ex*-lady's maid now. That's why I'm banished from London, remember?'

'Exactly.'

Samuel took a step back from the window and folded his arms again. He and Ralph had been friends at school, getting into all kinds of adolescent scrapes together, right up until the morning he'd walked out and never gone back, but the intervening years had taken them in different directions, the navy for him, university and the life of a *ton* bachelor for Ralph. Inevitably they'd lost touch and now he was starting to remember why. It wasn't *just* because he'd been busy fighting Napoleon. He liked to think that he'd grown up during the past ten years, but his old friend still seemed to have few interests beyond gambling, drinking and women. If it hadn't been for Bath being so quiet at this time of year, he might have avoided renewing the acquaintance entirely.

He stifled a sigh, wishing he'd taken up Admiral Northcott's invitation to visit his house that afternoon instead. A few hours of discussing naval tactics and studying nautical charts with a retired septuagenarian sounded infinitely preferable to helping Ralph conduct yet another flirtation. If flirtation was really *all* he intended... That morning, however, Northcott's invitation had made him far too melancholy. It was bad enough feeling homesick for a ship, but the idea that his naval career might be over barely a year after he'd achieved the long sought-after rank of Captain was depressing beyond words. Maybe he oughtn't to have put his uniform aside so soon, after all. At least wearing it made him feel as if he still belonged somewhere. Instead, here he was, standing on a street in the middle of another aimless afternoon, trapped between two possible futures.

'We'll just wait for these customers to leave.' Ralph was already straightening his cravat and tugging at the lace trim of his cuffs.

'Will we?' Samuel drew his brows together,

jolted back to the present. 'I don't remember agreeing to help you. What exactly are your intentions?'

'My intentions?' Ralph's expression was almost ludicrously outraged. 'I say, when did you become so passé?'

'Around the same time I learned that actions have consequences. I won't help you to ruin the girl.'

'I've no intention of ruining anyone. All I'm doing is enjoying the view, so to speak. A man has to pass the time somehow in Bath.' Ralph leered. 'Now you distract the termagant so that I can have a few minutes alone with my nymph.'

'And how do you propose that I distract her? Especially if she's as fearsome as you say?'

'Flirt with her! You used to be quite good at that as I recall, even if all you talk about these days is boats. You know, if I'd spent most of the past decade at sea, I'd want to do a lot more than flirt when I came back on shore. Isn't there any woman in Bath who interests you?'

Samuel threw a quick glance back through the shop window. Yes, there was definitely one and the thought of distracting her was distinctly, apparently irresistibly, enticing.

'Just think of it as another battle. Imagine that she's…' Ralph paused thoughtfully '…what was the name of that French Admiral you trounced again?'

'Villeneuve.'

'Right. Imagine that she's Villeneuve and you need to keep her occupied while I break through her line like Nelson. It'll be just like Trafalgar all over again.'

Samuel felt a muscle twitch in his jaw. Comparisons to his former commanding officer aside, he had the distinct suspicion that Nelson wouldn't have approved of what they were about to do, either. On the other hand, what harm *was* there in enjoying the view? Just to pass the time for a few minutes?

'All right.' He flexed his shoulders, ignoring a prickle of conscience as he prepared for action instead. 'For King and Country...'

Chapter Two

'He's here again.' Anna Fortini waited until the shop door had closed behind the last customer before narrowing her eyes at the window and scowling.

'I know.' Her assistant Henrietta raised a hand to her head, patting non-existent stray hairs back into place and batting her eyelashes coquettishly. 'This is the third time this week.'

'Maybe we can persuade him to actually buy something this time,' Anna muttered, pushing her own very real stray hairs out of her face and wondering if she had time to carry a bucket of cold water up to the first-floor window and deposit it over the admirers below. Alas, she suspected not. In fact, she was quite certain the front door would open again the very moment she left the room and she had absolutely no intention of leaving Henrietta on her own. Tempted as she was to believe that her shop's recent popularity with the young male population of Bath was entirely due to her baking, she was well aware that it had far more to do with her new and attractive assistant. Barely a day went by when she didn't have to chase some lovesick swain or other off the premises, but this particular suitor was proving more persistent than the others. He was becoming an irritation.

'There's another gentleman with him this time,' Henrietta murmured, coming to stand close beside her.

'So I noticed. Another of your admirers, no doubt.'

'Actually, he's looking at you. Quite intently, too.' Henrietta giggled. 'He's very handsome. I wonder who he is.'

'If he's anything like his companion, then I don't care. They look like gentlemen.'

'You always say that like it's a bad thing. What do you have against gentlemen anyway?'

'Plenty! And no giving biscuits away this time. Those samples are for customers, not— stop it!' Anna looked around sharply, making a grab for her assistant's arm as she started to wave. 'You shouldn't encourage them.'

'Why not? It's just a bit of fun. There's no harm in that, is there?'

'It depends on what kind of fun you both have in mind. I very much doubt it's the same thing. Honestly, didn't you learn anything from your last employment?'

The hurt expression on the girl's face made Anna regret the words instantly. Henrietta had lost her position in a dressmaker's shop after her employer's son had formed a passionate, but unrequited, attachment towards her. She hadn't done anything to encourage him, Henrietta had assured Anna when she'd first applied for the position as her assistant, only she was afraid that she might have acted naively by not immediately rebuffing his attentions, but then she hadn't wanted to be rude, either... The inevitable result was that she'd been dismissed without references.

'I'm sorry.' Anna winced. 'I didn't mean it like that.'

'I know.' One of Henrietta's most endearing qualities was her ability to forgive and forget. 'And I'm sorry for waving, but I was only being friendly. You don't think I'd be silly enough to fall for a gentleman, do you?'

Anna dropped her gaze to the biscuit samples set out on a plate in front of her. *Yes*, she thought silently. Yes, she did think that Henrietta was capable of having her head turned by an aristocratic appearance and a few charming compliments, but she didn't want to say the words out loud. Over the past couple of months she'd become genuinely fond of the girl. She was certainly a far livelier companion than Mrs Padgett, her dour and disapproving predecessor. No one had ever come into the shop to see *her*. All in all, Henrietta's hard-working and sunny disposition would have made her the perfect employee if it hadn't been for her propensity to be *friendly* with every man who as much as glanced in her direction—and men were *always* glancing in her direction. To be fair, it would have been hard for someone so pretty not to attract male attention— Anna only hoped it wouldn't lead her into doing something foolish one day.

'Just remember that no matter how honourable they might *seem*, gentlemen like that don't regard women like us as ladies.' She threw another venomous glare in the direction of the window. 'They won't treat us like ones, either.'

'How can you be so cynical?' Henrietta made a tsking sound. 'Sometimes a gentleman really is a gentleman.'

'But most of the time he's a wolf in sheep's clothing.'

'Good gracious, anyone would think...'

Henrietta bit her lip, leaving whatever anyone would think unspoken as the bell above the shop door jingled again and the two men entered finally.

'Perhaps you could finish the window display, Henrietta?' Anna gave her assistant a none-too-subtle nudge in the ribs. 'While I deal with these customers.' Then she lifted her chin, bracing both of her hands on the countertop before putting on her brightest, most insincere smile. 'How may I help you, gentlemen?'

'Good afternoon.' The first man, the *irritant*, faltered mid-step, a lock of blond hair flopping across his face as his gaze followed Henrietta. 'My friend and I were just strolling past when we had a sudden craving for chocolate.'

'Oh, what a shame.' Anna heaved an exaggerated sigh. 'Unfortunately we don't work with chocolate, which you might have known had you asked about our merchandise on one of your previous visits. We sell biscuits, *just* biscuits. Perhaps you might try the shop on...'

'But I adore biscuits even more!' The man grinned, exposing a row of dazzlingly white teeth. *Definitely* a wolf. 'Perhaps your lovely assistant here might recommend something special?'

'I'm perfectly capable of recommending—'

'I'd like one of the big tins,' the other man interrupted before she could finish, addressing her in an amused-sounding baritone that none the less carried a distinct note of command. 'If it's not too much trouble?'

Anna turned her head to glower and then felt her stomach perform a strange kind of bouncing manoeuvre instead. She'd been so focused on the *irritant* that she'd barely spared a glance for his companion, though now she seemed unable to look away again. Henrietta was right, he was *very* handsome and yet a mass of contradictions, too, with hair the colour of mahogany and eyes so silvery pale they resembled icebergs. He might have looked austere if it hadn't been for his athletic build and a rugged aspect that seemed at odds with his finely cut and, she couldn't help but notice, perfectly tailored tailcoat, midnight-blue waistcoat and crisp white shirt. His face was lean and tanned, too, somewhat surprisingly for Somerset in March, yet despite his youthful appearance— surely he couldn't be any more than thirty?—there was already a web of fine lines around his eyes that crinkled when he smiled. Just as he was doing now, she realised, making her cheeks flush and her stomach bounce all over again.

'Trouble?' she repeated the word, trying to focus on what he'd just said. 'Of course not. If it were trouble, then I'd be in the wrong profession, sir. Just allow me a moment to fetch one.'

She turned to climb a set of steps set against

the shelves, glad to avert her face for a few moments while she berated herself, or more precisely her body, for its own foolish reaction. He was a *gentleman*! Albeit a handsome one and in an attractively *un*gentlemanly sort of way, far less foppish than his friend and with an air of self-possession and authority that surely accounted for all the stomach bouncing, but *still* a gentleman, and hadn't she just been warning Henrietta about those? Besides, he could hardly have made his purpose there any more obvious if he'd had it printed across his forehead. He was a decoy, enlisted to divert her attention while his companion tried to seduce her assistant. Well, if he thought he could outwit or charm her so easily, then he could think again!

She reached for the nearest tin and started back down the steps, throwing a surreptitious glance towards the window as she descended. As expected, Henrietta was already deep in conversation with the first man, who was standing far too close for decency. Both details meant that *she* had to hurry.

'Here you are.' She deposited the rectangular-shaped tin in front of him with a clatter. 'It contains an assortment of biscuits, sixteen in total, each individually wrapped in tissue paper.'

'Just sixteen?' Her customer rested one forearm on top of the counter, regarding the tin as if it posed some kind of dilemma. 'May I see inside?'

'If you wish.' Anna removed the lid, struck with the uncharacteristic impulse to neaten her hair as he leaned closer. Not that there was any point in doing so when long experience told her the curls would only tumble straight out of her bun again, and not that she cared what this gentleman thought of her hair either, even when he was standing close enough to see every wild tendril, but something about the deep timbre of his voice made her self-conscious. She found herself tucking a stray coil behind her ear before she could stop herself.

'There you are.' She unwrapped one of the bundles of tissue paper, unveiling a cream-coloured round biscuit for his inspection, then waited in silence for several long moments until she couldn't wait any longer. 'Is something the matter?'

'Not exactly. I suppose the tin just looked bigger from a distance.' He rubbed a hand across his chin as if he were considering the problem. There were bristles there, she noticed, another ungentlemanly contradiction, though she supposed it *was* nearing the end of the day. They were the same dark auburn shade as his hair and looked softer than she would have expected bristles to look, positively strokeable, in fact... She gave a startled jolt and lifted her gaze determinedly back to his eyes, irritated that any gentleman could have such a distracting effect on her.

'I'm afraid this is the biggest tin we do.'

'Ah. Pity.' He laid his hand down flat on the counter beside hers, so close that their fingers were nearly, but not quite, touching. To her surprise, his skin was rough and weathered-looking as if, despite being a gentleman, he was used to manual labour. 'They're for a special lady, you see, and I wouldn't want to appear churlish.'

'Indeed?' She tugged her own hand away, heat rising in her cheeks. 'Then perhaps you might want to consider two tins? Or a different present altogether?'

'But these look delicious.' He seemed undeterred by her sarcasm. 'And of course some would say that quality is more important than quantity, only I'm afraid that this particular lady is rather...' he paused, lowering his voice to an intimate undertone '...*voracious* in her appetites.'

'I'm sure she'd be delighted to hear you say so.' Anna straightened her shoulders, feeling her temper start to escalate. How dare he talk to her about appetites, voracious or otherwise? No gentleman would *ever* speak to a lady in such an unguarded fashion! The words encouraged her to be indiscreet, too. 'Well, I suppose that size matters to some people. Perhaps you've disappointed her with something small before?'

She put her hands on her hips with a look of defiance, expecting him to storm out of the door in an offended rage, surprised when he burst into loud laughter instead.

'The tin it is.' He pushed himself up off the counter, eyes glinting with humour. 'And I'll just have to bear whatever criticism my lady friend makes. Are the biscuits inside all the same?'

'Only in shape.' Anna rearranged the contents and replaced the lid quickly, trying to ignore the way his laughter seemed to vibrate through her body, like a breeze stirring ripples across a lake. It seemed to cause a strange quivering sensation in her stomach, too, lower down than before and somewhat alarming in its intensity. It made her feel even *more* agitated. If only he'd stormed out! Then she could have forgotten his existence and turned her attention back to Henrietta. Instead, annoyingly, she found herself wanting to hear him laugh again... 'We make three types of Belle. Vanilla, cinnamon and rosewater.'

'So the biscuits are called Belles?'

'Precisely.' She pushed the tin across the counter, shooting a pointed look from beneath her lashes. 'You're very quick, sir.'

Despite the insult, he laughed again. 'Which is your favourite?'

'None of them. I started baking when I was eight. After sixteen years, I can honestly say that I've lost my sweet tooth.'

'But if you had to choose a favourite? So that I can particularly recommend one to my lady friend?'

'She's *your* lady friend.' Anna pursed her lips disapprovingly. 'If she's so special, then I would have thought you might know her tastes better. Here…' She picked up the plate of samples. 'Try one.'

'Thank you.' He selected the darkest-coloured biscuit and took a bite, eyebrows lifting as he chewed. 'Cinnamon? It's delicious.'

'You sound surprised.' She lifted her own eyebrows to mirror his.

'I am. I'm not usually fond of biscuits, but I could eat a dozen of these. Definitely my favourite.'

'You haven't tried the others.'

'I don't need to.' He rapped his knuckles decisively on the countertop. 'I'll recommend this one whatever the consequences.'

'Consequences?' she couldn't resist asking. 'Are you likely to face those?'

'Oh, yes. She's quite a tyrant in her own way.'

'Of course she is.'

'But open-minded, too.' He popped the last of the biscuit into his mouth. 'I admire that in a person. Being judgemental is such an unattractive quality, don't you think?'

'I think it depends. There's a difference between being judgemental and having high standards. Now, if that's all, that will be four shillings.'

'Ribbon?'

'That costs more.'

'Ah, but she's worth it.'

'Naturally.' Anna narrowed her eyes, reaching under the counter for a roll of blue ribbon and then coughing loudly as she saw Henrietta's companion touch her elbow.

'That sounds nasty.' Her own customer sounded amused. 'Perhaps you ought to consult a physician about it.'

'I'm perfectly well, thank you.' She narrowed her eyes even further, though it was difficult to do so without actually closing them.

'I'm relieved to hear it. Otherwise I'd have to suggest a visit to the Pump Rooms to take some of the waters, and it's not an experience I'd recommend.'

'Indeed? Then I wonder what you're doing in Bath, sir?' She gave the ribbon an aggressive snip with her scissors. 'Isn't it the start of the London Season soon? Perhaps you ought to be there, preparing yourself for balls at Almack's and picnics at Vauxhall Gardens?'

'Perhaps I should be.' He gave a careless-looking shrug. 'But what can a man do when his grandmother summons him?'

'Your grandmother?' She paused in the act of curling a ribbon.

'My *special lady*, yes.' The corners of his mouth curved upwards. 'Who did you think I was talking about?'

'I…' She cleared her throat, willing the sudden onslaught of heat across her cheeks to subside. 'Your wife, perhaps?'

'Alas, I haven't found a woman willing to put up with me yet. Hard to believe, isn't it?'

'Unfathomable.' She finished curling the ribbons, trying to ignore an unwelcome frisson of excitement at the words. 'There you are. I hope that your grandmother enjoys them. They were baked fresh this morning.'

'Do you bake them yourself?' He seemed in no hurry to be leaving, extracting a few coins from his coat pocket.

'I do everything here myself. It's *my* shop.'

'You're the proprietor?' He looked impressed.

'Yes.'

'And the baker?'

'And everything else.' She lifted her chin proudly. 'I do whatever needs doing.'

'Then I compliment you, Mrs...?'

'*Miss* Fortini.'

'Miss Fortini.' He repeated her name, his eyes lingering on her face in a way that made her wish she might plunge her head into a bucket of cold water. 'Do you have a first name, too?'

'Doesn't everyone? But I share it with acquaintances, not customers.'

'Ah. In that case it's been a delight talking to you, Miss Fortini.'

'Quite.' She inclined her head and then twisted it pointedly to one side, focusing her attention back on Henrietta's companion. 'Now have you finished getting recommendations, sir, or did you only come to grace us with your presence *again*?'

'Actually I've decided I'm not so hungry, after all.' The *irritant* spun around with another wolfish grin. 'However, I've just invited your charming assistant here for a walk, what with it being such a beautiful afternoon.'

'So it is.' Anna spoke quickly before her 'charming assistant' could agree to anything. 'Unfortunately, as you may or may not have noticed, we have a business to run. Our customers can't serve themselves.'

'But we close soon,' Henrietta interjected. 'Couldn't we leave just a little bit early for once?'

'We still have cleaning up to do.' Anna shot her a warning look.

'Then perhaps I might wait and escort Miss Henrietta home? I'd be more than happy to do so.'

'I'm sure you would.' Anna gave a tight-lipped smile in return, reluctantly conceding that she'd been outwitted. Her own customer had already picked up his tin and tucked it neatly under his arm, though his expression was noticeably less triumphant than that of his friend. There was actually a small furrow between his brows as if he were displeased about something. It made a striking contrast to the way he'd smiled across the counter a few minutes before. No doubt that had just been a charming mask, one he felt able to drop now that his task as decoy was complete, but if he thought the matter was concluded, then he was very much mistaken. She wasn't defeated yet!

'Do you know…?' She walked around the counter and across the shop floor to place a protective arm around Henrietta's shoulders. 'Now that I think of it, an evening stroll sounds most pleasant, after all. We'll meet you in Sydney Gardens beside the grotto in half an hour, after we've tidied. That way we can escort Miss Gardiner home *together*.'

Chapter Three

Samuel marched up and down a picturesque-looking pathway between rows of willow and ash trees, ardently wishing that he'd been out when his old friend had called to visit him that afternoon. As amusing as he'd found his encounter with the pretty and prickly Miss Fortini, his conscience was bothering him quite considerably. No matter how tedious he found life on shore, he should never have gone along with Ralph's plan. It had felt dishonourable somehow, his behaviour that of a rake, or even worse, his father! This walk struck him as a monumentally bad idea, too, but he was involved now whether he liked it or not. To his own chagrin, it was too late to walk away.

'I say!' Ralph called out to him from the bench where he was lounging, arms thrown wide as if he hadn't a care in the world. 'Why are you in such a bad mood?'

'Because I don't appreciate being dragged into your romantic exploits, that's why!' Samuel practically exploded. 'That whole scene felt underhand. You said it was just a little harmless flirtation, nothing about walks in the park.'

'Well, I call that very ungrateful. Here I've arranged a promenade with two very attractive young ladies and all you can do is complain.'

'An hour ago you described one of them as a termagant.'

'Yes, she is, isn't she?' Ralph chuckled unrepentantly. 'I thought she was going to spit actual feathers when I offered to walk Henrietta home.'

'You don't need me to be here, too. You and the termagant can squabble over the girl together.'

'Don't you believe it. If it's just me then she'll plant herself between the two of us and I won't get a word, let alone anything else, in edgewise. You can just tell she's the sort who wants to stop everyone else having fun because she's an old maid.'

'She's hardly an old maid.'

Ralph made a snorting sound. 'I doubt she's ever had a day's excitement in her whole life.'

'Leave her alone.'

'Why? Do you like her?' His old friend draped one leg over the other and regarded him thoughtfully. 'Well, she's attractive enough, I suppose. If I wasn't so smitten with my nymph, then I might have considered her for myself. After all, her name's practically famous in Bath. She'd be quite a conquest.'

Samuel stopped pacing abruptly. *Attractive enough* wasn't exactly the phrase he would have chosen to use. *Exceedingly pretty* was more like it, with porcelain skin, a stubborn chin and eyes dark and deep enough for a man to drown in, which given his nautical background was a dangerous metaphor indeed. They'd turned out to be an even darker brown than he'd expected, only a shade away from black, and sharper than Ralph had given her credit for. She'd known perfectly well what they'd been up to from the moment they'd entered the shop, her hackles well and truly raised from the start. *He* certainly hadn't deceived or charmed her.

Truth be told, the experience had been somewhat galling. He'd never been much of a lady's man, but he'd flattered himself that he still possessed a reasonable degree of charm, on the rare occasions he chose to display it, that was. He'd favoured Miss Fortini with his most dashing smile and she hadn't been swayed for a second. Teasing hadn't worked, either. She'd given as good as she'd got and more, rebuffing his advances with flashing eyes and a dry wit that had amused him considerably. Her protective attitude towards her assistant had impressed him, too. Her concern for the girl was both laudable and touching, making him feel even guiltier by contrast. She certainly deserved better than to have to spend her time guarding against men like Ralph. It was no wonder she behaved like a termagant. Which she wasn't.

'What do you mean, famous?' he asked finally.

'Mmm?' Ralph paused in the inspection of his fingernails. 'Oh, she's Belle. *The* Belle. Anna*belle* Fortini.'

'Annabelle.' He felt inordinately pleased to discover her first name at last. 'But aren't the biscuits called Belles?'

'Yes,' Ralph yawned, 'but they were named after her. The whole shop was, in fact. Her parents set up the place just after she was born, so Henrietta says, and they named both it and the merchandise after their baby daughter. It's ironic really, such a sweet name for such a shrew.'

Samuel folded his arms, choosing to ignore the last comment. 'What happened to her parents?'

'Oh, the father died a few years ago, but the mother's still around. She doesn't work any more, something to do with ill health apparently, but *she's* even more famous than the daughter. Notorious, actually.'

'I don't listen to gossip, Ralph.'

'It's not gossip, it's fact. Do you remember the old Duke of Messi—?'

He was prevented from saying any more by the appearance of the ladies themselves, walking with varying degrees of enthusiasm along the footpath towards them. They were still dressed in their shop clothes, in matching yellow empire-line dresses, though now they both wore bonnets and shawls, too. The nymph's headwear was pink, bringing out the slight strawberry tint of her hair, while Miss Fortini's was light brown, contrasting with her dark curls to give her a coffee-and-cream appearance. Damn it if he didn't crave a cup at that moment...

The younger woman walked straight up to Ralph with a small skip in her step, taking his arm with an enthusiastic smile. Too enthusiastic, Samuel thought privately, and certainly too trusting. Her yellow dress and hair gave her the appearance of a daffodil, her golden beauty blending in perfectly with the spring foliage around them. It gave him a twinge of unease. Such innocence could so easily be stamped on by the wrong kind of person. In natural daylight, moreover, she looked even younger and more vulnerable than she had in the shop, making him wish that he'd challenged Ralph on his intentions more thoroughly.

'Shall we?' He offered an arm to Miss Fortini, but she ignored it, sparing him only a cursory glance before starting along the path on her own.

'So your name is Belle?' he tried asking again, lengthening his stride to catch up with her quick pace.

'Annabelle.' She gave him a sharp look. 'Although, as I believe I mentioned earlier, my customers call me Miss Fortini.'

'Forgive me, I didn't intend to be overfamiliar, but I only just discovered that you're the original Bath Belle.'

If he wasn't mistaken, she gave a soft sigh. 'For what it's worth, yes, I am, or at least my parents presented us both to the world around the same time. It's actually short for Annabelle Claudia Teresa Fortini, but I prefer Anna.' She glanced sideways at him, the evening sunlight bathing her face in a reddish-gold glow. 'So now you know *all* of my names, which is a great deal more than I can say about you and yours. Do you make a habit of being mysterious, sir, or am I simply not important enough to warrant an introduction?'

'Ah, forgive me again.' He drew his brows together in consternation, belatedly realising that she was right. Despite asking for her name, he hadn't mentioned his own at all. 'Captain Samuel Delaney at your service.'

'*Captain* Delaney?' Her footsteps faltered and then stopped, her prickly manner disappearing at once. 'You're a captain? In the army or navy?'

'Navy.'

'But you're not in uniform.'

'No.' He flinched at the reminder. 'I'm trying to accustom myself to not wearing it.'

'Are you on shore leave?'

'Something like that.' He shrugged as she continued to regard him inquisitively. 'I sustained an injury during a recent skirmish and the Admiralty has no more need of me at present. I don't know when, or whether, I'll be able to return to active service.'

'It must have been serious.' Her dark eyes swept over him as if she were searching for evidence of a wound.

'Shrapnel.' He touched a hand to his collarbone, his lips twitching with amusement. He couldn't remember the last time he'd been inspected so thoroughly, especially by a woman. 'But it's mostly healed.'

'I'm glad.' She dug her top teeth into her bottom lip, a small frown puckering her brow as if she were considering telling him something. 'My brother, Sebastian, is in the navy,' she said finally.

'Indeed?' He felt strangely honoured by the confidence. 'What vessel?'

'The *Menelaus*. He's a lieutenant.'

'That's a good ship. I know Captain Marlow well.'

'You do?' Her brown eyes widened with enthusiasm, riveting on his face so intently that she didn't even notice when Ralph touched a hand to her assistant's cheek up ahead. 'Is he a good man?'

'Very. We served together on the *Asia* six years ago when we were both lieutenants. He can make buttons out of cheese and he doesn't like fish.'

'Fish?' She blinked. 'You mean to eat?'

'To do anything with, I imagine. Other than that, he's a fair man with an uncanny ability to sense bad weather. Your brother couldn't ask for a better captain.'

'Thank you. I appreciate your saying so.' For the first time since they'd met her smile didn't contain the faintest hint of sarcasm. 'You must be good, too, Captain Delaney. To reach such a high rank by the age of...' she looked him up and down again '...thirty?'

This time he couldn't stop himself from smiling. 'You're very direct, Miss Fortini.'

'Yes, I know.' She seemed unperturbed by the comment. 'It's a failing of mine, I suppose, but the problem is that I can never understand why. If I could, then maybe I could do something about it, but as it is...' she shrugged '...I like to get to the point. It was only an observation, however. I didn't mean to offend you.'

'I'm not remotely offended, although I'm afraid your observation is slightly out. I'm a weather-beaten twenty-six, but you're correct about my rank. In peace time, it would have taken a great deal longer to gain such a promotion, but things work differently in war.'

'I suppose so.' She nodded sombrely as they started to walk again. 'Do you enjoy it? Being a sailor, I mean?'

'I do. I've always loved the water. Swimming, sailing, fishing, even looking at it, so the navy suits me. I like the routine on board ship, too. It can be tedious, but it gives me a sense of purpose and it's calming.'

'Do you often need calming?' She gave him a quizzical look.

'On a daily basis at the moment. I've been on

shore for four months and it feels like an eternity. I'm afraid of losing my sea legs.'

'Sebastian loves the navy, too, but I wish he might come home for a while. The last we heard his ship was somewhere off the coast of South America, but I'm afraid of another big sea battle.'

'It's extremely unlikely. Napoleon doesn't have enough ships left to risk another naval assault and it's doubtful he'd want to anyway. Trafalgar was the longest day of my life, but at least the victory was decisive.'

'You were there?' Her head spun towards him so quickly he almost jumped. 'Is that where you were injured?'

'Yes.'

'You called it a *skirmish*!'

'A *big* skirmish.'

'A big...' She stared at him with an expression of bewilderment mixed with curiosity. 'I read that you were outnumbered. Thirty-three French and Spanish ships to twenty-seven British.'

'That's right. More than forty thousand men, all told.'

'What was the name of your ship?'

'The *Colossus*.'

'But I've heard of that!' Bewilderment turned to outright amazement. 'It was in the middle of the action.'

'Yes, unfortunately. Our yardarm locked with that of the *Argonaute*. We were trapped together for ten minutes before the sea swell drove us apart.'

'And then the *Swiftsure* surrendered to you?'

'Eventually, after we gave her a full broadside.'

'*And* the *Bahama*. You destroyed her mainmast.'

He lifted an eyebrow. 'You know your sea battles, Miss Fortini.'

'I don't see why a woman shouldn't read about such things as well as a man.'

'Neither do I, especially when that woman has a brother in the navy. Ask me anything you like.'

'All right.' She paused as if to gather her thoughts. 'What was the battle really like? The reports all make it sound so well ordered, but how do you stay in formation?'

'With many hours of practice, although what Nelson did at Trafalgar hasn't been done often before. Instead of the fleets facing each other, he divided ours into two columns. We cut through the enemy line instead of confronting them head on. It took them by surprise and gained us the advantage.'

'Did you know you were winning?'

He shook his head. 'At close quarters, it's hard

to see anything that's happening beyond your own ship. There are shards of timber and metal flying all around and you can't hear because the boom of so many cannons drowns out everything except the ringing inside your own head. You're aware of men shouting and screaming, but you can't make out the words. Meanwhile, the smoke burns your lungs so that you can't answer back, either. Most of the time, you're just fighting to stay alive.' He stopped, afraid that he might have said too much, but she seemed to be hanging on every word.

'It must have been terrifying.'

'It was. A few other words come to mind, but in essence they mean the same thing. Being responsible for so many lives is frightening enough, but I believe that every man is terrified going into battle. There's always the chance that you won't make it out again, but there's no use in showing it or giving in to the fear, either. And being with your crew and part of the fleet gives you courage.'

'Sebastian said something similar in one of his letters. He said it was like having a second family.'

'That's true. At sea, we all depend on each other for survival. You have to rely on your men to do what they've been trained for.'

'Did the fighting really last three hours?'

'It did, then the weather that night nearly finished us off. We were in a poor enough state after the battle, but the storm was even worse. Many of us spent the night on deck, waiting to see if we'd be scuppered on the rocks. A number of ships didn't make it to morning.'

'And you'd lost your commander.'

'Yes.' He clenched his jaw at the memory. 'During the battle, Nelson refused to go below deck for safety. He wanted to fight alongside us and he said the men needed to see him. Unfortunately a French sharpshooter in the rigging of the *Redoubtable* saw him, too. The musket ball entered his left shoulder.'

'It was a great loss.'

'It was. I remember when we got word of what had happened. The whole fleet fell silent. We'd won, but it felt like defeat.'

'Maybe all battles feel like that in the end.' She sounded pensive as they emerged out of the trees and on to a wide pathway leading up to a stone pavilion. 'It all seems like such a terrible waste.'

'It was. Thousands of men died that day. The waves were red with...' He stopped midsentence. 'My apologies. I shouldn't have said that.'

'Why not? Because I'm a woman?' She gave him a pointed look. 'There's no need to apologise, Captain Delaney. I like to be told the truth, not be sheltered from it. I appreciate your honesty and...' she hesitated and then stopped walking again, folding her hands tightly in front of her '...if you were to hear any news of my brother's ship, good *or* bad, I would appreciate hearing about that, too.'

'Very well. If I hear anything, I'll be sure to inform you.'

'Thank you.' She cleared her throat, turning her head to watch a squirrel as it ran about on the lawn beside them. 'I believe I owe you an apology, Captain.'

'I don't think—'

'But I do,' she interrupted him firmly. 'I behaved rudely towards you earlier. I made certain assumptions about your character, but I was mistaken. I had no idea what kind of a man you really were.'

What kind of a man...? Samuel froze, struck with a fresh pang of guilt. 'I'm not sure I understand you, Miss Fortini.'

She made an apologetic face. 'When you came into my shop earlier I assumed that you were just another bored, indolent member of the aristocracy with too much time on his hands. I didn't believe that you were really there to buy biscuits for your grandmother. I thought that you had an ulterior motive. Now I know I misjudged you. You're a gentleman who also works for his living, a man of purpose and honour and bravery.'

'Ah.' Samuel rubbed a hand around the back of his neck. Under other circumstances he might have been pleased by such a heroic portrait, but it was hard to swallow when she'd been right the first time. His earlier behaviour had been decidedly *un*heroic.

'You don't like the aristocracy, Miss Fortini?' He decided to focus on a different part of her speech.

Black lashes fanned over her cheeks as she dipped her gaze evasively. 'I'm sure there are some perfectly fine examples of gentlemen among the upper classes, but in my experience not many. Take your friend.' Her lip curled with distaste as she glanced towards Ralph. 'His sole purpose in life at the moment seems to be the pursuit of my friend.'

'I thought she was your employee?'

'Can't she be both?' Her gaze shot back to his. 'Sir, you accused me of being direct earlier so I won't mince words. I believe that we both know what he wants from her, and that when— *if*—he gets it, he'll abandon her as he already has countless others, I'm sure. I've lived in Bath my whole life and I've seen it happen more times than I can remember. Gentlemen may visit for the Pump Rooms, but they find other ways to pass their time and they see women like us as fair game. *That's* the reason your friend feels entitled to call into my shop whenever he feels like it without buying anything, why he thinks it acceptable to ask Henrietta to walk without a chaperon, too. He would never behave in such a way with a lady.

'Well, she is *not* fair game, Captain. She's eighteen years old and far too sweet-natured to understand what he really wants and, if you're truly a man of honour as I believe you to be, I beg you to dissuade him from pursuing her.' She took a step forward and placed a hand on his arm, her tone entreating as her fingers curled gently around his wrist. 'No good can come of it.'

Samuel listened in silence. By the end of her speech she was flushed and breathless and he was feeling somewhat mortified, not by her bluntness, but by the truth behind it. Every word she'd just spoken filled him with shame, the touch of her hand on his arm like a burning hot iron. Every word was true, too, except for the part when she'd called him a man of honour.

An honourable man would never have entered the shop and helped Ralph in the first place. An honourable man would have turned around and walked away. Which meant that all he could do now was try to put things right and behave like the man she thought him to be. Her impassioned speech and those soulful dark eyes made him *want* to be heroic again. Nearly as much as they made him want to kiss her, too. Quite suddenly and unexpectedly, right there in the middle of the park, in a way that *definitely* wouldn't improve her opinion of gentlemen...

'You look tired, Miss Fortini.' He pulled his arm away before he could do something he might regret. Now that they were standing so close he could see her face clearly and in truth she looked a stage beyond tired. She looked exhausted, her brown eyes ringed with dark shadows that made them appear even bigger. 'You ought to go home and rest.'

'Didn't you hear me, Captain?' She sounded dismayed.

'I did.' A new suspicion occurred to him. 'I wondered if you were speaking from personal experience?'

She took a step backwards as if he'd just threatened her, her face blanching visibly. 'What difference would it make if I was?'

He clamped his brows together. She was right. Her past experiences, whatever they were, made no difference at all to their current situation. As much as he wanted to know the answer, it was none of his business.

'Tell me, then…' he said, swallowing a different question '…does your friend usually walk home on her own at this time of evening?'

'Yes.' Her expression was guarded now. 'Although one of her brothers usually meets her on Pulteney Bridge.'

'Good. In that case, give me five minutes and I'll remember an urgent reason for myself and Mr Hoxley to be elsewhere. You have my word as a naval officer and…' he paused, resisting the urge to grimace '…a gentleman. If you'll trust me, that is, Miss Fortini?'

She didn't answer at first, holding on to his gaze for a few intense moments, her expression turning gradually from indecision to conviction to something that made his pulse start to accelerate.

'Thank you, Captain Delaney,' she said, nodding finally. 'I believe that I do trust you. Five minutes, then.' She dipped into a curtsy. 'And the next time your grandmother would like some biscuits, I'd be more than happy to deliver a tin myself.'

'I'll be sure to tell her.' He made a formal bow, but she was already turning away, waving a farewell to her friend before walking briskly towards one of the park gates.

Samuel felt an unexpectedly warm glow in his chest, followed by a pang of regret as he watched the subtle sway of her hips across the lawn. It was a pity that his future was so unsettled, otherwise she was exactly the kind of woman he would have been interested in: intelligent, capable and strong-willed. He'd *almost* fallen back into old ways that afternoon, the ones he thought he'd left behind when he'd joined the navy, but somehow Miss Fortini had stopped him. He'd been perilously close to steering off tack and she'd set him back on course. He actually felt grateful to her.

He heaved a sigh as she turned out of the gate and disappeared from view. It was *really* a pity... but it was also pointless to dwell upon what-might-have-been. Apart from anything else, she'd made her opinion of the aristocracy abundantly clear and, if she found out who he was besides a naval officer, who he *might* be anyway, then no doubt she'd walk away from him again even faster.

On the other hand, if events unfolded the way he wanted them to and he remained *plain* Captain Delaney, perhaps he might permit himself to visit her shop again one day. Not with Ralph obviously, especially since they were about to have the kind of full and frank discussion that would undoubtedly ruin their friendship for ever, but on his own and with honourable intentions this time. In another couple of months, perhaps, when the matter of his possible inheritance was settled…

In the meantime, it was probably best to keep away. He was developing an unfortunate appetite for biscuits as it was.

Chapter Four

Anna closed and latched the window shutters, drew two iron bolts across the shop door and then trudged up the back staircase to the parlour, wearily untying the ribbons of her bonnet as she went. A walk through Sydney Gardens had been the last thing she'd needed after a day that had started twelve hours before. Her neck felt stiff and her feet ached with tiredness, even more so than usual, but at least now she could rest.

From a shopkeeper's perspective, however, she couldn't complain. It had been another profitable day. She oughtn't to complain at all, she chided herself, especially when she had so much to be grateful for—an honest and reliable source of income, a warm and dry home, and independence to boot. The shop that her parents had founded almost twenty-five years earlier had become so popular with the spa visitors of Bath that they'd eventually been able to buy the whole building on Swainswick Crescent, narrow and compact as it was. There were three floors: the shop and kitchen below, a parlour in the middle and two small bedrooms in the attic. The parlour was the biggest room overall, with one large window where her mother liked to sit and watch the comings and goings on the street below. No doubt she would have seen Captain Delaney and his irritating companion earlier. Anna wondered what she'd thought of them, not to mention her and Henrietta's unprecedented early departure...

'Good evening, Mama.'

She found the scene just as she'd expected, her mother sitting in her customary armchair with an open book in her lap.

'Good evening, dear.' Elizabeth Fortini looked up from her reading with a smile. 'I was starting to wonder where you'd got to.'

'Henrietta wanted a walk in the park so I said that I'd join her.' Anna dropped down onto a sofa, telling herself that it wasn't a lie exactly, even if it wasn't the whole truth, either. 'It was nice to get some fresh air.'

'I'm surprised you had the strength after such a long day.' Her mother tipped her head to one side sympathetically. 'You work too hard, my darling. I wish I could help more.'

'It's not your fault, Mama.' Anna gestured towards her mother's swollen fingers. 'I know you're in pain.'

'It pains me to see you looking so exhausted, too.' Her mother stood up, wincing as she put weight on to her ankles. 'I'll make us some dinner.'

'It's all right, I'll do it in a few minutes.'

'You will not.' Her mother limped slowly across the room. 'I may not be much help in the shop any more, but I can still be useful in other ways. Now you have a rest and I'll be back soon.'

Anna smiled gratefully, too tired to argue. She was almost too tired to eat, although she knew that she had to. More than that, she was tired of simply *being* tired, but there seemed to be no way around it. There was always so much to *do*. When she wasn't baking, she was wrapping or stacking or cleaning or sweeping or preparing tins or doing one of the hundred other tasks that seemed to require her constant attention. Henrietta was an able assistant, but she only arrived at seven o'clock in the morning when the baking was already done and left again at four in the afternoon. Anna couldn't afford to pay longer hours, which meant that any remaining jobs fell to her and they were...*relentless*.

Yawning, she tipped her head back and closed

her eyes. Things hadn't been so bad while her father was still alive. After the swelling in her mother's joints had started ten years before, first in her fingers and toes, then in her hands and feet, Anna had taken on more and more of her responsibilities in the shop and enjoyed them, too. She'd enjoyed running a business, unlike Sebastian who'd gone off in search of adventure the moment he'd turned seventeen. *She'd* been the one to suggest they start making cinnamon and rosewater-infused biscuits and to start offering tins as well as cloth-wrapped bundles.

In return, her father had taught her everything he knew, which was a great deal, but unfortunately not how to find extra hours in the day or how to go without sleep, either. His sudden heart failure had left her with a shop to run as well as an ailing, grieving mother to take care of. Not that she resented either task, but it was hard sometimes *not* to feel trapped in an endless cycle of monotonous chores. No matter how much she saved, it still wasn't enough for a holiday—just a few days, or weeks preferably, to break free of the routine and maybe travel a little. It didn't have to be far, just somewhere different. Somewhere to enjoy a little free time to read or to walk or to simply lie around daydreaming…

For some reason, the thought of daydreaming

conjured up an image of Captain Delaney. His hair, somewhere between chestnut and auburn, those startling pale eyes and that deep voice that made her insides feel curiously soft and malleable, like an undercooked biscuit. He'd looked so handsome waiting for her and Henrietta in the park that she'd *almost* been tempted to take his arm when he'd offered it to her, but common sense had prevailed. She'd known better than to trust a *gentleman*.

As it turned out, however, she'd been wrong about him. She'd been so certain that he'd been trying to distract her in the shop, but apparently he really *had* been there to buy biscuits. She'd assumed the worst and discovered the exact opposite. Aristocratic though he obviously was, he was also a naval captain and not just any naval captain, but a national hero, a brave and honourable man instead of the rake she'd assumed. Their conversation in the park had been genuinely interesting and without any of the mocking undertones she'd detected earlier. Instead, his manner had been open and honest, enough that she'd felt able to appeal to his better nature to save Henrietta. Admittedly, he'd seemed somewhat taken aback by the request at first, so much so that for a few moments she'd thought he'd been offended on his friend's behalf, but to her relief his words had eventually proven otherwise.

Only the severity of his expression when he'd asked if her comments about gentlemen were based upon personal experience had unsettled her, conjuring up memories she preferred to forget. Then his gaze had seemed to bore into the back of her head, giving the uncomfortable impression that he could read all of her secrets. Thankfully he hadn't persisted in his questioning, asking her to trust him instead, and his gaze had softened then, causing a warm, tingling sensation in her chest. The feeling had actually been quite pleasant, as if some kind of unspoken communication were passing between them. It had made her decide to trust him, although she still couldn't help but wonder if she'd done the right thing by leaving Henrietta.

Whether she had or hadn't, however, she was far too tired to think about it now. But she liked his name, she thought sleepily. *Captain Samuel Delaney.* It had a nice ring to it, an authoritative ring, and it was nice to know that a few *real* gentlemen still existed in the world, even if it was unlikely that she'd ever see him again. Gentlemen who looked even more attractive when they turned out to be captains and bought biscuits for their grandmothers…

* * *

'I have a present for you.' Samuel deposited the tin he'd been carrying for the better part of two hours into his grandmother's narrow lap. 'Don't say I never give you anything.'

'Except for white hairs and anxiety, you mean?' Lady Jarrow regarded the offering with an air of suspicion. 'What is it?'

'They're Belles... *Biscuits*,' he clarified as his grandmother stared at him blankly. 'I'm told they're famous in Bath.'

'I've never heard of them in my life.'

'I have.' His grandfather's steel-rimmed spectacles peered over the top of a newspaper opposite. 'They're something of an institution, actually.'

'Do you mean to say you've eaten them before?' His grandmother sounded as shocked as if her husband had just announced an illegitimate child.

'Dozens. I discovered them a few years ago and now I insist upon having one every morning when I'm in town. Two, sometimes.'

'Then why haven't I eaten one before?'

'I'm sure you have, my dear.' The newspaper lifted again. 'Only you were probably busy thinking about a new saddle or something.'

'Harumph.' Lady Jarrow made short work of

the ribbon. 'I have a perfectly good collection of saddles, as you very well know. If anything, I'd be thinking about riding boots. I could do with a new pair.' She removed the lid and tossed it at Samuel. 'Well, this looks very pretty, I must say. I'll ring for tea. I can't abide sweet things without it.'

'I'm glad that you approve, Grandmother.'

Samuel sprawled in an armchair, looking between his grandparents with a combination of amusement and affection. Aside from his mother and half-sister in Cumberland they were the only family he had, not that he'd ever had a great many family members to speak of. Thanks to his father's notoriety in gambling, drinking and generally throwing away his inheritance, no one from the paternal side of the family had ever deigned to acknowledge Samuel, too afraid he might prove to be a chip off the old block. They'd all thought of him as tainted, refusing to budge from that opinion no matter how hard he'd tried, during the past ten years anyway, to prove otherwise.

Fortunately, his maternal relations had been made of sterner stuff, refusing to let the sins of a detested son-in-law influence their feelings for his offspring. His grandmother in particular had always been a force to be reckoned with, a renowned beauty in her youth as well as an heiress, though she'd always preferred spending time with her horses to listening to recitations of love poetry from her many admirers. She'd sat doggedly on the shelf until the shockingly great age of eight and twenty, until the day she'd set eyes on the bookish and shy Lord Jarrow. Seven years her junior, the young Baron had been as surprised as anyone by her sudden interest. Somewhat alarmed, too, since, as he frequently remarked to his grandson, when it came to a battle of wills he'd known he hadn't stood a chance. Where Georgiana had a will, she got her way. Their marriage had gone ahead with almost indecent haste and they'd immediately retired to the country to build a new block of stables and restock the library. *He'd* had his books, *she'd* had her horses, and they'd lived in perfect contentment for fifty years ever since. It was, in Samuel's opinion, an excellent example of a happy marriage. Quite unlike that of his parents.

'Have you been to the Pump Rooms today?' he enquired of the newspaper.

'Of course he has,' his grandmother answered, as was frequently the case, for her husband. 'It's the reason we're staying in this wretched city, after all.'

'There are still parks for riding in, Grandmother.'

'Pshaw! It's hardly riding when one's constantly expected to stop and make conversation. You'd think that horses were simply chairs! If people don't care about their animals, then they'd be better off using their feet.'

Samuel chuckled, though the very fact of his grandmother's presence in Bath made him uneasy. On every other occasion when his grandfather had come to take the medicinal waters she'd remained at their home in Rutland. The fact that she'd joined him this time suggested the seventy-one-year-old Baron's health was worse than either of them were letting on.

'I thought we might all go together on Monday,' his grandfather commented, folding his newspaper as the tea tray arrived. 'We could make a family outing of it, so to speak.'

'I'd be delighted, Grandfather.'

'Well, *I* wouldn't, but I will because I'm a good wife.' The Baroness lifted her eyebrows provocatively, though neither Samuel nor his grandfather were foolish enough to contradict the statement. 'But only on two conditions. One, that I don't have to drink any of that disgusting liquid. Two, that Samuel wears his uniform.'

'Grandmother…'

'Yes, I know, you're officially on sick leave, but you're still a captain until this whole inheritance matter is resolved and you look so dashing in uniform.'

'Let him be, Georgiana.' The Baron's bushy white eyebrows gave his frown a somewhat ferocious aspect. 'You know it only makes him feel worse about the whole business.'

'How anyone can feel worse about potentially inheriting an earldom is beyond me. Most reasonable people would be thrilled by the prospect.'

'Because of the entail.' His grandfather shook his head. 'It's a bad business altogether. Cruel, really. We just have to wait and see whether the widow has a boy or a girl.'

'Well, I wish that she'd hurry and make up her mind.' Lady Jarrow snorted contemptuously. 'I had a boy first and a girl second because that's what I wanted. It's all a question of mind over matter.'

'In which case, she'll have a boy for certain, my dear.'

'Only if she has a strong enough will, which I doubt. I met her once and she seemed insipid. No interest in horses at all. She hasn't even had the decency to reply to Samuel's letter.'

'What could she say, Grandmother?' Samuel

shifted in his seat uncomfortably. 'The letter I sent was one of condolence.'

'She might still have acknowledged the situation. Yes, the entail makes things awkward, but you should be allowed to visit Staunton at least. If the estate turns out to be yours, then you need to know how it's run.'

'I've no wish to visit Staunton.'

'Well, somebody should. She could be undermining your inheritance as we speak.'

'Since it might be her son's, then I doubt it.'

'The whole situation is completely ridiculous. Your injury's recovered, but your life is on hold while we wait for some insipid woman to give birth.'

'It's far worse for her. She's lost her husband and now her whole future depends on the gender of her baby.' Samuel reached into the tin of biscuits with a sigh. For some reason, the rows of tissue paper looked comforting. 'I don't want the inheritance anyway. I just want everything to go back to the way it was a year ago.'

'A year ago Trafalgar hadn't happened. You'd still be blockading the English Channel and giving me new wrinkles from worry.' His grandmother sniffed. 'Personally I'm glad the Admiralty won't let you go back to sea until matters are settled. They're probably worried about drowning a peer of the realm.'

'It's not just that.' Samuel took a bite of biscuit, surprised to find that he liked rosewater flavour even more than cinnamon. 'The Admiralty thinks that the war at sea is over and all the fighting will be on land from now on. They're trying to get captains off the payroll, no matter what they say about my *duty* to Staunton.'

'None the less, I'm afraid they're right about it, my boy.' His grandfather threw him a sympathetic look. 'If you do inherit, then you have a duty to look after the estate, not to mention all the tenants who live there. You're the last man standing, so to speak, on your father's side of the family anyway.'

Samuel rubbed a hand over his forehead. 'That's what's so strange about it. My father's father and brother never wanted anything to do with me. They've practically disowned me since birth, yet now I'm the heir to some cousin I've never even met.'

'Stranger things have happened.'

'If they didn't want it to happen then they should have had more sons themselves!' There was an iron glint in his grandmother's eye. 'This is all their own doing.'

'Perhaps they oughtn't to have died either, my

dear. That was rather weak-willed of them, too, don't you think?'

Samuel made a wry face as his grandfather winked at him. 'Their lawyers must have scoured the entire family tree looking for somebody else to inherit.'

'Perhaps, but the law's the law. You're the heir, whether people like it or not.'

'*If* it's a girl.'

'Well, I for one hope that it is,' his grandmother declared. 'It'll be a poke in the eye for anyone who ever cut you in society. I might not have approved of your father, which is a ludicrous understatement, but I always said that my daughter was free to make her own choices, however unutterably stupid.' Her face softened. 'But their marriage did give us you so I suppose it wasn't all bad. Now we just need to get you established and breeding heirs of your own.'

'Grandmother,' Samuel groaned. 'I'll inherit the earldom if I really must, but I draw the line at starting a dynasty.'

'You'll have to someday.'

'Not necessarily and definitely not straight away.'

'Pshaw, now you're being selfish. All I want is another little boy like you, even if I'll be too old to raise him myself this time.'

Samuel smiled affectionately. For all his grandmother's strong opinions, he couldn't have asked for a better surrogate mother. 'In that case, how can I refuse to wear my uniform on Monday? Just this once.'

'Excellent.' Lady Jarrow looked satisfied. 'And I wouldn't be surprised if the Pump Rooms are slightly busier than usual. News of a certain eligible bachelor's presence in Bath has already spread. I should imagine that several debutantes are on their way here as we speak.'

'Good grief, aren't there enough prospective husbands in London?'

'Not enough to go around, apparently. Besides, the Season hasn't started yet.'

'Well, I'm not eligible, not yet anyway.'

'True, but I imagine a few of them will want to get in the running early, just in case.'

'Then that makes them gamblers and you know how I feel about those. They remind me of Father.'

'You could always go to Staunton.'

'Grandmother…'

'Oh, all right, I'll settle for the Pump Rooms. We'll cut quite a dash with you in uniform.'

'And forget all about me, I suppose.' The Baron dipped his hand into the tin of biscuits.

'I say, all three types. It's hard to know where to begin.'

'Have one of each,' Samuel suggested.

'He will not!' His grandmother sounded outraged. 'We're here to make him fit and healthy again, not to fill him with treats.'

'I'm not a horse, my dear, and some things are a lost cause.' Her husband gave her an inscrutable look.

'Not if I have anything to do with it. You may have *one* biscuit and that's all.' She took a bite of her own, screwing her face up as if preparing to spit it out again, before nodding approvingly. 'Quite tasty. What did you say they were called again?'

'Belles. That's the name of the shop, too. It's a charming little place.'

'Indeed it is.' The Baron scooped up another biscuit before his wife could stop him. 'Have you met the eponymous Annabelle? A delightful young lady.'

Samuel lifted an eyebrow in surprise. *Was* she delightful? Prickly and forthright seemed like a more apt description, except for during those last few minutes in the park when she'd appealed to him for help. Then she'd been fairly inspiring...

On the other hand, maybe she *was* delightful in a way. If they'd met under different circumstances, then he might have thought so, too, from the start. She was definitely unique, or at least he didn't think he'd ever met anyone quite like her before. She wasn't impressed by rank, that much had been obvious by the contemptuous way she'd spoken to him and Ralph, seeming far more likely to lift her nose in the air than to bow or scrape, and she certainly knew how to stand up for herself. He liked both of those things about her, just as much as he liked her bouncy dark curls and the swirling depths of those wide coffee-brown eyes. She wasn't as obviously beautiful as the employee she called her friend, but in his personal opinion she was a hundred times more appealing. He even liked her voice, with its hint of an accent he couldn't quite place. It wasn't that of Bath, though it contained hints of the west country and even an occasional Italian inflection. It was…unique. He kept coming back to that word. It seemed like the perfect way to describe her. Not that he was about to tell his grandparents any of that.

'I met her briefly, yes,' he answered when he realised his silence had gone on a few moments too long. 'She seemed pleasant enough.'

'Aye, very pleasant. Do you know, we once talked about bees for half an hour?'

'Bees?'

'Yes, I thought that they looked like a pair of bees, her and that other girl in their yellow dresses, and that put me in mind of the hives at home. Before I knew it I was telling her all about them. I completely lost track of the time.'

'Poor girl.' The Baroness batted his hand away from the box as it drifted back again.

'She seemed interested, my dear.'

'She's a saleswoman. She had to seem interested or you might not have bought anything.'

'Ah…you may have a point. None the less, Miss Fortini makes excellent biscuits.'

'Fortini?' His grandmother's voice sharpened abruptly.

'Yes.' Samuel lifted an eyebrow. 'What's the matter with that?'

'I'm not sure. There's just something familiar…' She pursed her lips and then shook her head. 'Well, never mind. I'm sure it'll come to me eventually. When I'm out riding most likely. In any case, I approve of her biscuits. You may bring me a tin whenever you wish.'

'I'll remember that.' Samuel popped the remainder of his own biscuit into his mouth and reached for his tea. Unfortunately, the beverage itself was disappointing. Tea was all well and good, but he still felt a powerful craving for coffee.

Chapter Five

'Are you honestly telling me that you feel better?'

Samuel winced as his grandmother's contralto tones boomed out across the Abbey courtyard. At least twenty heads turned in their direction as they emerged from the Pump Rooms and made their way towards Bath Street.

'Yes, actually.' After five decades of practice, his grandfather was unruffled by either his wife's deafening volume or her cynical pronouncements.

'I don't know how you can bear to drink something that smells so revolting.'

'It's a natural spring, my dear. That's how it smells when it comes out of the ground.'

'Well, they might try to mask the odour somehow.' The Baroness took Samuel's arm and gave him a nudge in the ribs. 'I've heard that sailors always carry a flask of rum wherever they go. I'd far rather drink some of that.'

'I'm afraid I must have forgotten mine today, Grandmother, although I do know a rather good hostelry close by. I'm sure you'd fit right in.'

'Your grandmother doesn't fit into places, my boy, you know that. She simply takes over wherever she goes. If she'd been born a man, she would have been a general the day after she joined the army.'

'Or, better still, an admiral in the navy,' Samuel pointed out. 'We could have won Trafalgar in half the time.'

'You both know very well that I would have led a cavalry regiment.' The Baroness looked down her nose at them reprovingly. 'And made a damn fine job of it, too.'

'Naturally.' Samuel started to laugh and then stopped, his attention drawn by the sight of a woman's head peering out from behind one of the pillars of the colonnade up ahead. She seemed to be hiding in the shadows, or trying to anyway, but there was something familiar about her profile and that mass of wild curls... Miss Fortini? He came to an abrupt halt, bringing his grandmother up short.

'Samuel?' The Baroness looked at him as if he were a disobedient horse. If she'd been wearing spurs, he wouldn't have been surprised to find himself prodded. 'What on earth's the matter?'

'Forgive me, Grandmother, but I've just seen an acquaintance I need to speak to. You both continue without me.'

'Will be you back at the house for luncheon?'

'I think so.'

'You *think* so?' This time she looked as if she were considering a swift kick to his flanks. 'Well, don't expect us to wait if you're late.'

'I wouldn't dream of it. Unless you'd care to take pity on me, of course.'

He grinned as she gave a contemptuous snort, waiting until she and his grandfather were a few feet away before weaving his way through the other pedestrians, heading for the covered walkway at the side of the street and then curving around so that he approached the pillar from behind. Miss Fortini was still there, still peering out from the shadows, her hands clutching hold of the stone pillar as if she were poised and ready to dart behind it. She wasn't wearing any gloves, he noticed, or even a bonnet, just a shawl thrown haphazardly over her shoulders as if she'd come out in a rush. She was also clearly unaware of his presence, allowing him a moment to study the nape of her neck and the escaped dark ringlets framing each side of her head. They looked so soft and springy that he was tempted to curl his fingers around them.

'Miss Fortini?'

He said her name gently, though she still performed a mini-pirouette, bumping the back of her head against the pillar as she let out a startled, albeit quickly muffled shriek.

'Captain Delaney?' She put a hand over her chest, her bosom rising and falling erratically as her expression turned from surprise to relief to embarrassment in the space of a few short seconds. 'Good day.'

'Are you all right?' He started to reach for her head and then stopped himself. 'That was quite a bump. I didn't mean to startle you.'

'Oh, it's nothing.' She waved her other hand dismissively. 'I'm sure it looked worse than it felt.'

'Ah…good.' He studied her for a few moments in silence, struggling to make sense of her now guilty expression, before gesturing out at the busy street. 'It's a pleasant morning for a stroll.' He tried to sound as if there were nothing unusual about her behaviour. 'Is your shop closed today?'

'No… I mean, yes. That is, just for a few minutes. I had something important to attend to.' She lifted her chin, worrying her bottom lip between her teeth in a way that made her mouth look redder and distinctly plumper all of a sudden. Positively juicy, in fact.

'Ah.' He glanced enquiringly at the pillar and then back again. 'Anything I might assist you with?'

'Assist me?' She blinked, her dark gaze moving over his uniform as if she were just noticing it for the first time.

'Yes.' He smiled. 'You know, you remind me of my first Captain, Miss Fortini. He was a tyrant for inspections. Do I pass muster?'

'Oh.' Her eyes shot back to his, her cheeks reddening to match her swollen mouth. 'I'm sorry, I was just thinking.'

'About my offer of help? It was quite genuine, I assure you.'

'Thank you. And thank you for what you did the other night. Henrietta told me that you took Mr Hoxley away like you promised.'

'You're welcome.'

'Only… I'm afraid the situation involves her again.' She seemed to come to a decision, beckoning for him to come closer before pointing around the edge of the pillar. He looked dutifully. Her apprentice was standing next to a market stall at the far end of the street.

'She told me she was unwell. A headache.'

'And you didn't believe her?' Samuel pulled back, feeling vaguely ridiculous to be peeking out from behind a pillar in broad daylight.

'No. She's been acting strangely for days and she's a terrible liar. I could tell that she felt bad about deceiving me, too, so I knew something was going on.'

'So you closed up your shop and followed her? That doesn't sound very good for business.'

'Some things are more important.' She gave him a narrow-eyed glance. 'I expect you think that it's nothing to do with me.'

'I wouldn't say that exactly...'

He made a face. In his personal opinion, what her employee did in her own free time *was* nothing to do with her, let alone him, but if the girl was supposed to be working, then it *wasn't* strictly speaking her free time...and it *was* Miss Fortini's business that she'd been lied to. Frankly, he was starting to think that her assistant was more trouble than she was worth, but Miss Fortini obviously cared about her. Most employers would have dismissed her on the spot for lying.

'What is it that you suspect her of?'

'I think that she's come to meet someone.'

'Someone being Mr Hoxley?' He frowned, already anticipating the answer.

'Yes. He's been in the shop every day this week. I know he's your friend, but…'

She let the words trail away, although Samuel didn't finish them. Instead, he took a farther step back into the shadows, thinking. He hadn't seen Ralph since the evening he'd practically manhandled him out of Sydney Gardens, delivering a stern lecture about his behaviour on the way. He'd warned him off visiting the shop on Swainswick Crescent again, too, although he'd stopped short of actually threatening him. They'd been close companions once and he hadn't wanted to ruin the memory of their friendship entirely. Unfortunately, it seemed that he'd been too easy on him.

'I'm sure it's all perfectly innocent in Henrietta's mind,' Miss Fortini went on, 'only she has romantic ideas.'

'Is that so terrible? Surely a few romantic ideas are a good thing?'

She gave him a look that implied she'd expected better. 'I live in the real world, Captain, as I'm sure so do you. Gentlemen like Mr Hoxley don't marry girls like Henrietta. He might offer to set her up as his mistress, but that's all.'

Samuel arched an eyebrow, thinking it was a good thing he'd grown up with his grandmother or he might have been shocked to hear a woman speak about mistresses quite so openly. Not one of the well-bred young ladies he'd met in the Pump Rooms that morning would have ever contemplated using the word. Quite a few had probably never even heard of it.

Miss Fortini, on the other hand, stated it as a matter of fact, which, he had to concede, it probably was. Ralph's position as the third son of a minor baronet meant that he needed a rich wife and, unfortunately for his nymph, a shop assistant was never going to be that.

'There!' Miss Fortini uttered a sudden cry of dismay, pointing down the street to where the man in question was just now swaggering around the corner. Samuel leaned forward again, half appalled, half intrigued by the scene. Surely even Ralph wouldn't conduct a liaison in one of Bath's most famous streets? His reputation was disreputable enough, but this was outrageous even for him.

'He's walking right past her!' Miss Fortini whispered indignantly, seemingly afraid of being overheard despite there being at least ten feet and a dozen people between them and Ralph. 'Oh! He's looking this way!'

She shifted backwards, the rounded curve of her bottom bumping forcefully against Samuel's groin before she spun around and flattened herself against the pillar, her eyes wide with a look of alarm. 'Do you think he saw me?'

'I don't think so.' Although he'd certainly see *him*, Samuel thought, if he didn't move completely into the shadows, too. He could hardly have made himself look any more conspicuous in his naval uniform. There was nothing he could do but take a step closer towards Miss Fortini, bracing his hands on the pillar on either side of her waist.

It was a slender waist, he observed, though not so slender that he was afraid she might snap in a strong wind, flaring out into perfectly proportioned hips. She was reasonably tall for a woman, too, with legs long enough that when she'd stepped back against him he'd found it momentarily hard to think straight, a flood of heat rushing straight to the lower part of his body. He was still feeling somewhat befuddled now since the front of his trousers was only a few inches away from the legs and hips in question and their close proximity was doing nothing to diminish the effect.

Fortunately, Miss Fortini appeared blissfully unaware of his body's reaction. Unaware of him altogether, in fact, so taken up with the idea of saving her friend that she seemed oblivious to the impropriety of their position. He had her pinned up against a pillar in broad daylight, for pity's sake! A swift glance over his shoulder showed there was no one else under the covered part of the colonnade, but anyone who cared to look deeper into the shadows would take *him* for the rake, not Ralph. And how he was supposed to care about that when her breasts were heaving so tantalisingly close to his chest he had no idea!

'What's happening?' she whispered, her large brown eyes darting from side to side as if she could somehow see behind her. 'Is he going back to meet her?'

'Mmm?' For a moment, Samuel had no idea what she was talking about, his gaze transfixed by the flawless bow shape of her mouth. He hadn't paid her lips enough attention before, he chided himself, distracted by her many other attractive qualities, but now he found himself wanting to explore them in slow and intimate detail.

'Is he going back to Henrietta?'

'Oh…wait a moment.' Samuel gathered his scattered thoughts with an effort, sucking in a deep breath before stealing a look around the edge of the pillar. 'No.' He frowned. 'He's walking this way and she's following him. They must have arranged to meet like this.' His frown deepened with every word. It was typical of Ralph to flaunt his position so blatantly in front of the girl. He seemed to be stopping every few seconds to speak to some acquaintance or another, making her wait each time. It was just the kind of egotistical, self-aggrandising joke that he would enjoy.

'I need to do something!' Miss Fortini started forward, but Samuel kept his arms in place, restraining her against the pillar.

'Do what exactly?'

'Talk some sense into her!'

'Something tells me that you've already covered the subject quite thoroughly.'

The way her eyelashes fluttered confirmed it. 'Then what do you suggest I do? I can't just let her go with him!'

'No, but if you interfere now then they'll only arrange something else. You'll only delay the inevitable.'

'Then what *can* I do?'

He held on to her gaze, his whole body pulsing with an awareness of hers. Every one of his nerve endings seemed to be tingling and straining towards her. She looked so fierce and determined that he was seized with the same near-overwhelming urge to kiss her that he'd felt in the park. Which was quite possibly the stupidest idea imaginable under the circumstances. It certainly wasn't a solution to their current problem. He had no idea what to do about that... And then he did, the answer coming to him in a blinding flash as he glanced along the street and saw that Ralph wasn't the only person who'd stopped to talk. His grandmother was holding court amid a gathering of acquaintances.

He pulled one hand away from the pillar to rub across his chin, considering. It wouldn't be the most honourable course of action, but it might be the most effective. Non-violent, too, which would save him from having to pummel some decency into his former friend.

'Stay here and don't let your assistant see you.' He took a step away from her. 'I know someone who can help us.'

'Wait!' Miss Fortini lifted a hand so quickly that it collided with his chest, her palm pressing flat over his heart. He stopped at once, feeling as if every muscle in his body had suddenly gone into spasm.

She must have felt something similar because her eyes widened and then dipped abruptly, a small gasp escaping her throat as she jerked her hand away again. 'Forgive me, it was nothing.'

Nothing. He swallowed thickly. Whatever else it was, it was definitely *not* nothing. His heart was thumping a painfully rapid tattoo against the walls of his ribcage and his lungs seemed incapable of dragging in enough air. The pillar, the street, the crowd of people standing just a few feet away…all of them seemed to disappear and there was only her and him and a gathering heat that seemed to sear the very air between them… His gaze focused on the delicate flutter of her pulse at the base of her throat and, without thinking, he lifted a finger to touch it, rubbing his hand gently across the silky soft skin of her neck before sliding it around the back of her head and into the dark mass of her hair. He wanted to see her curls loose, he thought, swallowing again at the feeling of luxurious spirals against his fingertips. He wanted to see them wild and free, tumbling over her naked shoulders and breasts…

He cleared his throat, surprised by the vividness of the image in his mind's eye. 'There's nothing to forgive, Miss Fortini. Leave this to me.'

Anna sagged back against the pillar, willing her breathing to return to normal and for the cold stone to have a cooling effect on her body. What had she been thinking, reaching out to Captain Delaney in such an intimate way? In that moment she hadn't even cared that he was a gentleman! She'd simply acted by instinct, not wanting him to leave despite his offer of help, pressing her fingers against the solid wall of his chest as if *she* were the one there for a private assignation!

Not that he seemed to have minded. On the contrary, he'd touched her back, the gentle caress of his fingertips against her bare skin setting off a series of small fireworks inside her body. The expression on his face hadn't been one of disapproval or disgust, either. It had been surprised, arrested…hungry?

Hungry for what?

Whatever it was, she'd wanted it, too. She *still* did, though the empty, tugging, tremulous sensation in her stomach felt more like an ache than hunger. On the other hand, maybe she was just confused. She certainly felt confused. Her skin was covered in goose pimples though she was red-hot all over and her mind was spinning so fast she felt giddy.

With a gargantuan effort she forced her mind back to the situation with Henrietta, peering out from behind the pillar again. What was Captain Delaney doing? He wasn't heading towards his friend. Instead, he was striding purposefully towards an elderly-looking couple standing arm in arm at the end of the street. The woman in particular was striking, swathed from head to toe in dark purple with white hair, an upright, confident bearing and a long aquiline nose that tilted upwards as he approached.

She threw a swift glance towards Henrietta, wondering if she'd noticed him pass by, but it seemed not. Her friend was standing a few paces behind Mr Hoxley, apparently searching in her reticule for something, though in reality waiting for him. Anna felt her cheeks burn with indignation. How dared he! Not just try to seduce her friend, but to demean her like this? Forcing her to wait in the street as if she were his servant or some other female paid to do his bidding. It was just the kind of arrogant, entitled, *aristocratic* gesture that made her blood boil!

She curled her hands into fists, tempted to march out into the street and tell him exactly what she thought of him and his whole domineering class, but Captain Delaney had told her to wait and after asking for his help she ought to at least see what he planned. Of course *he* was a member of the same upper class as his friend, but there were exceptions to every rule. *He* was a rarity, a pearl among swine, almost too good to be true and even more strikingly handsome in his uniform than he was in his everyday attire. When she'd first noticed what he was wearing she'd felt an obscure urge to salute. His white trousers were practically moulded to his legs and his dark blue tailcoat, complete with epaulets and gold embroidery around the collar, encased his broad shoulders like a second skin. It was strange that Sebastian's lieutenant's uniform had never made her feel quite so tremulous inside, but then Sebastian was her brother and Captain Delaney was... Well, there was nothing remotely brotherly about the way she'd just reacted to him.

The older woman, however, *must* have been some kind of relation because he stepped right up to her without preamble, speaking into her ear as if he were sharing some kind of confidence. As Anna watched, the woman stiffened, but he laid a hand on her arm, saying a few more words before removing it again. Whatever it was obviously did the trick. Anna had the distinct and faintly startling impression of a powerful energy being suddenly unleashed, like a lightning bolt striking down from a cloud. The moment his hand fell away the woman launched forward, waving her walking stick out in front of her like a weapon, though the martial gleam in her eye was enough to make most bystanders dart out of the way.

The only person who appeared oblivious to her wrathful approach was Mr Hoxley himself. He had his back turned towards her, laughing with a group of fashionable-looking young dandies. It was only at the last moment that he appeared to sense his impending doom and turned to find himself nose to nose with what Anna could only describe as a force of nature.

'Lady Jarrow.' Mr Hoxley attempted to make a bow, though the endeavour was thwarted by the fact that her face was so close and he could hardly do so without butting her in the head.

'Hoxley.' The woman looked him up and down in a manner that suggested he was little more than a worm beneath her feet. 'I am *appalled*!'

Anna caught her breath and then clapped a hand over her mouth, repressing a strong urge to giggle. Lady Jarrow, as he'd just called her, wasn't making the slightest attempt to be discreet, every word she uttered clearly audible to their now captivated audience. A trumpet, an entire marching band even, would have made less of an impact.

'Madam.' Mr Hoxley looked as if he'd just developed some kind of fever, his cheeks flushing a vivid shade of crimson. 'I can't imagine what I've done to offend you.'

'Can't you? Because I've been hearing rumours about you. Disturbing rumours. Lechery! Wantonness! *Debauchery!* You ought to be ashamed of yourself.'

'I can assure you...'

'And with your mother's own lady's maid! Never mind how hard it is to find decent maids these days, but I hear the poor woman was dismissed after her indiscretion with you. Have you no shame?' She lifted her stick and prodded one end into his chest. 'Well? Defend yourself if you can!'

For an infinitesimal moment, Anna felt sorry for the victim of the harangue. He was producing a series of strangled-sounding gurgles, though he appeared to have nothing coherent to say for himself.

'If I were you, Hoxley...' Lady Jarrow took another step closer, seeming to grow in height while further diminishing his, forcing him to stagger backwards '...I would go home to the country and take some time to reflect on the virtues of a quiet life. You have a reasonable head upon your shoulders, boy. You ought to try using it once in a while instead of distressing your poor mother and father and *before* you get some other poor girl into trouble.'

As she uttered the last words her gaze flickered past Hoxley towards Henrietta, whose face was even redder and more stricken than his. Anna tightened her grip on the pillar, resisting the urge to rush out and comfort her, though she could see that the woman's words were having the desired effect. Henrietta was already backing away, fleeing the scene before Hoxley could say or do anything to stop her.

'Well, now.' Lady Jarrow's lips curved into a satisfied-looking smile. 'I believe that my work here is done.'

'My lady…'

Hoxley continued to splutter ineffectually as she turned her back on him, marching away as briskly as she'd come. Anna's gaze travelled with her, past the now busily gossiping audience to where Captain Delaney stood with his shoulders rigid and arms folded in front of him. He looked… *What* did he look? Angry, regretful, sombre? Somehow his expression suggested all three at once. Judging by the furious look that Hoxley was shooting in his direction, their friendship was well and truly over. And it was *her* doing. She'd asked Captain Delaney to side with her over his friend and he had. He'd saved Henrietta for her and she had no idea why.

She was still wondering when he unfolded his arms and looked straight at her, tipping his hat in a gesture of farewell before taking the older woman's arm and walking away.

Chapter Six

'Well, now, am I allowed to enquire what all that was about?' Samuel's grandfather spoke first, his tone faintly bewildered. 'You certainly sent that fellow away with his tail between his legs.'

'I was saving a damsel in distress, Hector.' The Baroness looked eminently pleased with herself. 'Even if she wasn't aware of it.'

'A damsel who didn't know she was in distress? How extraordinary. Well then, good show I'd say.'

'I couldn't have put it better myself.' Samuel threw her a grateful look. 'You're one in a thousand, Grandmother.'

'Is that all?'

'A million, then.'

'It was rather bracing, actually.' She chuckled. 'I never did like that Hoxley boy. What on earth persuaded you to take up with him again?'

'Old times' sake, I suppose.' Samuel shrugged. 'Only it turns out we don't have a great deal in common any more.'

'I'm relieved to hear it, but now I think it's time that you explained *why* you askcd mc to denounce the man in public. Not that I had any objections, but you don't usually ask others to fight your battles for you.'

'No.' Samuel frowned at the reminder. 'I wouldn't have done so today, except that it struck me as the most persuasive course of action.'

'I presume it had something to do with that very pretty blonde-haired girl hovering in the background?'

'Yes. She was intent on going with Ralph and I couldn't think of any other way to stop her.'

'And why exactly is her virtue any of *your* concern?' His grandmother fixed him with an interrogatory stare. 'I hope that you don't have similar designs on the girl yourself?'

'None at all, but I was asked to intervene by an acquaintance.'

'What kind of acquaintance?'

'Just somebody I met the other day.'

'Male or female?'

Samuel heaved a sigh. His grandmother was doing her best impression of a bloodhound, which meant that there was no escaping telling her the truth now. 'Miss Fortini, the owner of Belles, if you must know.'

'The bee girl?' His grandfather perked up at once. 'I didn't see her anywhere.'

'She was hiding behind a pillar.'

'Behind a pillar?' His grandmother sounded mystified. 'Then tell me, why were you intervening on behalf of a woman you only met a few days ago?'

'Because the situation was partly my fault. It's complicated. Suffice to say, I went along with a scheme of Ralph's that I shouldn't have and it was my responsibility to put things right.'

'And this Miss Fortini is *just* an acquaintance?'

'Yes. There's really nothing more to it.'

'Pity.' His grandfather stopped to rest on his cane. 'I would have applauded your good taste if there had been.'

'Hector!' his grandmother scolded. 'Good taste or not, *she* is a shopkeeper and *Samuel* might be an earl in another two months. If you're suggesting that he conduct some kind of dalliance then I shall have no qualms about denouncing both of you in public, too. As for anything more serious, she's entirely unsuitable.'

'Oh, I wouldn't say *entirely*.' The Baron sounded

unperturbed. 'Not when you consider who her mother is.'

'Who's her mother?' Samuel and his grandmother spoke at the same time.

'Oh, you know, the Duke of Messingham's youngest daughter, the one who ran off with a footman.' He scratched his head with his cane. 'It must be twenty-five years ago now. An Italian fellow, as I recall. It caused quite a scandal at the time.'

'You mean Elizabeth?' The Baroness looked confounded. 'Hector, do you mean to tell me that she's been living in Bath all this time and running a *biscuit* shop?'

'Aye, that's right, Elizabeth, that was her name. I say, you were quite close with the old Duchess once upon a time, weren't you?'

'Yes, although I thought she acted stupidly about the whole thing and I told her so. Of course she took umbrage, but I said my piece. There was no need to denounce the girl and cut her off completely. I'm sure she and that pig-headed husband of hers came to regret it, but of course, the rest of society took its cue from them.'

'Wait.' Samuel put a staying hand up. 'Are you telling me that Miss Annabelle Fortini is the granddaughter of the Duke of Messingham?'

'Oh, yes.' His grandfather nodded serenely.

'The former Duke, anyway. The new one's her uncle, I suppose, but there's no doubting the relationship. She has all those glorious curls just like her grandmother had. Her mother still has them, too, I expect, though I've only caught glimpses of her in the upstairs window.'

'And did it *never* occur to you to mention any of this before?' The Baroness sounded exasperated.

'Come to think of it, I did mean to say something once, but it must have slipped my mind. Then I probably thought I'd already told you.'

'Honestly, Hector! Where is this shop? I must go there and visit at once.'

'Why?' Samuel felt an ominous sense of dread.

'Because I want to see Elizabeth, of course. I remember her quite well, as it happens. She was a pretty young thing. Not bad on horseback at all and—'

'Grandmother,' he interrupted, trying to be tactful. 'After twenty-five years of being ostracised by society, don't you think it might be a bit of a shock if you just march in there, demanding to see her?'

'I can't see why.'

'Well…' Miss Fortini's disparaging comments about the aristocracy flitted through his mind.

No wonder she'd been so emphatic '…it might be that she doesn't want anything to do with society any more.'

'Don't be preposterous!'

'It's possible.' Not to mention that if he saw Miss Fortini again then she'd probably want to thank him for what had just happened with Henrietta and his conscience wouldn't be able to stand it. Then he'd *have* to explain exactly *why* he couldn't stand it and he really didn't want to do that. Far better for their acquaintance to end with a tender moment against a pillar than for it to be ruined with the truth.

'Harumph.' His grandmother clucked her tongue. 'Well, in that case go and invite her for tea tomorrow. Both of them, the mother *and* daughter.'

'I'm not sure…'

'Samuel.' His grandmother's expression turned to granite. 'I did a favour for you. *And* Miss Fortini as it turns out. Now it's your turn to do one for me.'

He grimaced, throwing a pleading look towards his grandfather, who shrugged and dropped his eyes to the pavement. 'Oh, very well.'

'Good. Off you go, then.'

'Now?'

'Yes, Hector and I are perfectly capable of

walking home by ourselves. Tell Elizabeth that tea is served at four o'clock sharp and that I shan't accept no for an answer. If she vexes me, I shall turn up on her doorstep myself.'

'And get some more biscuits while you're there!' his grandfather chimed in. 'I've already finished the last ones.'

There were three customers waiting on the doorstep when Anna got back to the shop, though fortunately, judging from the lack of any sound from upstairs, her mother was napping and unaware that anything out of the ordinary had happened. She apologised profusely, sold two small tins and one medium-sized one, then headed into the kitchen to make a cup of tea. She needed something to steady her nerves and not just because of what had *almost* happened to Henrietta. Her meeting with Captain Delaney had shaken her considerably, too, so much so that after half an hour her nerves were no closer to recovering.

She hadn't expected to *ever* see him again after their walk in the park, but particularly not when she'd been hiding behind a pillar. The idea that he'd approached specifically to talk to her had been somewhat flattering, though now she thought about it, he'd probably just wondered what she was doing. It must have looked rather as if she'd taken leave of her senses and her subsequent behaviour hadn't exactly helped. *Indiscreet* would be the polite way of describing it. And yet he'd *still* helped her, a fact that made her heart glow.

The doorbell tinkled, and she carried her cup of tea back through to the shop, her pulse jumping and then doubling in speed at the sight of Captain Delaney. *Again.* And this time there was no doubting the fact that he'd come to see her. Which was even more flattering. Positively thrilling, in fact, even if his expression was oddly sombre as he removed his bicorne hat and tucked it under one arm.

'Captain?' She smiled a welcome, smoothing one hand over her apron as she felt her cheeks flush with pleasure. 'Have you run out of biscuits already? I'd be glad to give you another tin as a thank you for your help this afternoon.'

'I don't believe that gratitude is in order.' His voice sounded stern, too.

'But it is. I'm grateful to both you and the lady. Your grandmother, I presume?'

'Yes. Lady Jarrow.'

'Please give her my thanks. The way she upbraided your friend was most impressive.'

'Upbraided…' If she wasn't mistaken, he grimaced. 'Yes, I suppose that's one way to put it.'

'Because you asked her to…' she faltered '…didn't you?'

'In a manner. That is, I explained the circumstances to her and she took the rest upon herself. As I fully expected her to, so…yes.'

'Then I'm indebted.'

'Don't be.' This time the grimace was unmistakable. 'I'm not proud of what I just did. In fact, I'm not proud of anything I've done in regard to you, Miss Fortini.' He snapped his feet together and lifted his shoulders as if he were facing a court martial. 'I've come to make a confession.'

'A confession?' She pressed a hand against her ribcage as her heart started to thump heavily inside it. Whatever he was about to say, she had the sudden, inescapable conviction that she didn't want to hear it. 'I don't understand.'

'Regarding the first time I visited your shop.' He held on to her gaze steadily. 'All of those things you said in the park the other evening about what you'd assumed about me and my motives were true. I *was* helping Mr Hoxley in his flirtation with your apprentice. I *was* attempting to distract you. I *didn't* intend to help him seduce her, but if I'd stopped to consider the matter fully…well, I ought not to have acted so irresponsibly. All I can say is that I'm ashamed of the part I played that day and I apologise for it.'

For a few horrified seconds, Anna thought that she must have misheard him. Or at least she tried to persuade herself that she had. Unfortunately it was impossible to ignore the truth. *Tricked!* She'd been tricked! *I'm ashamed of the part I played that day...* The words were accompanied by a dull thrumming sound in her ears, one that seemed to get louder and louder until it filled her whole head. Which was strange because she hadn't realised that emotions had sounds before, but that was what the thrumming surely was, a whole range of emotions all clamouring to be heard. Surprise, hurt, humiliation and a self-righteous fury that made her want to hurl the contents of her tea cup all over his smartly pressed, gleamingly spotless uniform.

Worst of all, however, was the disappointment, not just in him, but in herself. Hadn't she *known* that this was how the aristocracy behaved, gentlemen especially? Hadn't she *known* better than to trust one of them again? She'd thought she was older and wiser, but she'd been just as stupidly naive as she had been eight years ago, a fool to think any differently of this man just because he was a naval captain, too. He was just as dishonourable as his friend! Although, a small voice at the back of her mind argued, if that were truly the case then surely he wouldn't have apologised? But why on earth was she making excuses for him?

She slammed her cup down on the counter, clenching her teeth as she struggled to maintain an outward appearance of calm. 'So it was all a scheme?'

'Of sorts, yes.'

'And all those other things you said in the park? About the navy and Trafalgar? Were they all lies, too?'

'I've never lied to you, Miss Fortini.'

'No, you allowed me to deceive myself! You should at least have corrected me when I called you *honourable*!'

He inclined his head. 'Perhaps I should have, but I did attempt to make amends by separating your friend and Mr Hoxley that evening. I kept my word about that.'

She tossed her head scornfully, refusing to concede any point in his favour at all. She could feel a hot stinging sensation behind her eyes, but she'd be damned before she let herself cry in front of him. 'Very well then, you've confessed. *Now* you may leave. Forgive me if I ask you not to return.'

'As you wish, although I'm afraid there's one

other matter.' He looked uncomfortable. 'I've been sent with a commission from my grandmother. It seems that she and your mother are old acquaintances.'

Anna was vaguely aware of her mouth dropping open, though it took her a few moments to close it again, then a few more to actually think up an answer.

'I doubt that.'

'Her name is Elizabeth, is it not? Lady Elizabeth Holden, the Duke of Messingham's daughter?'

'Her name is Elizabeth Fortini.'

'Of course. I meant her maiden name.'

'That was twenty-five years ago. It's not a name she cares to be associated with any more.'

'I understand, but having only just discovered her identity my grandmother is eager to see her again.' He paused. 'She'd like to invite you both to tea tomorrow afternoon.'

'*No.*'

He lifted an eyebrow at the speed of her refusal. 'You don't wish to consult your mother about it?'

'I don't need to. I know what she'll say. No.'

'I see.' He looked as if he were about to say something else and then changed his mind. 'In that case I respect your decision, Miss Fortini, but I should warn you that my grandmother isn't very good at taking no for an answer.'

'Of course she isn't.' She allowed herself a small, cynical laugh. 'She's an aristocrat. You're all used to getting your own way, aren't you, especially with people like us? Well, for once she'll have to make an exception. If she wants to see my mother then she'll have to get through me and I'm not as easily frightened as Mr Hoxley.' She folded her arms. 'My mother and I don't want anything to do with you or any member of her old life.'

'Very well.' His gaze seemed to harden. 'Whatever you might think about me, however, I believe that my grandmother means well.'

'I've no interest in what she may or may not mean.' Anna stormed towards the door, flinging it open so hard that it bounced back off the wall. 'Now if that's all you have to say...'

'Just one more comment.' He came to stand in the doorway, putting his hat back on with one firm push. 'I believe that you spoke of a debt to my grandmother earlier. This seems like a curious way of repaying it.'

'So you think you can blackmail us into visiting her?'

'No, I just wanted to remind you of your own words.'

'They were spoken under a false estimation of your character!'

'None the less, my grandmother did you a good service today. As for your friend, Mr Hoxley would have continued to pursue her whether I'd accompanied him to your shop or not. In some ways, it was my involvement that saved her.'

'You have a strange sense of logic, sir.'

'Perhaps, but the situation has been resolved, has it not?'

'Get out!'

'I'm leaving.' He stepped out onto the street. 'However, in case you change your mind, my grandmother is currently renting a house on the Circus. Number Twelve. Tea is at four o'clock sharp.'

'A time when many of us are still working!' Anna threw him a look that she hoped conveyed a suitable degree of contempt before slamming the door in his face.

'Don't you like your mutton?'

'Mmm?' Anna looked up from the plate where she was absently pushing her food around with a fork. 'Oh, I'm sorry, Mama, it's good. I just have something on my mind.'

'Anything I can help with?'

'I'm not sure…' She glanced towards the clock

on the mantelpiece. It had been five hours since Captain Delaney had visited and revealed his true colours. Time enough to decide what to do, but her thoughts had been too much preoccupied with reliving their conversation, hearing his words over and over in her head. She still felt as angry as she had when she'd heard them the first time, but now the sense of humiliation was even worse. The horrible familiarity of it all made her feel sick.

She didn't want to mention the invitation he'd brought either, but judging by what she'd witnessed of his grandmother, she doubted she had any choice. She couldn't risk her mother being caught off guard and she could hardly barricade her upstairs if the old battle-axe came calling, which seemed a strong possibility. And she *did* owe her a debt of sorts. Perhaps just telling her mother about the invitation would be enough to discharge it…

'Mama, have you ever met Lady Jarrow?'

'My goodness, what a strange question!' Her mother lowered the fork that was halfway to her mouth. 'Yes, I knew her when I was a girl. She and my mother were friends. She used to visit the house and encourage us all to go riding. Why ever do you ask?'

'Oh…' Anna sliced a potato somewhat over-vigorously with her knife. 'I saw her today, that's all.'

'Really? I didn't think she ever came to Bath.'

'Well, she's definitely here now. She invited us to tea on the Circus tomorrow.'

'What?' Her mother looked taken aback. 'Just like that? Why?'

'It's a long story. Her grandson brought the invitation. Somehow she's found out who you are and she wants to see you again.'

'Goodness gracious.' Her mother's face brightened with a look that was both nostalgic and affectionate. 'Yes, that does sound like her. She never cared about anyone else's opinion, least of all the *ton's*. Was her grandson that man in naval uniform I saw leaving earlier? He was very handsome.'

'I didn't notice.' Anna shrugged dismissively. 'Anyway, I told him we wouldn't go.'

'But I'd be delighted to see her again!'

'What?' Anna pushed her plate away, her appetite vanishing completely. 'After the way society treated you and Father, why on earth would you want to spend time with any of them?'

'Because society as a whole might have treated us badly, but *she* didn't. She wasn't even in London at the time.'

'But won't it be upsetting to stir up old memories again?'

'*Very* old memories, dear, and I think I can manage.' Her mother reached across the table to pat one of her hands. 'I know that you've always tried to protect me from anyone I knew before my so-called disgrace, but there's really no need. I knew exactly what I was doing when I eloped *and* what the consequences would be. I'm not as delicate as you think. If I was, then your father and I would have chosen somewhere a lot less conspicuous than Bath to set up shop.'

'Yes, but…'

'Then it's decided. I'd very much like to see Georgiana again and you can close the shop early for once. If nothing else, a visit to the Baroness ought to be entertaining.'

'*Baroness?*'

'Yes. Didn't her grandson mention that?'

'No, he didn't.' Anna slumped down in her chair, her spirits sinking to new depths. *Of course* she'd be a baroness… 'Are you really sure about this?'

'Perfectly.' Her mother was positively beaming. 'I'm already looking forward it.'

Anna managed a wan smile in return. Her only hope was that a certain naval captain *wouldn't* be there.

Chapter Seven

'There—what did I tell you?' Lady Jarrow gave a nod of unabashed smugness at the sound of a knock on the front door. 'I've told Pearson to show them straight up, and they're on time, too, I'm pleased to say. You know how I despise tardiness.'

'I believe that you've mentioned it once or twice before.' Samuel put aside his copy of *Lyrical Ballads* with a wry smile. 'Although it might not be them.'

'Well, of course it's them. Who else would it be?'

He stood up, his gaze already travelling towards the drawing-room door. Personally he had significant doubts about the identity of the new arrivals, although he couldn't help but hope for another chance to apologise to Miss Fortini. Her refusal had been definite, to say the least, but then perhaps her mother had decided otherwise and it *did* seem unlikely to be anyone else. His grandmother's forthright opinions were notorious enough to put off all but the most thick-skinned of callers.

He'd barely had a chance to wonder, however, before the butler opened the door and Miss Fortini herself appeared. To his surprise, she looked comparatively neat for once, her dark hair scooped up into its usual high bun, though with the addition of two red bands across the top to hold stray curls in place. She was wearing a smart-looking dress, too, in the same practical style as her shop gown, but in a shade of light pink that perfectly complemented her complexion, making her skin glow with a luminous sheen.

The lady who entered behind her, meanwhile, looked nothing at all like someone who'd allegedly *ruined* herself. On the contrary, despite walking with a slight limp, she was tall and elegant, with chestnut-coloured ringlets and a remarkably youthful, unblemished countenance. She was also smiling, in contrast to her daughter, who looked as if she was only there under sufferance. Which, given her protestations of the previous day, was probably the case. Miss Fortini certainly didn't look in a very forgiving mood. He made her a formal bow, which she pointedly ignored.

'Elizabeth Holden.' As usual, his grandmother got straight to the point. 'So it is you.'

'It is, Lady Jarrow.' The older woman smiled and dipped into a stiff, but still graceful, curtsy, one that was belatedly copied with an air of reluctance and significantly less grace by the younger. 'May I present my daughter, Miss Annabelle Fortini?'

'The famous Belle, I presume?' His grandmother's gaze swept up and down appraisingly. 'I believe that you already know my grandson, Captain Samuel Delaney?'

'We've met.' Although judging by the belligerent tone of her voice, she wasn't overly thrilled by the fact.

'Lady Jarrow.' The mother spoke again, her voice sounding even warmer by contrast. 'What a pleasure it is to see you again after so many years. I was delighted to receive your invitation.'

'Indeed.' His grandmother's eyes lingered briefly on the daughter, making it obvious that her tone and reluctance to curtsy hadn't gone unnoticed. 'You must have been all of eighteen the last time I saw you.'

'I believe I was nineteen.'

'Well, take a seat beside me. We have a lot to

talk about and, as you can see, tea is all ready.' Her gaze shifted back towards Miss Fortini. 'Perhaps your daughter will be good enough to pour? If she'll oblige me, that is?'

Samuel winced, struck with the ominous mental image of two bulls locking horns. One of the bulls had youth, vitality and a decidedly obstinate chin, but the other had experience, indomitability and the advantage of home territory. There was a lengthy pause before the younger finally succumbed, appearing to grit her teeth as she spoke.

'It would be my pleasure.'

'It would be my pleasure, *my lady.*'

'Miss Fortini.' Samuel stepped forward, blocking her view of his grandmother's gloating expression, though unfortunately not her words. 'I'm pleased that you chose to accept the invitation after all.'

'Yes. Who would have poured the tea otherwise?'

'*Anna.*' Her mother's murmur was reproving. 'We're guests here.'

Fortunately, before anyone else could speak, the drawing-room door opened again and his grandfather entered the room, his arrival drawing a gasp from Miss Fortini.

'The bee man!' Her confrontational attitude fell away at once.

'Miss Anna.' His grandfather made a surprisingly gallant bow. 'How delightful to see you here. Not wearing yellow today, eh?'

'No, but…' She looked between him and the Baroness with an expression of consternation. 'Forgive me, but I had no idea…'

'That such a delightful old man was married to a harridan like me?' His grandmother's tone was even more gloating than before. 'Yes, most people are surprised when they find out. Hector, come and meet Elizabeth.'

'I hope that you haven't closed your shop up especially for us?' Samuel tried interceding again.

'Of course I—' Miss Fortini stopped midsentence, digging her teeth into her bottom lip as if she were actually biting back words before shaking her head. 'We close at four o'clock anyway. It was only a little early.'

'None the less, we really can't ask you to serve us after you've been working all day. I believe that I'm perfectly capable of wielding a teapot.' He gestured towards a sofa, waiting until she'd sat down before proceeding to pour and hand out the teacups himself, stifling a smile as she shot a particularly pointed look across the room towards his grandmother.

'There we are.' He took the last cup for himself and then headed towards the sofa. 'May I join you, Miss Fortini?'

'It's not my house. You may sit where you like.'

'True, but I thought perhaps we might be civil to each other.' He sat down, pretending not to notice the way her body tensed beside him. 'Would you care for a piece of cake?'

'No, thank you.'

'Naturally we wanted to serve Belles, but I'm afraid they've all been eaten. I'm not sure who ate the most, me or my grandfather.'

'Well, at least I can't fault your good taste.'

He inclined his head, wondering if she were ever going to relent. 'May I ask what changed your mind about coming today?'

'*I* didn't. It was my mother's decision.'

'Ah. Then I'm glad you told her about the invitation. I wasn't sure that you would.'

She gave him a sharp look. 'I admit I was surprised that she wanted to come, but she remembered your grandmother and thought it might be entertaining.'

'She obviously remembers her well. She likes you, by the way.'

'Who?' She looked surprised. 'Your grand-mother?'

'Yes. That was her being welcoming.'

'Welcoming?' Her expression was so incredulous that he smiled.

'Trust me, if she didn't like you then she would have found a way to get rid of you by now. She never lets anyone she doesn't like even sit down.'

'How does she stop them? By asking them to pour tea instead?'

'Usually she talks about ticks and worms and how she thinks she might have brought them in from the stables. Or, if she's not sure about a person, she mentions fleas.'

'Are they better than ticks and worms?'

'No, but horses don't get fleas. If the person knows that, she gives them a second chance. If she's in a tolerant mood, that is.'

'How generous.' Her gaze narrowed. 'Perhaps she's just tolerating me because she wants to speak with my mother?'

'That still wouldn't stop her from throwing you out.' He tipped his head forward and lowered his voice. 'So now I know why your mother is here, but why did *you* come, Miss Fortini?'

'To give her support, of course…' her shoulders stiffened '…and to make sure that she isn't upset.'

'Ah.' He glanced across to where Mrs Fortini and his grandmother were already deep in conversation. 'Fortunately she seems quite happy at the moment. In fact, you're the only one who looks *un*happy. Is it so very terrible being invited for tea?'

'That depends. Do you think I ought to feel honoured?' She lifted her cup to her lips and took a sip. 'I concede the tea itself is quite pleasant.'

'So it's just the company you find displeasing, then?' He leaned back on the sofa, throwing one leg casually over the other. 'The indolent aristocracy in their decadent lair?'

'I never said so.' She gave him a cutting look.

'Some words don't need to be spoken aloud. Your face is remarkably vocal. And of course you gave me the full force of your opinion yesterday.'

'It's not an opinion I apply to everybody. I find your grandfather, for example, to be quite charming.'

'Yes, I believe he's rather taken with you, too. I understand that you share a common interest in bees.'

'No-o.' An almost-smile danced about the edges of her lips. 'But I've learnt a great deal from him. About butterflies, too.' She glanced sideways and the smile vanished again. 'He's a *true* gentleman.'

'Unlike myself, obviously.' Samuel made an impatient gesture. 'You might be right, but I've already admitted and apologised for my ungentlemanly conduct the other day, Miss Fortini. I prefer not to be lectured ad nauseam.'

'I don't believe that I'm keeping you here, Captain. There are several other vacant chairs.'

'Yes, but since we're talking about behaviour, you tempt me to make certain ungallant observations.'

'Such as?'

'Such as that your mother's, for instance, is *exactly* what I would expect of a lady.'

'My mother was born a lady. *I* was not.' Her eyes flashed. 'Perhaps *I* don't care whether I behave like one or not.'

'Well then, you can rest easy, but perhaps neither of us has acquitted ourselves well of late.'

'I'm perfectly at ease with *my* behaviour, Captain.'

Samuel sighed, tempted to take her advice and go and sit somewhere else instead. Apparently she had no intention of forgiving him, in which case he had better things to do than drink tea and be insulted, but he made one last attempt anyway. 'How is your assistant? I hope that she wasn't too upset after yesterday.'

She gave him a sidelong look, the combative glint in her eye fading slightly. 'I believe she was, but she seems to have recovered from the shock. She came to work early this morning to help me with the baking. I think that she feels guilty for lying.'

'She ought to. It's fortunate she isn't in the navy.'

'Why?' She sounded reluctantly interested. 'What would the punishment be?'

He took a mouthful of tea, wondering how graphic he ought to be with his answer. 'Well, that would depend on the size of the lie. Answering back to an officer, for example, is punishable with a gagging. That means tying the offender up with an iron bar in their mouth. The same would follow for a small deception, but anything bigger and they'd be clapped in irons.'

'Irons?'

'Chained to the deck for everyone to see, at the mercy of the weather and waves.'

'How cruel.'

'That's one of the most minor punishments, actually. Some captains tie men to the rigging for days. Then there's flogging and "flogging around the fleet.".". That's the worst punishment of all, but it's reserved for the worst crimes, too.'

'It sounds barbaric.'

'It can be,' he agreed. 'There have been times when I wished I could have turned a blind eye to some misdemeanours, but a ship needs order.'

'You make me glad that I only run a shop. I wouldn't want to put Henrietta in irons just for one small lie. People make mistakes.'

He lifted an eyebrow, wondering if there was some hope of forgiveness for him after all. 'You know, there's a nautical term, Miss Fortini—to *parley*. It means a cessation of hostilities in order to discuss the terms of a truce. Perhaps we might consider something similar?'

She looked at him steadily for a long moment, then across the room towards her mother and his grandmother. 'Perhaps we should since they're getting along so well. Only that would imply the possibility of an eventual truce.'

'Well…' He sat forward, putting his tea aside and spreading his hands out in a conciliatory gesture. 'If we *were* to discuss terms, since we've already discussed what happened with your assistant, perhaps you might be persuaded to accept my apology?'

Her whole body seemed to bristle at the statement.

'Or…' he hurried on '…to accept that I mean it, whether you can forgive me or not?'

'All right.' She spoke slowly, as if she suspected some kind of trick. 'I can accept *that*, since you *did* make amends.'

'Thank you. In return, I shall ignore all your insults about the aristocracy.'

'You can ignore them all you want. It doesn't mean—'

'Ahem,' he interrupted her. '*Parley*, Miss Fortini.'

She pursed her lips. 'Oh, very well, but in that case we should simply agree to a state of parley *without* trying to establish an actual truce. We'll never agree on terms.'

'You might be right.' He felt a twinge of disappointment, though under the circumstances a tentative cessation of hostilities was probably the best he could hope for. Perhaps it was for the best, too. The more time he spent looking into those brown eyes, the more entrancing he found them. The more he found himself interested in her, too. Given her feelings about the aristocracy, however, he very much doubted the feeling was mutual, and if she ever found out about his possible inheritance then he suspected that even *parley* would be impossible. She'd probably turn away from him on the spot. On balance, it was probably best *not* to be entranced… 'That sounds like a compromise.'

'But I'm only agreeing for my mother's sake.'

'Naturally.' He leaned back against the sofa again. 'Speaking of your mother, I understand that she suffers from some kind of illness?'

'Yes. She has stiffness and swelling in her joints. It's not so bad at the moment, but it can be very painful for her.'

'I'm sorry to hear it.' He glanced discreetly across the room. 'I presume that she's seen a physician?'

'Yes. He tried blood-letting and leeches, all the usual things, but none of them did any good. Now he just prescribes the waters. He says that the symptoms can only be alleviated, not cured.'

'It must be very difficult for her.'

Her chin jutted upwards defensively. 'She's perfectly content, Captain. My mother has no regrets about her choices in life, even despite her condition now. My father did everything he could to make her comfortable. Contrary to everyone's expectations my parents were very much in love and happy together.'

'I'm sure they were. Your father passed away, I understand?'

'Yes, six years ago.' A wistful look came

over her face. 'He and I used to do all the baking together.'

'Surely you don't do it all by yourself now?'

'Yes, first thing in the morning.'

'*Every* morning?'

'Six days a week.'

'That sounds tiring.'

'I like to keep busy.' She lifted her chin even higher, though with an air of defiance that suggested the words were more of a stock answer than the truth.

'It still sounds tiring.'

'It's just how things are. Sometimes we find ourselves in situations that we didn't expect or choose, but that we can't walk away from, either.' A small frown puckered her brow as if she were afraid she'd just said too much. 'But I do miss my father a great deal. He called us *una squadra perfetta*.'

'A perfect team?'

'Yes.' Her eyes widened with obvious surprise. 'You speak Italian?'

'I'm a sailor. In the navy, it helps to learn a little of every language, although I'm not sure I'd get very far in conversation. You're fluent, I presume?'

'Especially about biscuits. My father always made a point of speaking Italian to my brother and me so we grew up learning two languages at once.'

'Ho bisogno di una corda?'

She stared at him blankly for a few seconds. 'You need some rope?'

'Not at this precise moment, but that's the kind of subject *I* can talk about. Or if you prefer, *Dove posso comprare dieci bottiglie di vino rosso*?'

'Where can you buy ten bottles of red wine?'

'For the Captain's table, just as important as rope.' He smiled and picked up his teacup again, regarding her quizzically as he drank. She was still as prickly as a hedgehog, though under the circumstances he couldn't particularly blame her. Given the way her parents had been ostracised by society, the details of which his grandmother had expounded to him earlier, he could understand her dislike of the aristocracy, too. She'd made her prejudice abundantly obvious, yet here she was, drinking tea with a baron and a baroness in one of the grandest houses in the city. It had to feel strange.

'I say.' The Baron crossed the room to settle himself in an armchair beside them. 'I'm afraid that my wife's trying to get your mother riding again, my dear.'

'Riding?' Miss Fortini echoed as if she didn't know what the word meant.

'Yes, she was quite an accomplished horse-woman in her day, so I've been told. Repeatedly. I ought to have known that was the reason Georgiana remembered her. It's usually something to do with horses. Those creatures are the bane of my life.'

'My mother *rides*?'

'Well, of course she rides!' the Baroness answered, though bellowed would have been a more fitting description. 'Show me a lady who doesn't!'

'That doesn't mean all of them enjoy it,' Samuel cut in.

'Nonsense. If they don't enjoy it, then they're not doing it properly. What about you, Miss Fortini? Do *you* enjoy it?'

'I don't know. I've never tried.'

'You've never—' For arguably the first time in her life, his grandmother appeared to be at a loss for words. 'But how on earth is that possible?'

'Quite easily when you don't own a horse.'

'But how do you go anywhere?'

'I have two perfectly good feet.'

'Then how do you travel longer distances?'

'We don't.' It was Mrs Fortini who spoke this

time. 'I'm afraid that we haven't travelled a great deal at all. My husband always wanted to take us to Italy, to show us where he grew up and introduce us to the rest of his family, but unfortunately our circumstances never allowed it.'

'Perhaps once the war is over...' The Baron's expression was kindly.

'No.' Mrs Fortini shook her head. 'It was *his* dream. We talked about it so often that it wouldn't feel right now to go without him. It would be too painful.'

'I know exactly what you mean.' His grandmother sounded uncharacteristically sympathetic. 'If I ever lost Hector, I should never set foot in a library again.'

'I can't imagine that affecting your life too badly, my dear. You hardly enter mine now.'

'Then I would never pick up another book as a matter of principle.'

'In that case I'm touched. I'd make a similar vow about stables, but we both know I'd never last a day without you.'

'Absolutely right.' His grandmother nodded vehemently, though with a tremulous note to her voice that Samuel found unsettling. Not for the first time since he'd joined them in Bath, he had the distinct impression that she was hiding something. Although if she didn't want to tell him, he knew that wild horses would never drag it from her.

'Which area of Italy was your husband from, Mrs Fortini?' he asked instead.

'From the north, an old Etruscan town close to Florence famous for olive trees, vineyards and Roman ruins. He came from a long line of bakers.' She gave a bittersweet smile. 'He used to say that he came to England for adventure, ended up as a footman, met me and went back to baking again.'

'Infinitely more interesting than being a footman, I should say.' His grandmother sniffed. 'I often wonder what they find to think about, standing around all day.'

'Perhaps you ought to let them sit down?' Miss Fortini's voice sounded altogether *too* innocent.

'I don't believe there really is much standing around,' her mother spoke gently. 'From what my husband told me, there was always work to do in a big house.'

'Hmm.' His grandmother's gaze honed in upon Miss Fortini. 'Would *you* like to visit Italy, Miss Annabelle?'

'Yes, very much. I'd like to visit Rome most of all.' Her face seemed to light up at the suggestion. 'Perhaps I ought to stow away on your ship, Captain Delaney? Or are you one of those sailors who object to having women on board?'

'Not at all. I wouldn't necessarily recommend the experience of living alongside eight hundred men, but I'll be sure to stow an extra hammock just in case.'

'That would be most obliging, thank you.'

Her lips curved and he sucked in a breath, struck by how pretty she was when she let her guard down. If she ever sheathed her prickles completely, then she might be quite beautiful. He felt unusually relaxed looking at her, too, which was curious since he'd felt almost permanently on edge ever since he'd set foot on shore; even more curious that someone so prickly could make him relax, but somehow she was doing it. Maybe it was those entrancing eyes, as dark as the sea at night and just as unfathomable. As tempestuous, too, able to leap from one emotion to another in a heartbeat. He felt as if he could gaze into them all day...

'*If* he goes back to sea, which I am determined he shall not,' his grandmother declared, breaking the mood abruptly.

'But why wouldn't he go back?' Miss Fortini seemed to give a small start, her expression arrested as she looked from him to his grandmother and back again. 'You said you loved being a sailor.'

'I do, but unfortunately my circumstances are such that it might not be possible.'

'Your injury?'

'Not exactly...' He threw a swift warning look at his grandmother, but it was too late. Her mouth was already opening and long experience told him there was no way to make it close again, or to speak over it, either. He was heading for rocks and keeling over at the same time, just when he'd thought he might make it through unscathed. In short, he was doomed.

'Because my grandson isn't just a naval captain, Miss Fortini. He's the future Earl of Staunton.'

And there it was. Shipwreck. So much for *parley*.

Chapter Eight

Anna hadn't intended to stand up, or to put it more accurately, leap out of her chair as if she'd just discovered that Captain Delaney was Napoleon in disguise. She'd had no conscious intention of moving at all, only somehow she was on her feet before her brain had a chance to catch up with her body, which seemed to have been galvanised into action by the Baroness's announcement.

The future Earl of Staunton.

She was vaguely aware of four pairs of eyes all fixed on her face, though she seemed unable to move or speak, her mind still reeling from the words. Instead, she took a deep breath, mentally reviewing all of the conversations she'd had so far with Captain Delaney, but nowhere, not once, *never* had he said anything to suggest that he was, could be, or had any intention of becoming an earl. It was a *title*, one of a collection of words that she loathed above all others in the English language. And not *just* the English language, either. In all languages. *Conte, Comte, Graf, Conde…* If she could have thought of any more examples, she would have hated them, too. It was bad enough that she was here in a house on the Circus, drinking tea with a baron and a baroness, but now one of them turned out to be an earl-in-waiting! All she wanted was to get out of the room and house as quickly as possible.

'Anna?' Her mother's expression was shocked. Which was no surprise since she was being unforgivably rude, even more than she'd been when they'd entered.

'I'm sorry, Mama, I'm just feeling…tired.' She found her voice finally. 'The shop was very busy today.'

'Oh…' Despite a valiant attempt to hide it, her mother looked embarrassed. 'I suppose we ought to be taking our leave anyway.'

'Well!' Lady Jarrow's voice conveyed exactly what she thought of her behaviour. '*You* must come again, Elizabeth.'

'I'd be delighted, my lady, and thank you for the invitation. I've enjoyed our talk very much.'

Anna watched, horrified, as her mother bent to kiss the older lady on the cheek. Meanwhile, she was acutely aware of Captain Delaney standing beside her. He'd risen to his feet at the same moment she had, though she'd kept her gaze studiously averted. Even without looking, however, she could tell that he appeared sombre. Strange that just a few moments ago she'd been *almost* enjoying his company again, enough to agree to a parley. Despite all her anger and humiliation, she'd found herself noticing little details about him, too, the fact that one of his eyes was subtly darker in colour to the other, the way he tapped his foot on the carpet as he talked, as if he were full of excess energy, and the scent of his cologne, light and citrusy, with a hint of salt that made her think of the sea. Or was she just imagining that? Now she felt as though she'd been tricked yet again, as if every time she found herself relenting towards him he revealed something else detestable...

'It's been charming to see you again, my dear.' The Baron stood and made a polite bow, causing her a sharp pang of guilt, then Captain Delaney himself stepped into her line of vision and she felt another pang of something more like regret, not for her behaviour, but for what she'd just learned about him. If it hadn't been for that...

She refused to complete the thought. If it hadn't been for that, then *nothing*. They belonged in different worlds. No matter who her mother was, or had been, *she* was a shopkeeper and she ought never to have agreed to come here. She might have known it would only lead to trouble.

'Miss Fortini.' His voice was even graver than his expression, as if he knew exactly what she was thinking. 'I believe this is goodbye.'

'Yes.' For some reason, she had difficulty uttering the word. It sounded so final, yet it *had* to be final, didn't it?

'Thank you for coming.'

'It was my pleasure,' she lied, so obviously and blatantly that his lips actually twitched upwards.

'I think not.'

'My mother's, then, Capt—' She corrected herself. 'My lord.'

'Not yet.' His smile reverted to a frown instantly. 'And perhaps never. Whether I inherit the earldom at all remains to be seen. There's still one significant matter to be decided.'

'Oh?' She tried not to sound too hopeful. 'What's that?'

He quirked an eyebrow, as if he were surprised by the question. Even for her, she was aware it was too direct. Impertinent, even. Whatever the matter was it was absolutely none of her business and it wasn't as if it would make any difference to her anyway. Yet for some reason she still wanted to know.

'Such as the gender of the former Earl's unborn child. I'm the Earl presumptive, but since the estate is entailed it's being held in abeyance. Nothing can be formally decided until the baby is born. If it's a boy, he inherits. If it's a girl...'

'Then you do?' She felt genuinely shocked. 'I didn't know such a thing was possible.'

'Neither did I until a few months ago. Frankly, I wish I didn't know it now, but that's the law. So, you see, it's not as simple as *just* going back to sea. Sometimes we find ourselves in situations we didn't expect or choose, but that we can't run away from, either. Wouldn't you agree, Miss Fortini?'

His expression seemed far too pointed suddenly, so much so that she couldn't think of an answer. Instead, she turned on her heel and fled.

'What on earth...?'

'I know, Mama.' Anna put her hands up the moment they were outside on the street. 'You don't have to say it.'

'I might not have to, but I'm your parent and I *will* say it!' To her surprise, her mother stormed on ahead without taking her arm. 'Your behaviour was appalling! We were there as their guests! Whatever must they think of me now?'

'There was nothing the matter with you!'

'Your behaviour reflects on me. They'll think I taught you no manners at all!'

'I never wanted to go there in the first place! You knew that.'

'That's still no excuse.' Her mother whirled around angrily. 'Your father would have been ashamed of you!'

'What?' Anna sucked in a breath of dismay. 'That's not true. Father hated the aristocracy!'

'No, he hated the way my family treated me. He resented all the whispering and gossip from people who came into the shop, too, but he would never have behaved so rudely to anyone and as his daughter you represent him. You just reinforced all the mean-spirited, snobbish comments anyone ever made about us!'

'But...'

'I shall walk on my own, thank you very much. The Baroness offered her carriage to take us home, but I declined. I don't believe that we deserve it.'

'What about your ankles? You'll hurt yourself if you're not careful.'

'I'll manage somehow. At this precise moment, I'm far too angry to care!'

Anna stood on the pavement gaping after her usually serene and calm-natured mother for a full minute before remembering where she was.

The Circus itself was intimidating enough with its three curved terraces forming a perfect circle, but the thought of all the eyes behind the windows made her feel even more self-conscious. Barons, earls, *dukes*…those were the sorts of people who lived here and she ought never to have come. Now look what had happened! She'd never seen or heard her mother so angry, though it took her several increasingly mortified laps of the central garden to concede that her accusations were true. She *had* behaved shamefully.

Unfortunately, that also meant there was only one thing she could do to make it right, though it took her another five minutes to summon the nerve. If she wasn't careful someone would call a constable to shoo her away, she thought with bleak amusement as she finally trudged back across the road and stopped back outside the gold-hued frontage of Number Twelve.

The black door looked even bigger and more looming than it had the first time, the Palladian style more striking, too. The style of the house actually varied from floor to floor, Doric on ground level, Ionic in the middle and Corinthian on top, as if any one of those styles on its own wasn't impressive enough! Even the butler who opened the door seemed more menacing than before, though he showed no sign of surprise and made no comment as he let her back into the hallway to wait while he checked whether the family she'd just left were still at home. Part of her hoped they decided they weren't, but a few moments later he returned, allowing her to precede him back up the staircase.

The inhabitants of the drawing room were positioned almost exactly as she'd left them. Only Captain Delaney had moved to the window, standing with his face half-averted and his arms clasped behind his back. He didn't bother to look around as she entered and she baulked at the idea that he might have witnessed her quarrel with her mother, but there was nothing for it now but to continue.

'Miss Fortini? Have you forgotten something, my dear?' The Baron greeted her with his usual kindly manner, and she dropped into a low, and this time sincere, curtsy.

'Yes.' She fixed her eyes on the carpet, deciding to get the worst of it over with. 'My manners. I misplaced them earlier. In fact, I think I might have left them behind in the shop. My behaviour this afternoon was rude and ungrateful and I've come to apologise. I beg that you don't take my actions as a reflection on either of my parents.'

She lifted her gaze slowly when she'd finished, surprised to find that Lady Jarrow had already risen to her feet.

'Miss Fortini…' the Baroness's tone was stentorian '…I've never thought it fair to judge children by their parents or vice versa and you strike me in particular as being very much your own person. I would never hold your mother responsible for your behaviour, ungrateful or otherwise. Come here and let me look at you.'

Anna took a few steps forward obediently, letting the older woman study her face in silence for a few seconds.

'You must take after your father in looks, although there's something of the Holdens about you, too. It's the curls, I suppose, *and* the stubborn streak. Still, I'm glad to see you have some spirit.'

'I still shouldn't have behaved so badly.'

The Baroness made a dismissive gesture. 'It was most diverting. I can't abide polite conversation. So many words and so little gets said. I presume that your mother just gave you a set-down? Well, if it makes you feel any better, I've had one, too. My grandson has just finished scolding me for chasing you away. He thinks that *I* behaved badly, if you can believe that.'

'Oh.' Anna glanced towards the window. Captain Delaney had finally turned around and was giving his grandmother a look that suggested his opinion on the subject hadn't much altered, though there was a glint of dark humour in his eyes, too. It made him look faintly sardonic, making her breath catch and the hairs on the back of her neck rise in a new and startling fashion.

'Perhaps we ought to agree that neither of us was at fault just to disprove them?' The Baroness gave her a nudge with one bony, but surprisingly powerful, elbow. 'Then we should become friends to spite them, eh?'

'I...' Anna felt her lips twitch despite herself. Being friends with a baroness wasn't something she'd ever imagined, but it was hard to resist the idea of this woman as an ally. 'I think that sounds like an excellent idea.'

'Good, then it's settled. We may consider ourselves friends. Although in that case, you'll have to learn to how to ride. All of my friends ride. I insist upon it.'

'But...'

'I'll provide lessons, of course.'

'Thank you, my lady...' Anna hastened to protest, 'but I'm afraid that it would be impossible. I have a shop to run and no free time for lessons.'

'Then we'll just have to make you some time.' The Baroness tossed her head imperiously. 'Mornings would probably be best.'

'I start baking at five o'clock, my lady.'

'Then I'll send a couple of my kitchen maids to you tomorrow. You can tell them what to do and then your mother can supervise, I suppose?'

'Well, ye-es.' Anna was surprised to find the idea decidedly tempting. She stole another glance towards the window, but Captain Delaney's expression was inscrutable. She had no idea what he thought of his grandmother's plan. Not that she cared about his opinion, either. It had nothing to do with him. With any luck she'd never have to see *him* again. He made her feel altogether too confused and distracted… 'But I wouldn't want to impose upon you.'

'Don't be ridiculous. I never allow anybody to impose, but if you *want* to be my friend…' the baroness gave her a look that dared her to contradict it '…then you must learn to ride or I shall refuse to receive you again. Now come to the house tomorrow morning at six o'clock sharp. You can have your first lesson and then tell me how you got on at breakfast.'

'Won't you be teaching me?'

'Good gracious, no. I have no patience with amateurs.' Lady Jarrow's eyes glittered with an expression that looked a lot like triumph. 'Samuel will teach you.'

Chapter Nine

'I can't.' Miss Fortini stared at the placid and sleepy-looking mount before her as if it were some kind of fire-breathing dragon.

'She's the most mild-mannered horse in the stables,' Samuel attempted to reassure her.

'I still can't.' She gestured at her skirts. 'I'm not properly dressed.'

He ran a hand over his chin and cleared his throat non-committally. There was really no disputing the statement, though he took the opportunity to steal a glance at her lower body anyway. Her dress was practical enough, but nothing like a riding habit, though it looked as if someone had attached some extra material to the skirts in a half-hearted attempt to conceal the fact. Of course if she didn't ride then presumably she didn't own a proper habit; something that he, or his grandmother anyway, ought to have considered.

'Horses don't care what you're wearing.' He looked up again before his staring became obvious. 'And we won't go outside the mews this morning. Today is just about getting you comfortable on horseback.'

'Today is a mistake.' She glared at the horse and then him. 'Surely your grandmother wasn't serious about what she said?'

'Does she strike you as a person who makes idle threats? She definitely won't receive you again if you don't even try.'

'Well, if this is some kind of punishment then it's not fair.'

He shrugged, though personally he was inclined to agree. It wasn't fair on *either* of them. Impressed though he'd been by her apology, which must have taken some considerable degree of courage, he hadn't been thrilled by the prospect of teaching her to ride, particularly after the way she'd reacted to the news of his possible inheritance. She'd seemed downright horrified at the time and apparently *still* was. She'd seemed determined to avoid looking him in the eye when they'd met on the Circus that morning, barely speaking a word until they'd reached the stables. Well, since she obviously found the company of an earl, even a potential one, so odious, the last thing he wanted to do was waste his time with teaching her. As usual, however, there was no gainsaying his grandmother, especially when she challenged him about *what else* he had to do. And when a small, contrary part of him still wanted to spend time with her... He shook his head at his own foolishness. If he searched the whole of England, he could hardly have found a woman more likely to reject him.

'Here, just stroke her. She won't bite.'

'How do you know?' Miss Fortini shot him a glance that suggested *she* might, though she did as he suggested anyway, placing her hand nervously on the mare's nose.

'That's it.' He nodded approvingly. 'Her name's Bramble and she's a sweet old thing.'

'How old?'

'Around thirty, I should think. I used to ride her when I was a boy before my grandmother insisted I have my own horse.'

For the first time that morning she looked him straight in the eye, her own curious. 'You seem very close to your grandparents.'

'I am. They practically raised me.'

'What happened to your parents?'

'Lots of things.' He gave her a pointed look. 'Don't think I don't know what you're doing. Stop trying to delay the inevitable.' He slotted his fingers together to make a step, putting an end to the subject of his parents. 'Now lean your shoulder against the saddle, put your foot in my hands and take it slowly.'

'Do you *promise* she's docile?'

'I doubt you could find a more docile creature in the whole of Bath. She's practically asleep on her feet right now.'

'All right...' Miss Fortini gave him a dubious look and then placed her right foot in his hands, exposing a length of shapely, be-stockinged calf all the way up from her ankle to her knee. Samuel looked before he could stop himself, so impressed that for an unguarded moment he was actually tempted to reach out and stroke *it*, too, though he had a feeling that would cause both her *and* the horse to bolt...

'There.' She placed one shoulder against the side saddle like he'd told her, sounding particularly pleased with herself despite the fact that one of her feet was still planted firmly on the ground. 'Now what?'

'Now grab hold of the pommel, keep your legs as straight as possible and pull yourself up.'

'Into the saddle?'

'That would be the general idea. I'll give your foot a push, too.' He lifted an eyebrow when she didn't move. 'Or I could just lift you if you prefer?'

'No.' Her answer came even quicker than he'd expected. 'I can do it.'

She closed her eyes, taking a deep breath before hoisting herself inelegantly into the saddle, exposing both of her calves and one thigh this time as she struggled to rearrange herself.

'Good.' Samuel made a show of adjusting the bridle, pretending not to have noticed. 'Now give her a nudge and we'll walk to the gate.'

'I thought you said we weren't going anywhere!'

'Miss Fortini.' He gritted his teeth, starting to lose patience. '*Must* we dispute every single detail? I said *to* the gate, not beyond it.'

'Oh... All right. How do I tell it which way to go?'

'*It* is a *her* and don't worry, I'll hold on to the bridle for now.' He handed over the reins, wrapping his fingers around hers for a brief, somewhat unnecessary moment, before leading them casually towards the gate. A quick sideways glance revealed Miss Fortini's expression to be one of sheer terror.

'Try to relax.' He rubbed a hand over Bramble's neck in case she sensed her rider's fear. 'And don't hold on to the reins too tightly.'

'I don't like being so high up.'

'You're really not.'

'I don't like wobbling from side to side, either.'

'You'll get used to it after a while. Try rolling with the movement. Imagine you're on a boat.'

'I've never been on a boat either and I *still* think this is unfair.' She sounded belligerent again. 'I apologised to your grandmother, I shouldn't have to risk my life, too.'

'You're not going to die, I promise.'

'What if I fall and break my legs? I suppose your grandmother *still* wouldn't receive me out of principle?'

'No one's ever accused her of being fair and reasonable.'

She made a harumphing sound. 'What about you? Are *you* fair and reasonable on board your ship, Captain?'

He looked around, surprised by the question. 'I hope so. I try to be.'

'Will you tell me more about life at sea?'

'What would you like to know?'

'Anything to distract me. Sebastian's a terrible correspondent.'

'Well, a lot of what we do can be quite monotonous and repetitive. Take the last two years, for example. We've spent most of the time blockading the French ports, stopping enemy ships from getting in or out, which meant a lot of time doing drills and preparing for battle, but not much real action.' They reached the gate and he started to lead them around in a half-circle. 'Although it paid off in the end. When it came to the battle, we were ten times better at reloading and aiming the cannons.'

'Wait!' Miss Fortini reached a hand out to stay him. 'We can keep going. Out of the mews, I mean.'

'Are you sure? I thought you were afraid of breaking your legs?'

'I still am, but if you can bear to live on a floating collection of planks for months on end then I can manage a short, *very short*, ride.' She looked down and then adjusted her skirts again. 'Just as long as you promise I'm not making a public spectacle of myself.'

'Not at all.'

'All right, then, let's go around to the Circus. If I can make it to the front door, then maybe your grandmother will say I've done enough.'

Samuel repressed a smile. If she thought that, then she really didn't know his grandmother very well. On the other hand, he had to admire her courage, *again*, although he really wished that he didn't. He glanced up as they turned out on to the street, just in time to see her twist her face away, a faint crease between her brows as if she'd just been studying him. The two of them must make a curious sight, he thought in amusement, her sitting stiff as a poker on horseback, him walking alongside like her groom, with one of his grandmother's maids following as a chaperon several feet behind. Not that he cared what anyone might think. He was just pleased that they weren't arguing any more. It felt like parley again, as if they might eventually come to terms after all…

'You're perfectly safe, Miss Fortini,' he reassured her. 'As for those floating planks, they're very well constructed.'

'That's what Sebastian tells me.'

'What made your brother join the navy?'

'The spirit of adventure, I suppose. He said he wanted to travel like our father had.' She smiled. 'Not that our father travelled *so* far, but Seb and I always loved listening to his stories when we were children. It was a sad day when we realised the ones about giants and dragons probably weren't true.'

'Didn't you crave adventure, as well?'

There was a significant pause. 'I'm a realist.'

'That wasn't the question.'

'It's my answer.' She jutted her chin into the air. 'What about you? Why did you join the navy? Was it a family career?'

'No, I'd never been to sea before I enlisted.'

'Neither had Sebastian. It didn't seem to worry him, but how could you possibly know whether or not you'd like it?'

'I didn't. I regretted the decision the moment we got out into open water.'

'Why?'

'Seasickness.'

She gave him an incredulous look. 'You get seasick?'

'Not any more, but to begin with…' he shook his head at the memory '…I was tempted to throw myself overboard a few times.'

'But how did you perform your duties? What did your Captain say?'

'Thankfully he was sympathetic. He said that he went through the same thing when he joined. A lot of sailors do. Even Nelson got seasick. It takes about three days, but eventually it settles down.'

'So if I stay on this horse for three days I'll start to feel better, too?'

'Perhaps, but I wouldn't put ideas into my grandmother's head if I were you.'

'Good point. She seems to think you won't go back to sea.'

'Only because she doesn't want me to. She was horrified when I joined the navy. I believe that my grandfather actually had to restrain her from visiting the Admiralty and demanding they release me.'

'So why *did* you join? If you didn't know whether you'd like it and your grandmother objected, why do it? It can't just be because water makes you feel calm.'

'No.' He looked around, surprised that she'd remembered that particular detail, though his other motives weren't something he particularly wanted to talk about. On the other hand, he had a feeling she wasn't about to drop the subject and he felt surprisingly comfortable talking to her. 'But I wanted a purpose in life and I was determined to make my own fortune. Which I did.'

'And now you might be an earl.' She was silent for a few moments. 'Why didn't you tell me about your situation before?'

'Why didn't you tell me your grandfather was a duke?' he rejoined. 'We all have secrets, Miss Fortini. Often they're things we don't care to discuss.'

Anna looked down at the reins twisted tight between her fingers. Captain Delaney was right, everyone had secrets and subjects they didn't like to talk about. She had no right to pry into his. She'd barely known him a week, after all, and yet somehow she couldn't seem to stop herself and it wasn't *just* to distract from the fact that she was sitting several feet above the ground...

'Don't you want the inheritance?' She couldn't seem to take her gaze off his face, either. 'You didn't sound very happy about it the other day.'

If she wasn't mistaken, his jaw clenched at the question. 'No, I don't want it.'

'Because you'd still prefer to make your own fortune?'

'Because of a lot of reasons.'

'What do the rest of your family think about it?'

He threw her an exasperated look. 'You ask a lot of questions, Miss Fortini.'

'I'm trying not to think about the horse.'

He rolled his eyes. 'Oh, very well. My grandparents *are* my family, all I've really known of it anyway. I have an uncle, too, my mother's older brother, but he spends most of his time in London. As for my parents, my father died when I was eleven and my mother married again a year later.'

'So you were never close to your father's family? That must be the side you've inherited from.'

'Yes, ironically, since they never wanted anything to do with me.'

'Why not?'

He sighed heavily. 'Because my father was the black sheep of his family. For very good reasons, I might add.'

'What were they?'

'Gambling and drinking mostly. Other vices, too, but I shan't offend your ears by listing them all. Suffice to say, he and Ralph have certain interests in common. His family disinherited him before he even met my mother.'

'Oh.' She tried not to sound too shocked. 'But she married him anyway?'

'He was very charming by all accounts. It was a whirlwind romance, though things soured quickly after the wedding. They had a very loud marriage.'

'Loud?'

'Turbulent. All of my earliest memories seem to involve shouting. It was a long time before I realised that wasn't how most people communicated. Eventually their marriage broke down and I barely saw him.'

'Did you miss him?'

'A great deal. He was my hero.' He glanced back over his shoulder. 'You have to understand, to a growing boy he was the best father you could possibly imagine, always ready to play games and make jokes. Completely irresponsible games, of course, and often dangerous, too, but I was happy. It was only much later that I realised his amusement came at the expense of everyone else around him. At the time, however, it was fun. There were no rules or constraints, so I ran wild.'

'What happened to him?'

'He ran away with another woman. Somebody else's woman, unfortunately. When the husband found them he challenged him to a duel. It was my father's fifth, but the first time he lost. He bled to death on Hampstead Heath all on his own.'

'I'm sorry.'

'So was I. In retrospect it was amazing he survived as long as he did, but at the time I was inconsolable. I decided the best way to pay tribute to my father was to emulate his bad behaviour so my mother packed me off to boarding school, which I hated.'

'How sad.' She gave him a sidelong look, sympathy now mingling with suspicion. His answers had become longer as he'd talked, as if once he'd started, he'd wanted to keep going. Overall she was starting to feel as though she understood him a bit better. As if she *liked* him more, too. The differences between him and Henrietta's would-be seducer were becoming more and more obvious, but he was *still* a gentleman. A possible earl, even if he didn't act in the way she expected.

'School is where I met Ralph,' he said, as if he'd somehow guessed the direction of her thoughts. 'We were close companions growing up.'

'I see.' She paused. 'In that case, I'm sorry for what I asked of you the other day.'

'It was the right thing to do for your friend.' He shrugged. 'In any case, I've barely seen him over the past ten years. One day I walked out of school and never went back.'

'You ran away?'

'I was sixteen and a barely average student. I doubt they cared very much. I went to London, but unfortunately I found that a life of dissipation didn't suit me. I didn't even enjoy it very much. Which is a long and roundabout way of explaining why I joined the navy.' He smiled. 'I've been a model of good behaviour ever since. Most of the time anyway.'

'What happened to your mother?'

He shook his head. 'You really *do* ask a lot of questions, don't you?'

'I'm interested. Families interest me.'

'She married again and moved to Cumberland to start a new family.'

'Brothers and sisters?'

'One half-sister, Susan.'

They rounded the corner of the Circus, and Anna looked up in surprise. Somehow their conversation had managed to distract her after all. So much so that she almost regretted it was coming to an end.

'Here we are.' Captain Delaney put a hand on Bramble's nose, bringing them to a halt. 'Without a single broken bone.'

'Only a few ragged nerves.' She smiled down at him. 'You do an excellent job of distracting a person, Captain.'

'With my tale of woe?' He raised an eyebrow ironically.

'It *is* a tale of woe,' she scolded him back. 'You may make light of it, but I know how terrible it is to be estranged from your family. I've seen how the experience affected my mother. I'm truly sorry for the situation with yours.'

'Thank you. Maybe we have something in common after all?' He held on to her gaze for so long that she felt heat start to spread up her throat and over her cheeks.

'Perhaps.' She tried to sound brisk. 'Now, how do I get down?'

'Here…' he reached a hand up, his voice husky '…jump down.'

'Just jump?' She slid her feet out of the stirrups, grabbing hold of his fingers and trying not to crush them.

'I'll catch you.'

'All right.' She launched herself into the air, flinging herself against him with such force that her bonnet smacked into his forehead.

'*Oomph*. I meant down, not outwards.'

'I'm sorry...but you said jump!' She clamped her arms around his neck as he staggered backwards.

'Maybe slide would have been a better word.' He laughed as he lowered her to her feet. 'Never mind, no harm done.'

She looked into his face, shocked by the sensation of his hard body against hers. She could feel the muscles of his neck and shoulders beneath her fingertips, large and thick and corded, *definitely not* parts of him she ought to be touching!

'Thank you, Captain.' She sprang backwards, remembering how many windows were facing towards them.

'You're welcome.' He bowed, though there was a look of something like regret on his face.

'I expect that your grandmother is waiting for me.' She shuffled one foot on the ground awkwardly.

'She doesn't wait for anybody. She's probably halfway through her bacon and eggs by now.'

'Will you be joining us?'

'I'll take Bramble back to the mews, but then I'll come and submit to coffee and a rigorous questioning. I ate breakfast an hour ago.'

'You must have been up early.'

'You're not the only one with an early rising profession, Miss Fortini.'

'Oh, yes, of course.' She felt her cheeks flush a vivid shade of crimson. 'Well, thank you for the lesson.' She started towards the front door, eager to get away before she looked like a beetroot. 'It was most instructive.'

'Miss Fortini?'

'Yes?' She turned back as he called after her, surprised to see a deep furrow between his brows.

'There's something I think you ought to know.' He paused as if he were giving her time to brace herself. 'My grandmother intends to re-introduce your mother into society.'

'What?' Her lips parted in surprise. 'How?'

'She intends to ask her to visit the Pump Rooms with her later this week.'

'But the scandal with my father…?'

'That was a quarter of a century ago. I believe that my grandmother intends to make a public show of accepting her and woe betide anyone who gets in the way.'

'Meaning me?'

'I hope not.' He gave her a searching look. 'No doubt she'll tell you herself at breakfast, but I wanted to forewarn you. If your mother accepts, then it's likely that word will get back to her— *your*—family, including the Dowager Duchess. From what I understand, she was never happy about the estrangement.'

'I see.' She swallowed, feeling as though all of her muscles were stiffening with tension. 'You mean you think that it might lead to a reconciliation?'

'It's a possibility. Although, considering that your mother accepted my grandmother's invitation to tea yesterday, it might be what she wants.'

'If it is, then I'll be happy for her.' Even to her own ears, the words sounded insincere.

'I'm sure your relatives would like to meet you, too.' His voice softened. 'You just said that estrangement was a terrible thing. Maybe it's a chance for you all to be reconciled.'

'Never!' she shot back before she could stop herself. 'They're aristocrats. I told you I don't want anything to do with any of them!'

'You already *are* one of *them*. You're more aristocratic than I am.' His eyes took on a hard gleam. 'As far as I'm aware, there are no dukes in my lineage.'

'How dare you?'

'You know, if you'd been paying attention, Miss Fortini, then you'd understand that I have about as much interest in being a part of the aristocracy as you do.' He spoke over her as she started to splutter. '*Unlike* you, however, I don't choose to dismiss a whole group of people out of stubbornness and prejudice.' He strode back to the mare, throwing the words over his shoulder as he walked away. 'Tell my grandmother I *won't* be joining you for coffee after all. As it turns out, I have better things to do.'

Chapter Ten

❧～～～～～❧

It wasn't that she resented her mother, Anna told herself, repeatedly and at great length, over the course of the following two weeks. She was glad to see her looking happy again, happier than she'd looked in years, in fact. Now she wondered if perhaps her mother had been lonely and *she'd* simply been too busy in the shop to notice. The change in her demeanour was striking. Elizabeth Fortini seemed like a whole new woman, a physically stiffer, but mentally refreshed version of her old self. She visited the Pump Rooms with the Baroness most days, took tea with her every afternoon and had even dined at the Circus on several occasions.

Anna had chosen *not* to accompany them. Firstly, because she had a business to run. Secondly, because she had a point to prove, even if it was hard to prove anything to a man she hadn't seen since he'd announced he had 'better things to do' and then abandoned her on his grandmother's doorstep. He hadn't visited the shop or given her any more lessons since, though as she hadn't gone back to the mews either she supposed she could hardly blame him for that.

It was as if he'd simply forgotten her existence. Which was *exactly* what she ought to do in return, Anna thought bitterly, except that her mind seemed to be working against her. Much as she hated to admit it, she already thought about him far too often for comfort. It was bad enough at night when her dreams were haunted by the image of a man with auburn hair and silvery eyes, but every time she sold a big tin or caught a glimpse of a naval uniform outside the shop window she found herself feeling alarmingly nostalgic.

It didn't help that her mother mentioned him quite so frequently, making it obvious that she *was* seeing him. *Such* a kind gentleman, *so* dashing and thoughtful and polite, and *such* a hero, too! Had she heard the story of his daring manoeuvre at Trafalgar? And what a bizarre situation to find himself in, especially when he yearned to go back to sea! But *surely* he'd make a very competent earl if it came to it… Anna listened with every outward appearance of composure, secretly thinking that if she heard the name Captain Samuel Delaney one more time, she would scream.

'Lady Jarrow intends to throw an evening party next week,' her mother finally announced one morning in the kitchen.

'Does she?' Anna paused in the act of spearing bread on to a toasting fork.

'Yes.' There was a telling pause. 'We're both invited.'

'Oh.'

'She's rather domineering, I admit, but her heart's in the right place.'

'Mmm…' Anna murmured non-committally. She hadn't seen the Baroness since that first breakfast when, still shaking with anger over Captain Delaney's accusations, she'd announced that she'd had enough of horses for ever. To her surprise, instead of delivering a dressing-down, Lady Jarrow had simply told her to come back when she was ready.

'I'm grateful for all the attention that she's shown me over the past couple of weeks,' her mother continued. 'I'd like to attend.'

'Then you should.'

'*With* you.'

'Mama…'

'Just wait a moment.' Her mother lifted a

hand. 'I *know* what you think of the aristocracy. You have a lot of ideas about who you are and where you belong. It's hardly surprising given our family's circumstances, but I'm afraid you may have become overly prejudiced, my dear.'

Anna lowered the toasting fork slowly. *Prejudiced.* It was what Captain Delaney had called her before he'd stormed away… She'd resented the accusation then and it still rankled. Not because it wasn't true, but because nobody, not even her mother, knew the real reasons behind it. As much as she resented the way her parents had been treated by society, she hadn't *always* detested the aristocracy, but eight years ago she'd learnt better than to trust them…

'If I am, then they deserve it.' She answered stubbornly.

'Do you forget that I was born *Lady* Elizabeth Holden?'

'You're different. You ran away from all that.'

'I still loved my family a great deal. It broke my heart to leave them, but I knew it was the only way I could be with your father. I only wish there had been another way. I miss them even now.'

'Mama, they disowned you!'

'That doesn't mean they were happy about it. My father was a proud man. I never expected him to accept or forgive what I did, but I do believe that he loved me, and continued to love me, in his own way. I wanted to go to his funeral, but your Uncle Anthony would have been horrified. They were always very alike.'

Anna lifted the toasting fork again, holding it close to the fireplace. 'What about my other uncle, your youngest brother?'

'Tobias? Oh, he was more like our mother. I think he would have forgiven me. With him and her, I think there might still be a chance of reconciliation, even after all these years.'

'So you *want* to see them again?'

'Yes.' Her mother didn't hesitate. 'Yes, I do.'

'What about Father? If you go back to that life, then it'll be like he never existed.'

'Except that I have you and Sebastian and many years of happy marriage to remember him by.' Her mother's gaze warmed. 'It's not a betrayal of your father to move on. He always felt bad about the rift with my family and if he were still here then I know he'd want me to be happy.' Her mother's hand curled around her arm, drawing the fork back before the toast burned. 'He would have wanted you and Sebastian to be reconciled with my family, as well. He always wanted to give you more in life.'

'He gave us everything we needed. You both did.'

'Yes, but there are other ways that my family could help you.' Her mother smiled hopefully. 'Come to the evening party with me. Let yourself have some fun. You work too hard.'

'I don't know...'

'Anna.' Her mother's voice turned slightly chiding. 'Sometimes it's easier to stay in our own little worlds than venture out, but prejudice has a way of shrinking the opportunities around us. If you aren't careful the person you end up hurting is yourself. Bitterness and resentment aren't very attractive qualities.'

'Maybe I like my life the way it is.'

'You can still like it and come to the party, too. Please, as a favour for me.'

Anna groaned, dropping the piece of toast on to a plate. Doing a favour for her mother was all well and good, but the thought of spending an evening with a group of people she'd spent years resenting gave her the shudders. On the other hand, maybe she *had* become too prejudiced. Maybe she'd let her feelings about what had happened eight years ago control her to the point that she really *had* become afraid to leave her 'own little world' as her mother called it? Maybe she'd overreacted when Captain Delaney had told her about his grandmother's plan, even if it hadn't been for the reasons he'd thought?

Maybe that was why she'd refused to forgive him for his behaviour when they'd first met despite his apology, too? And maybe she was holding him accountable for the sins of a man he'd never met and knew nothing about?

The memory of a letter and an innocent walk and an alleyway floated into her mind before she buried it quickly, deep down where it belonged.

'What would I even wear, Mama?' She tried a different tack instead. 'I don't want to waste money on a gown that I'll only wear once and, before you say anything, I don't want the Baroness's charity.'

'Neither do I.'

'So unless I can persuade someone to purchase a year's supply of biscuits in one go...'

'You won't need to. I have some money saved.'

'Not for a dress, Mama.'

'Yes, for a dress. We'll buy some material and make something new.'

'How? Your hands are too swollen for you to sew and I'm terrible at it.'

'I'm not.' Henrietta stuck her head around the doorway that led to the shop. 'I'm sorry, I wasn't eavesdropping, but I couldn't help but overhear. *I* could make you a dress.'

'I couldn't ask you to...'

'You're not. I'm offering and I'm good at

making clothes. Please let me. I want to make amends.'

'What for?' Anna offered her a piece of toast, but Henrietta only looked contrite.

'For something foolish I did a while ago. I lied to you about it, but I learnt my lesson and I'll never do it again. I want to make something of myself, just like you.' She took a deep breath, as if she were summoning her nerve for something. 'And you know that my brother's wife is having another baby? Well, it's getting crowded at their house and I wondered whether you might let me move in here with you? I don't mean upstairs. I could make a bed up in the kitchen every night so that I'd be here to help you bake in the mornings. If you can forgive me for lying, that is?'

'Of course I forgive you...' Anna smiled '...but I'm afraid I don't have any spare money to pay you.'

'You don't have to. Just letting me stay would be enough. And I have some new ideas for the shop we could try, like taking a basket out every morning and selling biscuits outside the Pump Rooms or on Pulteney Bridge? Or inventing a new variety and making a big announcement about its arrival?'

'Well...' Anna looked from Henrietta to her mother and back again '...in that case, what can

I say except yes? *And* no. That is, yes, you can stay here, but, no, you can't sleep in the kitchen. You can share my room.'

'Really?' Henrietta hugged her so enthusiastically that Anna had to drop the toasting fork in order to avoid a painful accident. 'Thank you. You won't regret it, I promise.'

'Of course we won't.' Her mother nodded approvingly. 'And we'll make the dress together. I'm sure there are still some tasks I can do.'

'We'll make the most beautiful dress you've ever set eyes on.' Henrietta clasped her hands together dreamily. 'It sounds just like a fairy tale. You're going to a ball.'

'An evening party, not a ball.' Anna felt a fresh burst of anxiety at the thought. 'What if someone recognises me from the shop?'

'Then you'll do as I do. Hold your head up high and be proud of who you are.' Her mother tossed her curls as if to illustrate the point. 'You'll say that your name is Miss Annabelle Fortini, owner of a *very* successful confectionery business.'

'They might say there's a bad smell in the air.'

'If they do, then *I* shall tell them what I think of them.' Her mother's eyes took on a martial gleam. 'Then I'll set Lady Jarrow on them, just for fun.'

'I still don't know…' Anna bit down on her bottom lip. She wasn't ashamed of who she was and she wasn't *really* afraid of being insulted, not in the Baroness's own house, but it all seemed so unbelievable. She was being invited back into society along with her mother. It was the opposite of anything she'd ever expected to happen, but perhaps her mother was right and she was only hurting herself by holding on to the past. Perhaps it *was* time to move on. And perhaps she wanted to see Captain Delaney again. Perhaps she could trust him, too?

Her heart gave a little leap at the thought.

Chapter Eleven

An evening party… Samuel groaned, his already depressed spirits sinking even lower as he descended the stairs of his grandparents' house on the Circus. It wasn't that he was inherently misanthropic, he reminded himself, just that he was altogether *too* aware of the whispers and curious glances that followed him whenever he appeared in public. As his grandmother had predicted, a number of ambitious parents had recently experienced an impulse to visit Bath before the start of the London Season, making a point of introducing him to their young and unattached daughters, all of whom expressed a profound admiration for the navy while being unable to name a single ship.

His mood that day hadn't been helped by the receipt of two letters, one from his lawyer advising him, yet again, to visit Staunton, the other from his friend Harry Cartwright telling him, somewhat apologetically, that he'd just been awarded a new command and was preparing to sail from Plymouth. As happy as he'd been for his old comrade, to whom he'd immediately sent a letter of congratulation, Samuel still couldn't help but feel jealous. If it hadn't been for the whole damnable situation over his possible inheritance, then he might have been in a similar position, about to leave England on his own command, but the chances of that *ever* happening were receding more each day.

He'd spent most of the afternoon riding over the Downs, trying to ease the feeling of restlessness that had seemed to grow stronger over the past couple of weeks. The purposeless hours were becoming harder and harder to bear, especially when his thoughts drifted so often towards a pair of brown eyes that both entranced and infuriated him in equal measure. Since he didn't want to waste his days with idle pursuits and there was only so much reading a man could take, he'd started trying to fill them with exercise instead, though unfortunately, today's ride had done nothing to soothe his spirits or distract his thoughts. He couldn't even call himself tired. He felt trapped between two lives, two paths and purposes, and there was nothing at all he could do about any of it for another month and a half but wait.

He crossed the hall with the enthusiasm of a man about to run the gauntlet. By the sound of it, most of the guests had already arrived, a hundred of them at least, all apparently talking at once. When his grandmother decided to do something, she did it properly and she was re-launching the Fortinis back into society with a vengeance. Mrs Fortini, whom he liked and admired, and Miss Fortini, whom he did not.

Strictly speaking, of course, that wasn't true. He *did* like her, only her prejudiced, prickly behaviour made it impossible to enjoy her company for long. As for admiring, well, obviously it was different from the way he admired her mother. *Very* different, in fact, and with a very different effect. The last time he'd seen her, he'd admired her legs and that brief glimpse of thigh so much that he'd found them impossible to forget. Typical that the one woman he was interested in was also the one most likely to spurn him!

He took a deep, fortifying breath outside the drawing room and then stopped abruptly, struck by the sight of the very legs in question. They were covered up, of course, but the light from the vast candelabrum behind her outlined the contours of what he now realised was a quite

spectacular body. The gown she was wearing
made a striking contrast to her practical shop
clothes, in periwinkle-blue and with a fashion-
ably high waist, a low scooped neckline, short
puffed sleeves and wisps of delicate lace around
the hem. Her arms, meanwhile, were encased in
white, tight-fitting gloves and a pair of turquoise
earrings hung suspended from her ears. With her
dark hair fastened into a low knot at the back
of her neck, though still with corkscrew ringlets framing the sides of her face, she somehow
managed to look understated, ethereal and stun-
ningly attractive all at the same time.

What the hell had he been thinking, avoiding
her company for three whole weeks?

He cleared his throat, willing himself to look
away, but his eyes refused to so much as blink.
In a room filled with dozens upon dozens of
people, he seemed unable to focus on anyone but
her. His heart was hammering so fast he actually felt slightly winded, panting with a sudden
onslaught of desire.

Despite that, he was aware of a feeling of irritation, too. After everything she'd said about
the aristocracy, she appeared to be deep in conversation with Augustus Lambert—a marquess,
no less. Not only that, but she was actually looking him in the eye and smiling. As if she were

enjoying his company! As if she weren't determined to argue at every available opportunity! As if she could smile at a marquess but not at a potential earl!

Her gaze shifted towards him suddenly, as if she'd somehow sensed the words in his head, her lips forming a small O shape and her skin flushing a dusky and becoming shade of pink. Even the tops of her breasts appeared to be blushing, he noticed, not that he ought to have noticed, except that somehow he couldn't help it. He felt as if his eyes were being dragged of their own volition down to the swell of her usually covered bosom. If he hadn't known how he wanted to spend his free time before, he certainly did now and it involved taking her straight upstairs…

'Samuel!' For once he was glad of his grandmother's booming voice, bringing him back to his senses. 'Have your feet stopped working?'

'Apologies, Grandmother.' He forced himself to smile, though it was hard to know what expression to adopt when his body was strung so tight. 'I thought you said this was a party, not a squash. No doubt the evening will be declared a great success.'

'Harumph.' His grandmother looked disgruntled by the compliment. Her own fashion choices were the direct opposite of understatement, a vision of copper-coloured fabric, diamond jewellery and tall peacock feathers. 'I had no idea so much work was involved. I've had to clear out nearly all of my furniture, pull up the carpets and spend a small fortune on food and wine. And *plants*!'

'Plants?'

'My housekeeper informed me that plants were a must. Why, I have no idea, but as you can see, for once I capitulated. It looks like a forest in here.'

'Yes.' He glanced around, noticing a surprising new abundance of shrubbery. 'It certainly looks greener than usual.'

'It's ridiculous. Goodness knows what I'm supposed to do with it all afterwards. I certainly shan't be throwing another party in a hurry.' She fixed him with a steely look. 'I expected you here earlier.'

'I went for a ride and stayed out longer than I intended.'

'If that's supposed to be an excuse, then I don't accept it. You ought to have been here on the receiving line.'

'My apologies. I didn't think that you'd need me.'

'Honestly, Samuel, you're getting as bad as your grandfather.' She gave him an exasperated look. 'Fortunately, despite your absence, things have been going well. Even Miss Fortini appears to be on her best behaviour.'

'Indeed?'

'Yes, she's barely rolled her eyes all evening. She's been much admired, too, although most of the gentlemen have been more discreet about it than you, I'm pleased to say. I was afraid your gaze might burn a hole in her dress.'

'Tactfully put, as always, Grandmother, but you're right, I shouldn't have stared. I was just surprised to see her.'

'Really?' His grandmother's voice was blatantly sceptical. 'Then I shall have to take care not to startle you in the future, Samuel, if that's the effect.'

'You stopped surprising me a good twenty years ago, Grandmother. Now if you'll excuse me, I ought to go and apologise.'

'Do that and fix whatever squabble you two have had while you're there.'

He tipped his head, refusing to either acknowledge or contradict the comment, before making a beeline straight across the room.

'Miss Fortini.' He bowed gallantly. 'I've just been admonished for staring. May I say how lovely you look this evening?'

'Thank you, Captain.' She bobbed a small

curtsy in return, her pupils widening a fraction as their eyes met, then to his surprise extended a gloved hand. He accepted it at once and pressed his lips lightly against her fingers, better prepared this time for the surge of desire that immediately raced through his body. It was like an oncoming tide, building in strength the closer he got to her. He wanted to get closer still, to touch a lot more than her hand, too, to gather her into his arms and...

'Lambert.' He let her go again reluctantly, turning towards her companion with gritted teeth and a forced smile. 'How do you do?'

'Very well, Delaney.' Fortunately the Marquess seemed unaware of any tension. 'But how could I not be in such charming company?'

'Indeed. Miss Fortini is very charming.'

'She's just been telling me that she's Belle. *The* Belle.'

'Just Belle.' The lady in question looked faintly embarrassed, though her gaze never wavered from the Marquess. 'Although I've always preferred the name Anna.'

'But that's far too plain!' Lambert put a hand over his heart. 'A beautiful woman should have a beautiful name and you're quite the most exquisite diamond in the room this evening, Miss Fortini.'

'I'd keep my voice down if I were you.' Samuel felt a primitive urge to raise his fists. The way Lambert was looking at her was altogether too appreciative. 'My grandmother takes offence very easily.'

'Ah.' The other man's gaze flickered with alarm towards the Baroness. 'Well, naturally I didn't mean to offend...'

'Your grandmother said you were out riding.' Miss Fortini came to the Marquess's rescue.

'Yes, over the Downs. It was such a beautiful day, I couldn't resist the sunshine.' He paused, waiting for some disparaging comment about the luxury of not having to work, but she only smiled.

'Then I'm glad you made it back in time for the party. It's nice to see a familiar face.'

'A friendly one, too, I hope?' He smiled back, suppressing a look of surprise. After the way they'd parted the last time, he'd expected her to still be angry with him. Or aloof at the very least. Instead, she seemed to have sheathed all her prickles, actually looking pleased to see him, as pleased as he was to see her. He was struck with the realisation that he really *had* missed her. Those gorgeous brown eyes, that low voice capable of leaping into sudden animation, that rarely bestowed smile, although she seemed to have been bestowing it quite liberally this evening... He felt an unwonted pang of jealousy.

'Of course a friendly one.' A mischievous gleam appeared in her eyes. 'I just thought you might have had something better to do.'

That time he had to stifle a laugh. 'At this precise moment, I can't think of anything else I'd rather be doing. Perhaps you'd care to join me for a stroll about the room?' He held an arm out, not that there was much possibility of strolling anywhere in such a crush, but he felt suddenly determined to separate her from Lambert.

'I'd be delighted, Captain. Excuse me, my lord.' Her black eyelashes fluttered as she dipped into another curtsy and then threaded her hand through his arm, allowing him to draw her along the side of the room.

'You seem different, Miss Fortini.' Samuel tilted his head towards hers as they walked, his lips grazing inadvertently against one of her curls, though he still had to raise his voice to be heard above the crowd.

'That's because I made up my mind to enjoy myself. According to my mother I don't do it often enough so I've decided to get out of my shop and start.'

'I'm glad to hear it. How are the riding lessons going?'

She gave him a startled look, as if she hadn't expected him to broach the subject. 'Your grandmother didn't tell you?'

'Tell me what?'

'That I never came back after...well, the last time. Only for some reason she still insists on sending her maids to help me with the baking every morning. I've told them they don't need to, but they say they daren't not.'

'Do you blame them?'

'Not at all. To be honest, it's quite pleasant. We get the work done in half the time, then we all sit around the table and eat breakfast.'

'Then I'm pleased you're enjoying a rest.'

'I am and I have to admit the extra sleep has been very nice.' Her expression turned faintly guilty. 'The other morning I stayed in bed until seven o'clock.'

'Well, Miss Fortini, I'm shocked...' He smiled, although the mention of bed made his breeches feel somewhat tighter. 'And how was the experience?'

'Wonderful.' Her lips widened and he felt a glow in his chest, as if her smile were actually warming his insides in several different locations now.

'In that case, I'm glad my grandmother is so domineering. Just this once.'

'Talking about me again?' The Baroness swooped down on them suddenly, peacock feathers waving on top of her elaborately arranged hairstyle.

'Only in the nicest possible terms, Grandmother.'

'I don't believe it.' She dipped a feather towards his companion. 'He's been in a perfectly foul temper for the past three weeks. I would have sent him away from Bath if I hadn't thought he'd take it as an opportunity to run back to sea again.'

'Well, he's being perfectly charming now.' Miss Fortini smiled. To his surprise, despite the fact that she claimed to have spurned further riding lessons, there didn't appear to be any friction between her and his grandmother.

'Then it must be thanks to your company. I insist upon the pair of you sitting together at supper.'

'Oh, I don't know…' She glanced towards him uncertainly.

'Unless you're promised elsewhere?' He lifted an eyebrow, almost wishing that he'd punched Lambert when he'd had the chance.

'No, but I wouldn't want you to feel obligated.'

'I'd be honoured.'

'Good. Then it's settled,' the Baroness announced with an air of finality. 'Now, where is your grandfather? If he's hiding in his library, then we shall have words.'

Samuel watched as she sallied forth again, struck with the distinct impression that his grandmother was matchmaking. Which was a ridiculous idea given the uncertainty of his current circumstances, only on this particular occasion he didn't seem to mind...

'Miss Fortini.' He took the opportunity to draw her into an alcove half-hidden behind a tall potted palm. 'I believe that I owe you an apology for the way we parted three weeks ago.'

'Anna,' she corrected him. 'You can call me Anna and I believe I owe you one, too. In fact, I owe you two. One for my behaviour that morning and one for not accepting your last apology about Henrietta. I should have forgiven you.'

The words caught him by surprise. 'Well then, perhaps our apologies cancel each other out? And *my* name, incidentally, is Samuel.'

'Samuel.' Her eyelashes fluttered. 'I thought about some of the things you said and I realised that you were right. I *have* been too prejudiced.'

'I still shouldn't have spoken so bluntly.'

'Yes, you should have. I'd be a hypocrite if I objected to plain speaking just because it was about me.'

'Are you suggesting some kind of parley, Miss Forti—*Anna*?'

'No.' She shook her head though her eyes were soft. 'I'm suggesting a formal declaration of truce, if you'll agree to one?'

'Then a truce it is, but I'm still sorry.'

'Apology accepted. And, while we're apologising to each other, I'm sorry if you've had a difficult time since. It must be very hard, waiting to find out whether or not you're going to inherit.'

'It is. I like visiting my grandparents, but my ship is my home. I miss having a sense of purpose, too. Waiting around like this makes me feel...'

'Adrift?'

'Something like that.' He made a wry face. 'Forgive me, I don't mean to complain, especially when my position is in many respects so enviable.'

'But it can be hard to remember how we *ought* to feel.' She put a hand on his forearm, her tone earnest. 'I do understand what you mean. Everyone wants to have control over their own life. I *have* a sense of belonging and purpose. My parents actually *gave* me a shop and yet sometimes I feel as if I'm drifting along, too, in a current I can't escape.'

'How so?' He let his gaze drift over her face. They were standing so close that if he moved his own forward just a little…

'Sometimes I wish I could have chosen a role for myself, as you did with the navy.'

'Indeed? What is it that you would have chosen?'

She lifted her shoulders and then dropped them again with a sigh. 'I don't know. I suppose I don't let myself think about it because there's nothing I can do to change anything. It was always just presumed that I would take over Belles, but if there was one thing I could change…' She stopped and bit her lip.

'Yes?'

'Nothing. It's not important.'

'It is to me.'

'Well…' She threw a quick glance over her shoulder as if she were afraid of someone overhearing. '*Baking!* I detest it. If I could avoid it, then I'd never bake another biscuit again in my life!'

'Baking?' He gaped at her in astonishment for a few seconds and then burst out laughing.

'Shh!' She gave his sleeve an admonishing tug. 'People will wonder what we're talking about.'

'But they'll never guess. Who *would* guess that the famous Belle of Bath doesn't like baking?'

'I can't help it. I never particularly enjoyed it, but I liked helping to run the shop with my father. Only after he died, my mother's hands were already too stiff for baking and I felt so... trapped, somehow. I know it sounds ungrateful, but it felt like more of a burden than a gift.'

He sobered instantly. 'Does your mother know how you feel about it?'

'No!' She looked shocked by the idea. 'She already worries about me. I've never told anyone else, not even Sebastian.'

'Then I'm honoured that you chose to tell me.' He pressed a hand over the one resting on his arm. 'Your secret is safe, I promise.'

'Thank you.'

'Anna...' He seemed to enjoy saying her name now, especially when he was staring deep into her eyes. They looked very big all of a sudden, even darker and more enticing than usual. So enticing that he felt as though he were being drawn towards them. Towards those full rosebud lips, too, the same shade of pink as her cheeks...

'Time for some music!' His grandmother's voice broke the spell, reverberating around the room with the force of a small cannon.

'Do you play the pianoforte?' He jerked upright again, surprised to find how close his head had just come to hers.

'I'm afraid not.' If he wasn't mistaken, she pulled away at the same moment. 'Or sing either, although my mother has a beautiful voice.'

'Is that true, Mrs Fortini?' Samuel led Anna out of the alcove, calling across the room to where her mother was standing in a crowd of what appeared to be gentlemen admirers. 'Do you sing? Shall we perform a duet?'

'It's been a while since I performed for anyone.' Mrs Fortini looked more than a little daunted by the idea.

'For me, too, but perhaps we can muddle through together? If you'll permit me to accompany you, that is?'

'Oh…' The look of determination that crossed Elizabeth Fortini's face at that moment was identical to that of her daughter. 'I'd be delighted, Captain Delaney.'

Chapter Twelve

Anna watched with a smile as her mother went to stand beside Captain Delaney—*Samuel*—at the piano. She was surprised by how well the evening was going. Even standing in the receiving line alongside the Baron and Baroness hadn't been as bad as she'd feared. A few of the guests were customers she'd recognised, but all had greeted her politely and her mother had seemed to enjoy herself immensely, even recognising a few friends from her youth.

The only blot on the evening had been Samuel's absence. After the first half hour she'd started to fear he wasn't coming at all, though when he finally *had* arrived, she'd felt oddly tongue-tied and light-headed. She still did. Since she'd decided to let go of the past and put her prejudices aside she'd been forced to admit to herself just how attractive she found him. It was positively alarming how handsome he looked to-night in formal evening attire, the silvery shade of his jacket, enhanced by a diamond pin in his elegantly tied white cravat, emphasising the vibrant paleness of his eyes.

Now, to top it all off, he was playing the piano and singing, his voice a rich baritone to her mother's clear and sweet-sounding soprano. Singing duets had been one of her parents' favourite pastimes, though her mother had barely sung a note since her father's death. Now Anna was glad to hear her voice again, albeit somewhat irrationally jealous. It made her wish that she'd inherited some of her parents' musical ability, but unfortunately that had all passed to her brother.

Irrational jealousy aside, however, Samuel and her mother made a fine pair, holding their audience's attention to the very last note.

'You have a beautiful voice, Mrs Fortini.' He was the first to offer his compliments, too, as the rest of the room started clapping. 'How about this as an encore?'

He tinkled a few more bars and Anna felt as if her heart had just clenched. It was an old Italian folksong, one that her father had often sung around the shop, the words as familiar to her as the alphabet. For a moment she didn't know whether to smile or cry, but then, seeing the look of mischievous enthusiasm on her mother's face, she laughed instead. It was a joke to everyone present, a good one, acknowledging who they were without making any apology for it. And Samuel had thought of it. She felt so delighted, she could have kissed him.

The thought made the smile freeze on her face. It wasn't *just* a thought, either. It was an image, too, and not a very discreet one. She wasn't envisaging a chaste peck on the cheek. On the contrary, it was far more intimate than that, all lips and bare skin and hands, all joined together and searching, exploring, feeling... Her heartbeat stuttered and then quickened with a burst of pure longing. If it hadn't been for the room full of people, she thought she might actually have acted upon it, might have marched across the room and thrown her arms around him.

That was the moment he chose to look up. Just as a tremor of excitement coursed through her body, he looked straight at her, his eyes flashing with surprise followed by recognition.

For a few seconds, she thought that something must have happened to the room. All of the candles seemed to flare at the same moment, making it hotter and brighter and so airless that she could feel her breath coming in soft pants. Yet despite the heat, she shivered, as if they were sharing some kind of intimate moment, her whole body feeling tighter and more exposed somehow.

The song came to an end while he was still looking at her, his gaze never wavering despite the applause that erupted around them. Anna gave a start, the rest of the room coming back into focus with a jolt, feeling as if she'd just been shaken to her core.

'What a clever idea for your mother to sing in Italian.' The Baroness appeared at her side again. 'She always was very talented.'

'Yes.' Anna stood up a little straighter, afraid of what the other woman might have just witnessed. 'Very talented.'

'Would you do an old woman a favour and escort me outside for some air? It's so stifling in here I can hardly breathe.'

'Of course, my lady.'

They made their way out onto the terrace at the back of the house, Lady Jarrow leaning on her arm for support, not that Anna was fooled by the performance. She'd never met anyone less frail. There had to be some ulterior motive behind the request and if the Baroness *had* just witnessed the look that had passed between her and her grandson, then doubtless it was connected with that. She was probably about to admonish her for looking at a possible earl in such an intimate way…

'Do you know why I'm in Bath, Miss Fortini?' Lady Jarrow dropped her arm the moment they were a few feet from the house, half-swathed in darkness.

'Why?' Anna blinked. It wasn't how she'd expected her to begin. 'I understood that it was for the Baron's health, my lady.'

'Quite so. It's far worse than people know. Hector is very ill, although he hides it well, even from Samuel and me.'

'You mean he hasn't told you he's ill?'

'No.' The Baroness fixed her with a hard stare. 'I imagine that when you look at us you see a curious pair, two very different individuals living separate lives under the same roof, but the truth is that I love my husband deeply. We understand each other. He suspects that I know about his health, of course, but if he doesn't wish to tell me outright then I respect his decision. It's the way he wants it to be.'

'So you think that he's…?' Anna couldn't bring herself to finish the sentence.

'Dying? Yes.' Lady Jarrow nodded firmly. 'I

know that he is. He's weaker now than when we arrived in Bath.'

'I'm sorry, my lady. I don't know what to say.'

'There's nothing *to* say, or to be done about it, either. I'm telling you in the strictest confidence, as a secret from Samuel especially, not for sympathy, but because I want you to understand why I *cannot* leave Bath. Otherwise I would have marched my grandson to Staunton a long time ago. He ought to go, but he refuses.'

'Staunton?' Anna drew her brows together. Nothing about this conversation was going the way she'd expected. 'That's the estate he might inherit?'

'Yes. In Derbyshire, a good two days away by coach.'

'But surely it's his choice whether or not he wishes to visit?'

'Pshaw.' The Baroness rolled her eyes. 'It's an earldom, Miss Fortini, not something he can just walk into. If the baby turns out to be a girl, then he will be thrown, quite literally, to the wolves. He needs to learn about the estate and his duties and responsibilities beforehand and without interference. The only reason he hasn't been overwhelmed with sycophants and even more matchmakers already is that they're waiting to see what happens.' She made a disgusted face. 'I cannot bear the idea of my grandson with some fortune-hunting debutante, but if this baby's a girl, they'll all pounce together. He'll probably end up marrying one just to get rid of the rest. In short, he needs to stop wasting his time here, pull himself together and get ready.'

'I suppose so.' Anna regarded the Baroness with trepidation. It made sense from a practical perspective, but why tell her?

'Naturally I've given him my opinion on all of this, but he refuses to disturb Clarissa, Percival's widow. It's some notion of gentlemanly propriety, I suppose, and if he finds out about his grandfather then he definitely won't go, but it won't do. And *she* doesn't help, the foolish woman. She ought to write and invite him directly, but since she won't, he needs to be convinced to go himself.'

'I understand, my lady, but what does it have to do with me?'

Lady Jarrow gave her a look that implied a great deal, but for once she said nothing.

'If you think that I have some power to persuade him, then I'm afraid—'

'I do.' The Baroness forestalled her protest. 'I saw the way that you were looking at each other just now. You may have more influence than you think.'

'I don't know what you mean.' Anna lifted her chin. 'I haven't even seen Captain Delaney for the past three weeks. Whatever you think you saw, I'm afraid you're mistaken.'

'If you say so.' The Baroness pursed her lips unconvincingly. 'By the way, I had a communication from your grandmother this morning.'

'What?' Anna drew in a sharp intake of breath. It was becoming hard to keep up with all the changes in subject. 'You mean the Dowager Duchess?'

'Yes. Ottoline and I were great friends once upon a time. She wrote to tell me that she'd be very glad to see her daughter again. *And* to meet her granddaughter.'

'Me?' Anna's mouth fell open. 'Wait, have you told my mother this?'

'No, I thought she had enough to deal with this evening, but I intend to tell her later.'

'Oh.' Anna drew her brows together, her thoughts whirling. Samuel had warned her that it might happen, but it had only been three weeks. How could gossip have travelled so fast? Unless... A new suspicion stole across her mind. 'It all seems to have happened very quickly, my lady. I mean, for news about my mother to reach my grandmother and then for her to contact you and extend such an offer… Which one of you exactly began the correspondence?'

The Baroness made a clucking sound. 'Details, my dear. What matters is that there is one. I'm quite certain that Ottoline would have heard about it and contacted me eventually, but when you get to my age, waiting is so tedious. I wrote to inform her of my contact with your mother after the first time you came for tea and she replied at once. She's most eager to see her again.'

'So she's coming here?'

'No. At her age such a journey would be inadvisable. I told her that you'd visit.'

'You told her *what*?' Anna burst out, resisting the urge to put her hands on her hips. 'That's out of the question. I have a shop to run.'

'Nonsense. My girls know what they're doing there now.'

Anna shook her head, annoyed with herself for having been so blind to the Baroness's machinations. 'That's why you sent them to me every morning? So that they could learn to take over?'

'I thought it might come in useful at some point.'

'I still can't go running off to…where does she live?'

'With your youngest uncle at his estate in the southern part of Yorkshire.'

'I am *not* going to stay with my grandmother in Yorkshire!'

'I never said that you should. No, these things probably ought to be done in stages.'

'Then where do you expect us to…?' Anna stopped mid-sentence as the answer occurred to her. 'Wait, the *southern* part of Yorkshire?'

'Very close to the border with Derbyshire, yes.' Lady Jarrow nodded placidly. 'Now the details have still to be arranged, but naturally I can't let you and your mother travel alone and Samuel has nothing else to do at present.'

'You seem to have it all worked out, my lady.'

'I usually do. And you have to agree that this works in everyone's favour. Samuel will be your escort and you'll be his chaperon at Staunton.'

'His *chaperon*? That might be the most ridiculous thing I've ever heard.'

'It may well be, but he can hardly stay in a house with Clarissa all on his own. Your being there will make the whole thing look perfectly respectable.'

Anna pressed her lips into a thin line, impressed despite herself. 'I thought that you truly wanted to help my mother?'

'If you're suggesting that I've been using her, then I take offence. I would have introduced her back into society anyway, though I admit the two purposes have dovetailed nicely. However, I took that as a positive sign.'

'And what about a chaperon for me? Don't you think it might start rumours if your grandson is seen to be escorting my mother and me around the country?' She lifted an eyebrow. 'People might talk.'

'Let them.'

'So you won't mind if your grandson, a possible earl, is spoken of in connection with a shop-keeper?'

'Who also happens to be a duke's granddaughter.'

'*And* a shopkeeper!'

Lady Jarrow let out an exasperated-sounding sigh. 'Do you know, the first time I set eyes on my husband was at an evening party like this one. He was the only man in the room with absolutely no interest in either my looks or my inheritance. It was the most exceedingly attractive quality. I decided to marry him right there and then.'

'Did you ever ask what *he* wanted?'

To her surprise, the Baroness laughed. 'I hardly remember, but it all worked out in the end. I'd like a similar partner for my grandson, a woman with her own mind, who doesn't care whether he inherits an earldom or not. In my personal opinion, you'd be a most excellent match for Samuel.' She held a hand up as Anna started to protest. 'Oh, for goodness sake, I'm not saying that you *have* to marry my grandson. I'm only asking you to travel with him to Staunton. Surely that's not so much to ask?'

'No, but…' She stopped as the other woman's gaze moved past her shoulder suddenly, towards the sound of approaching footsteps.

'Honestly, Samuel.' Lady Jarrow put a hand to her chest. 'You oughtn't to sneak up on people in the dark. You just frightened me half out of my wits.'

Chapter Thirteen

'I doubt it's so easy, Grandmother.' Samuel folded his arms over his chest, his eyes narrowing suspiciously as he took in the scene. 'I came to tell you it's time for supper, if you've quite finished scheming out here. What's going on?'

'I resent the word *scheming*.' Lady Jarrow drew herself up stiffly. 'I was just telling Miss Fortini about a letter I've received from the Dowager Duchess of Messingham. She's hoping for a reconciliation.'

'Your grandmother?' His gaze softened to one of concern as he turned towards Anna. 'I hope it hasn't upset you?'

'No-o.' She was touched by the almost tender expression in his eyes. He looked as if he genuinely meant it. 'If it makes my mother happy, then it makes me happy, too.' She paused ironically. 'I mean it this time.'

'I'm glad.'

'Only apparently she isn't well enough to travel to Bath so we have to go to her.'

'We?' He sounded surprised. 'Then you intend to go, too?'

'I think it's what my mother will want…'

'And I insist that they need an escort.' Lady Jarrow chimed in.

'Naturally. I'd be happy to accompany you wherever you need to go.'

Anna winced, catching a glimpse of the Baroness's gloating expression. 'I wouldn't speak too soon if I were you.'

'Why? Where does she live? The Outer Hebrides?'

'Close to Derbyshire.'

'Ah.' There was an extended moment of silence before his gaze slid slowly back to his grandmother. 'What a coincidence.'

'Isn't it?' The Baroness tossed her head imperiously. 'In fact, the estate is only a matter of miles from Staunton, but naturally a reconciliation takes time. These things shouldn't be rushed. Personally, I think it would be best for all concerned if Miss Fortini and her mother stayed with you at Staunton Manor for the duration of their visit. You'll be doing a service for each other.'

'But only if you're willing.' Anna threw a pointed look at the Baroness. 'If you really object, then my mother and I can stay at an inn. We're perfectly capable.'

'I shan't hear of it.' The Baroness stiffened indignantly. 'Not when...'

'Stay with me at Staunton Manor?' Samuel's voice was like granite. 'After I've told you, *repeatedly*, that I have no intention of visiting.'

'And I've told you not to be so foolish. Honestly, anyone would think that I meddled for fun and not for your own good. Now, I ought to return to my guests. In the meantime, I'll leave Miss Fortini to talk some sense into you.'

Anna clenched her jaw, waiting until the older woman had gone back inside before slowing sighing out a breath. 'I'm sorry. I'm not sure what just happened.'

'My grandmother just happened. It's not your fault.' Samuel twisted his head to one side as if he were trying to ease a crick in his neck. 'Are you really sure you want to go and visit yours? I'm starting to think they're overrated as a relation.'

She gave a soft laugh. 'I don't want to, no, but my mother will and I need to go with her.' She paused. 'Only I get the strange feeling that your grandmother's been planning all this from the start.'

'I wouldn't put it past her.'

'Although she might be right about your visiting Staunton.'

'You're *agreeing* with her?' His eyes glinted dangerously.

'Not necessarily, but I think she has a point about your learning about the estate beforehand, just in case.'

'While my cousin's widow is still in residence? You don't think that would be monstrously tactless?'

'It's…unfortunate, but it's not as if you'd be asking to see the accounts. You're just going to see the place so it won't be such a shock if you *do* inherit. I understand your reservations, but perhaps it's a necessary evil.'

He held on to her gaze for several long seconds before rubbing a hand over his face. 'Maybe it is, but if I had my way, I'd never set eyes on the place at all.'

'Why?' She took a step towards him. 'Why are you so against the idea?'

'I told you, that side of the family never wanted me. The idea of me being the one to inherit their name and estates was their worst nightmare. And maybe they were right to fear it. Maybe *you* were right, too, not about the aristocracy in general, but about some of us.' He frowned. 'My father was the worst kind of aristocrat. What were the words you used? Indolent and debauched. Well, that was him. He gambled and drank away every shilling he ever had and I have his blood. What if I turn out to be just as dissolute? What if I *can't* be trusted to inherit?'

'Oh.' She wasn't sure which part of his statement to address first. '*Do* you drink and gamble?'

'In moderation and never.' He ran a hand through his hair. 'I don't even play whist.'

'Then why are you worried about that?'

'Because I haven't always shown good judgement. Do you know why I accompanied Mr Hoxley to your shop that first afternoon? Because I was bored. I'd spent months on dry land drinking tea and making calls and I was bored to tears. What if I inherit Staunton and I can't bear that, either?'

'If you inherit, then I doubt you'll have time to get bored. From what I understand, it takes a lot of work to run an estate.'

'Are you defending the aristocracy now?'

'No, just you, and you're not your father. You're a captain in the Navy. If you were so easily led astray, then you would never have made it to that rank.' She frowned. 'And it can't be boredom that really worries you. You said yourself that the navy was boring at times. No…' she shook her head '…there has to be another reason.'

He quirked an eyebrow. 'You think you know me so well?'

'It just doesn't make sense that you'd be afraid of turning into your father. You already know that you're not really.'

The skin across his jaw seemed to stretch with tension. 'Well, then, maybe some things can't be explained.'

'Or maybe you know, but you don't want to admit it?'

'Anna…'

'I could call your grandmother back out here.'

A flash of anger animated his face 'All right, maybe it's *not* because I'm afraid of turning into my father. Maybe it's because I don't see why I shouldn't! His family never even acknowledged my existence, let alone wanted to meet me. I'm the heir that nobody wanted, but if I inherit then I'm expected to just give up the life I built for myself, a life that I love, out of some kind of familial loyalty? Why should I? I never asked for their money and I sure as hell don't want it now. Why *shouldn't* I drink and gamble it all away just to spite them? How can I ever belong in a place where I was never wanted?'

She took another step towards him, feeling a burst of sympathy at the look of heartfelt anguish on his face. 'For what it's worth, I think it was your family's loss not to know you.'

'I could say the same thing about your grandfather, the Duke.' He looked deep into her eyes, his expression arrested and faintly wondering. 'It's strange, but you might be the only person in the world who *can* understand.'

She felt her pulse quicken at the words. It was the same thing she'd thought when she'd told him how she felt trapped, as if they truly *could* understand each other. As if maybe, despite everything, they might be a good match after all, just as the Baroness had said. The way he was looking at her now suggested he thought so, too, but how could that be possible? She was a shopkeeper and he was an earl...*maybe*. Or maybe not. There was an equal chance that he might remain a captain.

'I do understand.' She tried to keep her voice normal. 'Only my mother told me recently that bitterness and resentment weren't very attractive qualities. Shall I repeat her lecture?'

'Did it make you feel any better?'

'No, but it did make me think. Now I want

to let go of the past and move on, wherever it leads me.'

'*Wherever…?*' He echoed the word as he lifted a hand to the side of her face, his fingers sliding gently across the curve of her cheek and beneath her chin, tilting it upwards. The touch sent a thrill of heat coursing through her body, making her feel as if every inch of her skin was blushing. Thank goodness they were outside in the dark. Although they really shouldn't be. Not together and certainly not touching like this. No matter what he said about understanding each other, there were still too many obstacles between them. Only it was becoming hard to hold on to that thought.

'We ought to go in.' She swallowed nervously. 'You said it was time for supper.'

'Did I?' He moved closer, his jacket brushing against the front of her dress. 'I can't remember.'

'Yes. I don't think…'

Her words faltered as his arms closed around her waist, enveloping her in a feeling of strong masculine warmth. She didn't move or resist, too surprised to do anything as he leaned in towards her, his mouth moving slowly towards and then hovering above hers, so tantalisingly close that it was hard to believe they weren't already touching. She could feel the warmth of his breath as it skimmed across her cheek…and then there was a sensation of cold air as he moved to one side, gently grazing the edge of her mouth.

She gave a small jolt of surprise, vaguely wondering if he'd missed, though it was hard to imagine how that could be possible at such a close distance. Not that the sensation was unpleasant. On the contrary, her cheek seemed to be throbbing beneath the caress of his lips. No, he hadn't missed, she realised, as his mouth drifted down her neck and into the dip at the base of her throat, his tongue darting out in a way that made her breathing come to an abrupt and ragged halt. She lifted her hands to his shoulders to steady herself, her pulse accelerating to a dizzyingly rapid tempo as her fingers curled around the hard, solid mass of the muscles beneath his jacket. Was the whole of his body like this? she wondered. There was only one way to find out…

Tentatively, she lowered her hands, dragging them slowly over his chest, her breath returning in a series of too-loud, too-rapid gasps. Yes, she realised, he *was* the same all over. Emphatically so. Hard and honed and muscular. And *she* was touching him. Fondling him almost as his lips and tongue continued to trail a path over her throat. She tipped her head back and closed her eyes, mortified by her own behaviour and yet powerless to do anything to stop it. Her whole body was in thrall, alive with so many sensations that it was hard to hold on to reality. All she wanted was to keep on touching him like this, to keep on being touched, too…but they *had* to go back inside. If anyone found them like this, they'd be well and truly compromised…

One of his hands pressed against the small of her back, smoothing its way up the length of her spine until it cupped the back of her head. She opened her eyes to find his only a short distance away. They were watching her intently, possessed with the same look of hunger she'd seen when she'd reached out to him in the colonnade. Did she look the same? Probably. She could feel the same ache she'd felt that day, too, that odd empty, yearning sensation low down in her stomach.

Now, surely now, he was going to kiss her? She hoped so. Maybe then the ache would be satisfied and go away. Just one quick kiss and they could go back inside the house and nobody would be any the wiser. In the meantime, all her senses felt in danger of being overwhelmed. The silvery light of his eyes, the husky sound of his breathing, the warm touch of his fingers, the citrusy scent of his cologne… There was only taste left and, more than anything at that moment, she wanted to taste his lips, just to see what they would be like. She felt her own part in anticipation and saw his gaze follow the movement.

'Samuel?' She spoke his name in a whisper.

He answered by moulding his lips against hers, plundering her mouth with an intensity that only made her want more. So much for one quick kiss. If anything the aching sensation seemed to be getting stronger, but that couldn't be right, could it? This was nothing like the first time she'd been kissed. She'd never even imagined that a kiss could be so completely destabilising.

'Anna...' He pulled away again after a few moments, breathing as rapidly as if he'd been running.

'Yes?'

'If this is your idea of talking some sense into me, then I'm convinced.'

'Then you'll come with us?' The prospect seemed ten times more exciting all of a sudden.

'I will.' There was a sound of a gong being struck and he nudged his lips against hers one last time. 'Just as long as you know this conversation isn't over.'

Chapter Fourteen

He wished it were raining.

Samuel pulled the brim of his hat down over his face and scowled, silently resenting the sunshine that seemed determined to accompany them all the way on their journey from Bath to Derbyshire. It felt wrong to be arriving in Staunton on such a beautiful spring day when all he could feel was dread. There ought to be clouds. Big grey stormy ones preferably, filled with torrential rain and lightning and hailstones for good measure.

He threw a swift glance towards the carriage where Anna and her mother were ensconced while he rode on horseback. After two days of near-constant travel, they were both probably sick of the sight of the interior, but at least they were safely out of range of his thunderous glares. He'd joined them for some of the journey, but it had only made his mood worse. Sitting opposite Anna without being able to touch her had been more than his patience could bear. They hadn't been alone since his grandmother's evening party, but every time he looked at her he found himself wanting to kiss her again. Just the memory of her lips made his own tingle. Not to mention other parts of him. He wondered if she felt the same way, half-afraid that she might have changed her mind after the party, but unfortunately there had been no opportunities to find out...

'Is that Staunton?'

He looked around to see Anna's head poking out of the carriage window, one of her arms gesturing into the distance. His next impulse was to turn his horse and ride south again without looking, but since he couldn't do that, he braced himself to look in the direction of her hand instead.

He already knew the answer, of course. They'd passed through Staunton village a couple of minutes before so there was really only one house it *could* be. Her question was surely rhetorical, though the amazement in her voice suggested an element of disbelief, too.

Slowly, he looked up and understood why. Staunton Manor put even his grandparents' hall in Rutland to shame, though in fact there was not one, but two Staunton Manors, a huge red-brick mansion standing beside the ruins of a smaller, much older-looking stone building. Set amid perfectly maintained lawns and woodland, the old and the new were located side by side at the top of a south-facing incline that looked out over rolling hills towards a range of peaks in the distance. He'd been told the new building was Tudor, built during the latter half of the sixteenth century in a then-popular Renaissance style, but what it lacked in modernity, it more than made up for in extravagance. From their vantage point on the drive the afternoon sun reflected off a row of large, vertical windows, ten on each of the four levels by the look of it, making the whole frontage seem to sparkle.

He let his gaze roam over the assorted towers and cupolas and projecting bays, each of them emblazoned with intricate patterns of heraldic symbols and crests. It was impossible not to admire the attention to detail. Even the drive was impressive, lined with topiary in intriguing, though not always recognisable, shapes, all leading towards a large gravelled area in front of the house. The whole place exuded rank and ostentation, as he imagined it was supposed to, not to mention wealth and power, yet somehow it had all come down to *him*. Briefly, he wondered what its original owner would have thought about that. Nothing that bore repeating, he imagined.

To his horror, however, worse was to come. As they drew closer, he saw literally dozens of people start to gather on the front steps—the entire household staff, by the look of it—led by the butler and housekeeper, though there was no sign of anyone resembling the lady of the house. Which was one small mercy, at least. The last thing he wanted was an audience to watch his meeting with Percival's widow, though he couldn't help but wonder why she was absent.

Unfortunately, there was nowhere to go but forward and no way to arrive unobtrusively, either. He smothered a few choice swear words and jumped down from his horse reluctantly.

'Captain Delaney.' The butler executed a bow so low that his nose almost scraped along the gravel. 'It's an honour to meet you, sir. We received your request to prepare rooms for yourself and two others. May I present the staff?'

Samuel's first thought was no. No, he could *not* present the staff. The staff, for all he cared, could all go and take leaps into the nearest lake, but they were all staring expectantly at him...

'I'm not sure that would be appropriate.' He glanced towards one of the upper windows, where he thought he noticed a flicker of movement. 'Considering Lady Staunton.'

'It was her order, sir.' The butler looked embarrassed. 'She was most particular about it.'

'Ah. I see. Very well, then.'

He gritted his teeth, following the butler along an interminable line of staff and giving nods at appropriate places until the housekeeper finally came to his rescue.

'Perhaps yourself and your guests would care for some tea in the drawing room, Captain?'

'That would be most welcome, Mrs...' He racked his memory for the name he'd just been given.

'Minty.' Anna's voice murmured behind him.

'Minty,' he echoed. 'Will Lady Staunton be joining us?'

'I'm afraid that her ladyship has a headache.' The housekeeper's eyes dropped to the floor, though not before he saw a definite flash of panic. 'She said that she'll see you at dinner, Captain.'

'Ah. I see.' He glanced back at Anna with a look of gratitude and relief, extending an arm before leading her up the front steps towards a door set at a right angle in one of the projecting bays.

'The drawing room is just through here.' The housekeeper led them through a cavernous, stone-floored hallway, empty except for a collection of wooden chairs by the fireplace, then along a side corridor and into a large, oak-panelled room. 'I'll attend to the tea.'

'You did very well.' Anna squeezed his arm once the housekeeper had departed. 'That can't have been easy.'

He gave a tight smile. 'At least I'm used to inspections.'

'That's true.' She let him go and wandered across to one of the tall sash windows. 'I suppose that managing a large household is a bit like running a ship. And maybe an estate is like a fleet.' She glanced back at him thoughtfully. 'That would make you an admiral.'

'I appreciate the confidence.' He looked around at the elegantly decorated, cream-coloured drawing room. 'So here we are. It's a beautiful house.'

'It is.'

'You could fit a whole ship into that hallway.'

'And still have room for my shop in one corner.'

'Where's your mother?' Samuel twisted around, acutely aware that they were finally alone together.

'She said she wanted a stroll through the gardens after being cooped up for so long. I think she's nervous about tomorrow.'

'What about you?' He found his gaze riveted

on her slender figure as she stood, bathed in sunshine in the window. 'Are you nervous, too?'

'A little, but now that we're here, I'm glad. It's nice to get away.' She looked apologetic. 'Sorry.'

'Don't be. I'm glad that one of us is enjoying themselves.'

She gave him a sympathetic smile. 'Thank you for bringing us. I know that you didn't really want to.'

'You persuaded me, remember?'

'Oh, yes.' She bit her lip as the air between them seemed to become charged suddenly. 'So I did.'

He sat down in an armchair to stop himself from going to her. The urge to take her in his arms was as strong as ever, but somehow being in this house, a house he'd never wanted to see, let alone visit, made him doubly afraid that she might have changed her mind about him. It seemed so unlikely that she was here at all *or* that she'd altered her thinking about the aristocracy. He was half-afraid to believe it was true. Besides, the housekeeper, not to mention her mother, would be back any minute.

'I suppose the tea will be here soon.' She seemed to be thinking the same thing.

'I'd prefer rum.'

'It's too early for rum.'

'Maybe a little.' He sighed. 'Do you suppose that Lady Staunton really has a headache?'

'I can't judge that before I meet her. It *might* be true.'

'Or she might just be appalled at my poor manners in coming here?'

'You're not doing anything wrong.' She walked back towards him, stopping just in front of his chair. 'You've given her plenty of time. Her baby's due next month, isn't it?'

'Yes, although I don't know if that makes my behaviour better or worse.'

'It is what it is. It's the intention that matters and you didn't come here with the intention of hurting anyone.'

'Thank you, Anna.' He dug his fingernails into the arms of the chair, resisting the urge to pull her down onto his lap. 'I'm starting to wonder what I would do without you.'

The next morning dawned as bright as the last, the sky a breathtaking pastel orange and blue as the three of them sat down for breakfast, the earliness of which appeared to both shock and scandalise some of the staff.

Anna sipped at a cup of hot chocolate, looking between Samuel and her mother with a feeling of helplessness. Despite their outward appearances of calm, it was hard to tell which of them was more nervous. Her mother was drumming her fingers rhythmically on the tablecloth and Samuel's gaze kept drifting in the direction of the doorway as if he expected Lady Staunton to make an appearance, though since she hadn't come down to dinner, after all, sending another message to say she was still feeling unwell, Anna doubted they'd see her at breakfast, either. Her own sympathy for the woman was starting to wear thin. No matter how much she was grieving, she might still have shown her face, even briefly. Her continued absence only made Samuel feel worse.

There hadn't been any opportunity for them to resume the *conversation* they'd begun at his grandmother's evening party. Which was a good thing, she told herself, since it wasn't one that *ought* to be continued, no matter how enjoyable she'd found it at the time. It was undoubtedly better to wait and find out what the future would bring before resuming *anything*, even if the look on his face when he'd said he didn't know what he'd do without her the previous afternoon made her wish otherwise…

They made their way to her uncle's estate early, too, her and her mother in an open-topped barouche with Samuel riding alongside. She'd told him that he didn't need to accompany them any further, but he'd insisted, looking visibly relieved as they'd drawn away from Staunton Manor, seemingly engrossed in his own thoughts as they travelled in silence the miles between the two houses.

It took just over an hour to reach her uncle's house at Feversham. Compared to Staunton, it looked like the very height of modernity, built in an elegant Palladian style that seemed to spring up like a natural extension of the parkland around it. Anna felt her lips curl with self-mocking amusement. Up until a few weeks ago, she'd never been inside anything resembling a mansion before, yet now she seemed to be making a habit of it.

'This is it, Mama.' She clutched her mother's hand supportively.

'Yes.' Her mother's fingers trembled. 'I just hope I'm doing the right thing.'

'Of course you are. They invited you, remember?'

'Yes, but what if…?' Her mother leaned forward suddenly. 'Oh!'

'What's the—? *Oh!*' Anna echoed as she turned her head to see two people waiting for them on the drive, a small, silver-haired lady holding a cane beside a gentleman with greying curly hair. Her grandmother and uncle, she presumed. Even at a distance she could see they both bore a striking resemblance to her mother.

Samuel dismounted before the carriage had stopped, opening the carriage door and lowering the steps without waiting for a servant to help him.

'Mrs Fortini?' He offered a hand and her mother clutched it, descending the steps with a look of unmistakable trepidation. As her feet touched the gravel there was a heavy moment of stillness, disturbed only by the sound of a blackbird trilling in the background, followed by a sudden flurry of activity as she and the grey-haired man both moved at the same time, each of them throwing their arms around the other.

Anna watched, fighting a swell in her throat. Samuel held out his arm and she took it, stepping down onto the drive to find herself face to face with the silver-haired lady.

'You must be Annabelle.' To her surprise, the woman had tears in her eyes. 'I'm so delighted to meet you, my dear.'

'I'm pleased to meet you, too, your Grace.' She dipped into a curtsy.

'Curls!' The older woman peered under her bonnet. 'You have *my* curls!'

'Oh…yes.' Anna lifted her shoulders and then dropped them again, unsure how else to respond as the woman gave a stifled sob and then pressed a handkerchief to her face, bursting into a flurry of tears. Thankfully, her mother and the grey-haired man walked quickly to join them.

'I didn't say anything terrible, I promise…' Anna looked at her mother apologetically.

'I know, dear.'

'It's not your fault,' the man hastened to reassure her. His expression was kindly, though his eyes looked moist, too, she noticed. 'I'm afraid that my mother's been feeling somewhat overwrought this morning. You must be my niece.'

'Yes.' Anna nodded, feeling as though she were in some kind of bizarre dream. 'I suppose I must be.'

'I'm your uncle, Tobias Holden.' He extended a hand. 'Welcome to Feversham, Miss Annabelle. How do you do?'

'I…' She had the impression that her tongue was stuck to the roof of her mouth.

'Captain Samuel Delaney,' Samuel interceded, taking her uncle's proffered hand when she didn't move and shaking it warmly. 'Perhaps Miss Fortini and I might take a walk around your gardens while you and your sister get reacquainted? I'm sure that you have a lot to catch up on.'

'That sounds like a good idea.' Her uncle agreed tactfully. 'Though I'd very much like to talk with my niece afterwards. If that's agreeable to you, of course, Miss Annabelle?'

'Anna, and yes.' She finally managed a strained smile, clutching hold of Samuel's arm as if her life depended on it. 'Just give me an hour. Or two.'

Chapter Fifteen

To Anna's immense relief, Samuel led the way, drawing her around the side of the house as the rest of her family, as unlikely as it sounded to call them that, went inside.

'Thank you,' Anna said when her tongue felt normal again. 'I didn't know how to react when he offered me his hand. I felt as though my arm had just frozen.'

'I'm sure he'll understand. It's not an easy situation for any of you, but it seems to be going well.'

'Yes.' She drew in a deep breath and then expelled it again slowly. 'I don't know what I expected, but it definitely wasn't that.'

'Not how you pictured them?'

'I've never tried to picture them. I've always avoided thinking about them at all. But they seem quite…normal.'

'I suppose it just goes to show.' He sounded

philosophical and she lifted her face towards him curiously.

'Show what?'

'Just that things aren't always as they seem. Perhaps your grandmother really did regret the estrangement.'

'She might have said so at the time.'

The pressure of his arm against hers tightened. 'Not everyone is as forthright as you. Some people are afraid to say what they think. And who's to say that she didn't? Maybe she just couldn't defy your grandfather.'

'Maybe.' She pursed her lips. 'I suppose it does make you think about things differently. Maybe not everyone in your father's family wanted to shun him, either.'

'I'm afraid in my father's case he did a pretty effective job of alienating everybody.'

'Then maybe not everyone wanted to shun *you*?'

'Ah.' He was silent for a long moment. 'Maybe not all of them, no, but there's no way of knowing now. Most of my family are gone.'

They lapsed into silence, wandering along a side terrace and into a walled kitchen garden. Most of the flowerbeds were empty, waiting for warmer weather, all except for one long row of herbs that still defied the night-time frosts. The day itself, however, was cloudless, the chill of the breeze tempered by the heat of the sun. As long as they kept out of the shadows, it was a near-perfect temperature.

Anna closed her eyes, her nostrils filled with the scent of sage and rosemary, and began to relax. It was incredible how much her life had changed over the course of the past few weeks. It was bizarre enough that she was here, visiting the home of the family she'd always despised, even more bizarre to be in the company of a possible earl whom she'd kissed. But here she was, alone with him again. It felt as if the whole world had turned upside down.

'It's fortunate that your uncle's estate is so close to Staunton,' Samuel spoke again after a little while. 'You and your mother should be able to visit often.'

'Yes.' She reached a hand out, skimming her fingers along the branch of a honeysuckle. 'Although we've never discussed how long we'll be staying.'

'I thought I'd see how Lady Staunton responded to our arrival.' He gave her an ironic look. 'I'll have to let you know when I find out. In any case, we ought to leave before the baby arrives.'

'That would probably be tactful…' she nodded in agreement '…and I shouldn't stay away too long or else your grandmother might knock down my shop and turned it into a stables.'

'It's a possibility.' He laughed. 'She'll need a new project now that your mother's left. It's amazing she's stayed in Bath as long as she already has. Usually she hates the place.'

'Mmm.' Anna pretended to study a clematis on the wall to hide her expression of guilt. It was obvious that Samuel had no idea of the seriousness of his grandfather's condition and, since his grandmother had told her in confidence, she could hardly reveal it. Besides, telling him would only send him riding headlong back to Bath, the last thing either of his grandparents wanted.

'What's the matter?' He seemed to sense the conflict in her.

'Oh, nothing.' She forced a smile. 'It's just been a busy month, that's all. So much has happened.'

'For me, too. I thought that I'd put off seeing Staunton until I had to, *if* I had to, but I suppose my grandmother was right about preparing myself just in case. Not that I'll ever admit that to her.'

'I think she's trying to protect you.'

'From social climbers and debutantes? I know. She seems to think I'll be mobbed if I inherit. It's quite insulting how little she trusts me to defend myself from marriage traps.'

'I'm not sure I blame her. Fighting Napoleon is one thing, but debutantes can be very unscrupulous.'

He snorted. 'Then you agree that evasive action is called for?'

'Well…' She made a show of looking around, as if there might be fortune hunters hiding in the bushes. 'You ought to be safe enough here and at Staunton, but I wouldn't go anywhere else without a chaperon if I were you.'

'I thought that you were my chaperon?'

'Oh, yes, so I am. You're perfectly safe, then.'

'I wouldn't say that.' He gave her a significant look. 'About that conversation we started the other evening… Have *you* ever thought about marriage?'

'Me?' Her heart gave an unusually heavy thump, making her fingers clench inadvertently over his forearm.

'Yes. You must have thought about it.'

'Must I? Not every woman dreams of marriage.'

'No, but I can't believe you haven't had suitors. Not unless there's something in Bath's spa water that clouds men's minds.'

'Now you're trying to flatter me.'

'Only because I'm trying to get answers.' He

tilted his head towards hers, his voice huskier than usual.

'Well…' She felt her stomach quiver in response. 'I suppose there *have* been a couple.'

'But no proposals?'

'Four.'

'Four?' He stopped walking abruptly. 'You just said a *couple* of suitors.'

'Because the proposals were all from the same man, Mr Etton. He owns the shop next to mine.'

'He sounds tenacious. What kind of shop is it?'

'General goods. Sugar, flour, all the baking essentials. That's how we met.'

'But you turned down his proposals?'

'No, I married him…' She giggled. 'What do *you* think?'

His expression turned faintly petulant. 'You might have told him to come back in a year after you'd thought about it.'

'Four times? That sounds cruel.'

'So why did you say no?'

'Why?' She lifted an eyebrow at the question. 'Didn't you just accuse *him* of being tenacious?'

'Humour me. Didn't you like him?'

'Oh, I liked him well enough. He's very good natured.'

'Too old?'

'No. He was thirty-one the first time he proposed and that was five years ago so I suppose now he's...'

'Thirty-six.' There was a hard edge to Samuel's voice this time. 'Then what *is* wrong with him?'

'Nothing, I just didn't want to marry him. To be honest, I think he sees me more as a business proposition than a bride. He's never remotely bothered when I refuse him. He just says the offer's open if I ever change my mind.' She sighed. 'I suppose I could be Mrs Etton in a month if I wanted, but that wouldn't be a very romantic story to tell the grandchildren.'

'Hmmm. What about the other one?'

'What?' Her heart thumped again, even harder than before, though for a different reason.

'Your other suitor. What happened to him?'

'Oh.' She placed a hand over her stomach, turning queasy at the memory. 'That's not a very romantic story, either.'

'Anna?' Samuel's gruffness was replaced by instant concern. 'Are you all right? You've gone pale.'

'Yes...' She drew her arm away from his, going to sit on a small wooden bench set beside the wall. Her *other* suitor wasn't a subject she'd ever talked about with anyone and yet, now that Samuel asked, she found herself wanting to tell him.

'I'm sorry.' He crouched down in front of her. 'I didn't mean to upset you. I shouldn't have asked so many questions. It's just hard not to feel jealous.'

'Jealous?'

'Yes.' He gave a self-deprecating smile. 'That tends to happen after you've kissed someone, especially when you can't stop thinking about them.'

'Oh…'

His smile wavered. 'But if you don't feel the same way then I understand.'

'It's not that. There's just something I need to tell you.' She looked into his face, watching intently for his reaction. 'Do you remember that first day in Sydney Gardens when you asked if my attitude towards Henrietta and Mr Hoxley was based on personal experience? Well, you were right, it was.'

'A bad experience?' His brows lowered.

'Yes.' She nodded stiffly. 'It was the summer I turned sixteen. There was a gentleman who used to visit the shop every morning. He was the youngest son of…well, an important person. He was always so charming and polite and friendly, I could never understand why my father didn't like him. Then one day he passed a note to me across the counter. It said that he was in love with me, obsessed with me even, that he could barely sleep because his heart ached so badly. Then it asked me to meet him that afternoon, to go for a walk in the park and spend some time together.' She couldn't bear to look at Samuel any longer, twisting her face to one side. 'Stupidly, I decided to go.'

'Didn't your father stop you?'

'I didn't tell him. I said I had some errands to run and went off in my best dress and bonnet.' She swallowed against a tight, burning sensation in her throat. 'I was so excited.'

Samuel stood up abruptly, placing one foot on the bench beside her as if he were bracing himself. 'What happened?'

'Nothing at first. We met at the end of the street like he'd suggested, only he took me in a different direction from the park. I thought he must have made a mistake, but when I asked where we were going he just gave me a funny look and said he was taking me to meet his family.'

'But you didn't believe him?'

'I'm not *that* naive. I told him I wanted to go back home, but he wouldn't listen. He got angrier and angrier, accusing me of flirting with him and saying that I'd led him to expect certain…things.'

'Did he touch you?'

She jerked her chin up, alarmed by the note of raw anger in his voice. His expression was furious, his jaw clenched so tight that she could see the pulse of a vein in his neck.

'Yes.' She dropped her gaze again, feeling a rush of shame as she remembered the way he'd grabbed and fondled her breasts. 'But he didn't get what he wanted. I knew where to kick him so I did. As hard as I could.'

'Good.'

'Then I ran.' She shook her head, trying to remove the memory of that run, thinking that her heart might actually burst with panic, that he might catch up with her at any second. 'I was terrified for days afterwards that he'd come back to the shop, but thankfully he didn't. I never saw him again at all. Then, after the fear had passed, I felt so stupid and humiliated and dirty. I'd thought that he'd genuinely liked me, but he barely saw me as a person.' She gave a bitter laugh. 'So you see, when you accused me of blind prejudice it wasn't strictly true. There was a reason. I didn't always hate gentlemen, either. I was just scared of being tricked and deceived again.'

'And I tricked you that first day...' Samuel dropped his boot back to the ground, muttering a series of barely distinguishable oaths before sitting down beside her. 'Anna, I'm so sorry.'

'What you did was different.'

'Not *that* different. I'll never deceive you again, I promise.'

'I know. I trust you and I accepted your apology, remember?'

He reached for her hand, folding his fingers around it. 'If I'd known, I would never have accused you of being prejudiced.'

'But you were right. I blamed the whole of the aristocracy just because I couldn't blame him. I couldn't tell anyone.'

'You didn't tell your parents?'

'No. I knew that my father would have done something foolish and Sebastian would probably have joined him. Then they'd both have been hanged.'

'So you never told anyone?'

'It was too shameful.' She tried to pull her fingers away, but he wouldn't let her, his own tightening as she tried to withdraw.

'You've no reason to feel that way. He's the one who ought to feel ashamed of himself.'

'I know, or at least my head knows that. It's just hard convincing the rest of me sometimes.' She looked up at him anxiously. The lines on his face showed he was still tense, though he seemed to be looking inward rather than out. 'Don't you judge me?'

'For being an innocent young woman who thought she was going for a walk?' His gaze softened. 'You trusted the wrong person, but you've nothing to blame yourself for.'

'Thank you.'

He lifted her hand, pulling her fingers gently to his lips and holding them there. 'What was his name?'

'What?' She gave him a startled glance. 'Why?'

'I want to know.'

'So you can do what?'

'Ever hear of running the gauntlet?'

'Ye-es.' She opened her eyes wide. The horrible practice of leading a man at sword-point between two rows of sailors while they whipped at him with frayed pieces of rope had made her doubly afraid for Sebastian when he'd joined the navy. As if storms and cannons hadn't been enough to worry about... 'But I thought the practice was banned now?'

'I could make an exception.'

She let out a shuddering laugh. 'I appreciate the thought, but I've put what happened behind me. It took a long time, but I have.'

'You shouldn't *have* to just put it behind you. He should be made to pay for his behaviour.'

'He did. There was a scandal involving another woman a few months later and he was sent off to the army. I've no idea what happened to him, but I should think going to war was sufficient punishment.'

'Still not enough.'

'Samuel.' She pulled her thumb free from his grasp, rubbing it gently across the tops of his fingers. 'It spoiled my life for a long time, but I don't want to think of it any more. I didn't tell you so that you could take some kind of revenge. I told you because...' she hesitated '...well, because I wanted to explain why I felt the way I did about the aristocracy.'

'All right.' He nodded slowly. 'No revenge, if that's truly what you want.'

'It is.' She lifted her spare hand to her face, swiping away the tears that seemed to have leaked out from the corners of her eyes. 'So, in answer to your original question, no, I've never seriously thought about marriage. I don't want to marry just for business reasons and I'm fortunate that I don't need a husband to take care of me. My shop gives me independence and security.'

'But you don't enjoy it.'

'I never said that.'

'You said you'd be happy if you never baked another biscuit in your whole life.'

'Well...yes...but I *do* enjoy the business side of it.'

'Doing accounts?' He looked sceptical.

'Yes. I like working with figures. Accounts, prices, haggling, all of that. It's just the baking that doesn't suit me.'

'So what if you had a baker to do that part for you? Then you could just do the things you enjoy.'

'I'd have to pay a baker.'

'But if you had a husband who was willing to help you? One who didn't see you as a business proposition, but wanted you to be happy?'

'I don't know.' She felt colour wash over her cheeks. 'I told you I've never really considered marriage.'

'Neither have I until recently. Only now I can't seem to stop thinking about it. It's a curious feeling.'

'Samuel...'

'Do you know what else is curious?' he went on, looking down at their still-joined hands. 'That I spent my first four months on shore wishing I were back at sea again and yet recently I've thought about it less and less. Hardly at all for the past few days.'

'Oh.' She felt her pulse flutter at the implication.

'The only reason I can think of is you.'

'We weren't even talking to each other a week ago!'

'But we are now.' The side of his thigh nudged against her leg. 'You're the most honest and loyal woman I've ever met. You're also the only person who understands how I feel about my family and this inheritance. It makes me wonder whether we might be compatible in other ways, too. I think we would be.'

Anna caught her breath at the words. They made her wonder, too. *Could* they be a good match? But surely he couldn't be suggesting what it sounded as though he was suggesting, especially when so much was still undecided... She felt her temperature rise and then plummet again abruptly.

'Wait, is this because of your grandmother?'

He looked confused. 'What do you mean?'

'All this talk about marriage. Did *she* suggest that you ought to propose to me?'

'No. Why? Did she suggest it to you?'

'She said that she thought it was a good idea.'

'Oh, for pity's sake... When I get back to Bath, she and I are going to have a serious talk.'

'She did add that I didn't *have* to marry you.'

'How decent of her.' He sounded terse. 'I'm sorry.'

'It's all right. It was actually nice to know that she approves, although I told her I'd be completely unsuitable. I mean, maybe not for a captain, but if you inherit, how could *I* ever be a countess?'

'Haven't we been over this? How could I be an earl?'

'Exactly! One of us at least ought to know what we're doing.'

'But if I were a captain you would consider it?' He rested his forearms on his knees and gave her a long look.

'I don't know…perhaps.' She was surprised by her own answer. 'But what would you do? Go back to the navy and leave me behind?'

'Not necessarily. Maybe I'll decide on a career in baking instead. That's something we would decide together. I've saved a reasonable amount of prize money over the years so I wouldn't have to go back if you didn't want me to.'

'But I thought you said you belonged there?'

'I said that it gave me a sense of belonging, but maybe belonging doesn't have to be with a ship.' His gaze latched on to hers. 'Maybe it could mean with a person instead. Maybe it already does.'

'You should still wait and see what happens.'

'Why? If we belong together, then what does it matter who I am or where we are?'

Anna clenched her jaw, refusing to consider the possibility. 'Are you always so impulsive?'

'I joined the navy on impulse. That was the best decision I ever made.'

'Well, I like to think things through.'

'That's why we're perfect together.'

'Except that you don't love me.' She spoke the words softly, trying her hardest to make them into a statement and not a question. She didn't want to sound as if she were trying to force him into a declaration. He hadn't said that he loved her, although his words were tantalisingly close. Did she love him? Everything had happened so fast that she hadn't had a chance to consider. Maybe it was *too* fast? What had he said about his parents' whirlwind romance? Maybe there was a danger of them repeating the same mistake. She didn't know. All she knew was that her blood was coursing so heavily that she could hear the rapid thud of her own heartbeat.

'Don't I?' He rubbed a hand thoughtfully over his chin. 'I've never considered the idea in a great deal of depth before. How would I know if I did?'

'I don't think I'm the person to ask. I've never considered it in depth before, either.'

'Then maybe we both ought to start considering.' He lifted his hands to either side of her face, twisting it slowly towards him and lowering his mouth against hers. His touch was featherlight and gentle, stroking and caressing rather than possessing. His lips were warm and soft, too, making her feel as if she were slipping into some kind of trance. Her mind, that was, since her body felt the exact opposite, thrumming with vibrations that seemed to reach down to her very core. Briefly, she thought of the piano he'd played in Bath, feeling as though she were the instrument. His hands seemed to be playing her just as skilfully, trailing a slow path over her throat, down her shoulders and around her back, down to the base of her spine, making every part of her quiver.

They came apart finally and he looked deep into her eyes, his own heavy-lidded with what, even to her inexperienced mind, looked like desire. Desire for her. The thought made her even more light-headed. If she wasn't careful, she might lose her grasp on reality altogether. She might forget who she was and where she came from and start to think that she belonged with him, too. And then what might she say...and do? It was madness to even consider marrying him and yet...she was.

'It's just something to think about.' He touched his forehead lightly against hers before moving away. 'You don't have to give an answer. Not yet.'

Chapter Sixteen

Samuel waited outside for an hour while Anna went to meet her family. It gave him some time to think about what had happened in the herb garden, which he had to admit, in retrospect, might have been somewhat misguided. They'd both been through enough emotional turmoil over the past few days without him bringing up the subject of marriage. He probably should have waited. On the other hand, he couldn't bring himself to regret it, either. The fact that she hadn't refused outright made him optimistic, too.

'I'm sorry for keeping you waiting,' a voice called out from behind. 'I hope you don't feel banished out here.'

'Not at all.' He turned to find Tobias Holden walking towards him. 'I'm sure you had a lot to talk about.'

'Twenty-five years' worth and we're not finished yet. I just wanted to thank you again for bringing my sister and niece back to us.'

'They were coming anyway.'

'But you came with them. My mother and I are both grateful.'

'Then you're welcome.' Samuel inclined his head with a smile. The other man had a kind face, a lot like his sister's, and greying curls that seemed determined to stand upright rather than flat on his head.

'We've wasted so many years.' Tobias sounded regretful. 'I always thought that Elizabeth must hate us for what happened.'

'I don't think she's the kind of person who hates.'

'Neither is our mother, although I'm afraid she never had the courage to stand up to our father. Neither did I, unfortunately, and after he died... Well, we assumed it was too late for a reconciliation.'

'Was he such a tyrant?'

'He wasn't a bad man, but he was very proud. Once he found out who my sister had eloped with, he forbade us from ever speaking about her again.'

'Did he know she lived in Bath?'

'I believe so. He had terrible gout, but he refused to go anywhere near the city.'

'And your older brother? What will he think about all this?'

'Anthony can think what he wishes. I won't let him spoil things.' The other man's expression turned resolute. 'Now, will you stay and have luncheon with us?'

'I don't wish to intrude. Perhaps I ought to leave the ladies here and return later?'

'I won't hear of it, Captain.' Mrs Fortini emerged out onto the terrace at that moment, Anna on one arm and the Dowager Duchess on the other. 'There'll be no more tears, I promise. We'll all be perfectly composed for the rest of the day.'

'Well, then…' Samuel smiled, though his eyes felt like magnets, drawn inevitably straight towards Anna '…how can I refuse?'

Mrs Fortini was as good as her word, Samuel reflected, as he, Tobias and Anna strolled in the grounds later that afternoon. The mood during luncheon had been warm and light-hearted, without any tears at all, as if nothing untoward had happened during the past twenty-five years. Even Anna had started to smile and relax in her new family's company, though she seemed subdued, too, as if her thoughts were elsewhere...

Her uncle Tobias, as it turned out, was another kind of seafarer, a member of the Royal Academy who'd been a member of several scientific expeditions to study ichthyology around northern Europe. It was a topic he enthused about over luncheon, insisting on taking Samuel and Anna to see what he referred to as his 'pride and joy' afterwards.

'There it is.' Tobias stopped beside a lake, around a hundred feet in length and only slightly less in breadth. 'Stocked with the finest examples of trout and perch I could find.'

'It's a beautiful prospect.' Samuel smiled as his gaze fell upon a small wooden jetty. 'You have a rowing boat.'

'Yes, I like a day's fishing now and again.'

'She looks like a sturdy vessel. Do you think I might be permitted to borrow it?'

'Of course.' Tobias looked surprised. 'Do you want to go fishing?'

'Not today, but I've been pining for the water over the past few months.' He exchanged a swift glance with Anna, wondering if he could convince her to join him. There was only one way to find out... 'And I'd like to show Miss Fortini here my navigational skills.'

'On a lake?' Her eyes lit up with amusement.

'At least you can be sure we won't get lost.' He grabbed her hand before she could argue, pulling her towards the jetty.

'Samuel!' Anna gave him a remonstrative look as they reached the boat. 'There's only one bench.'

'Then you'll just have to sit in the stern. It looks dry enough, but here...' He shrugged out of his jacket and laid it flat in the bottom of the boat. 'Use this.'

She lifted an eyebrow. 'Something tells me you wouldn't ask a real lady to sit there.'

'You *are* a real lady, although if you mean some timid debutante just out of the schoolroom then you're right, I wouldn't. But then I wouldn't have asked her to come with me in the first place.' He held out a hand and gave her a quick wink. 'Fortunately, I know you're not likely to have a fit of the vapours.'

'I might surprise you.'

He grinned as she accepted his hand and stepped down from the jetty, staggering against him slightly as she made her way to the stern.

'It's very wobbly.' She sounded anxious.

'I won't let you fall, I promise.'

'So far, so good.' She settled herself on his coat, rearranging her skirts and then opening up the parasol that her grandmother had insisted she carry in the sunshine. 'Do I have to address you as Captain now we're on the water?'

'Naturally. Unless you want to be put in the brig for insubordination.' He untied the rope that held them to the jetty and jerked his head towards the other end of the boat. 'It's over there and there's no coat to sit on.'

'Oh, dear.' She laughed. 'Well, then, whatever you say, Captain.'

Samuel looked away quickly, using one of the oars to push them off as a bolt of desire shot through his body. She looked so pretty leaning backwards, one hand trailing in the water while she twirled her parasol in the other, completely relaxed, too, definitely more than she had been at luncheon, as if she were happy that it was just the two of them again. Considering what they'd discussed that morning he took that as a good sign.

'What are you thinking about?' he asked as they glided out into the middle of the lake.

'Just that I could get used to this. It's so peaceful. All I can hear are birds singing and water lapping against the oars. Is this how it is at sea?'

'Not exactly.' He laughed at the idea. 'Ships are noisy places, especially ships with cannons and squadrons of marines on board. There isn't much time for quiet reflection.'

'I suppose not.' She gave him a quizzical glance. 'You look happy.'

'I told you, I like water.'

'Does Staunton have a lake?'

'I've no idea.'

'You ought to find out just in case you *do* inherit. What self-respecting captain can have a house without a lake?'

'I'd be a retired captain, but you're absolutely right. If there isn't, then I'll make it my first order of business to dig one. *If* I inherit.'

'I think you'd make a very good earl.'

'Based on?'

'On my own vast experience of running country estates, naturally.' She paused, her expression turning serious. 'And because you're a good man.'

'For a *gentleman*?'

'For any man.'

He felt a fresh stirring of desire, his blood heating at the words. 'You ought to be careful, Anna. That kind of praise might go to my head.'

'I've said enough insulting things about you. It's about time I redressed the balance a little.'

'Is that why you let me kiss you this morning? To redress the balance?'

'No.' A delicate pink flush suffused her cheeks. 'I let you kiss me because I liked it.'

'I liked it, too. If I thought I could get away with it, I'd do it again.' His gaze dropped to her lips. They were slightly parted and temptingly moist-looking. 'You know the far shore is a long way from the house. I could take you there and kiss you properly. No one would see. Not without a telescope anyway.'

'They still might wonder what we were up to. I don't want my uncle and grandmother thinking I have loose morals on the first day I meet them. Besides, we don't need a distant shore. I have this parasol. If we hide behind it, then nobody will see.'

'Is that an invitation?' His heart leapt at the thought. 'Does this mean you're considering my proposal?'

'I didn't say that.' Her lashes fluttered downwards for a second, obscuring his view of her eyes. 'But it might help me to decide.'

'Well, in that case…' He rested the oars on his lap and leaned forward, bringing his face down to hers.

'I *am* considering it.' She spoke softly, tilting the parasol so that they were both sheltered from any view of the house. 'Only I can't promise anything, not yet.'

'I understand.' He rubbed his nose lightly against hers. 'It's a big decision.'

'Not to mention sudden and impetuous and reckless. And anyone watching is going to get very suspicious if I keep my parasol here for much longer. You ought to hurry up and kiss me, Captain Delaney, or I'll have to do it myself.'

'Go ahead.' The words made him positively feverish. 'I'm not going anywhere.'

Brown eyes seemed to spark briefly before she kissed him, closing the remaining distance between them without hesitation or trepidation or the faintest hint of reticence. Her lips were soft and silky, tasting of the wine they'd drunk at lunchtime, intoxicating his senses more than a whole bottle of rum could have done. He kissed her back, sliding his tongue past the smooth line of her lips. She moaned softly and he went deeper, cupping one hand around the back of her head as he tasted the inside of her mouth. He could feel each of their heartbeats accelerating through both layers of their clothing, could feel the gasp of her breath as his own emerged in increasingly short bursts. Unfortunately, he could also feel the oars slipping away from his lap.

'You're a fast learner.' He ended the kiss reluctantly, making a grab for the oars before they fell into the water.

'You're a good teacher, Captain.' She tipped the parasol back behind her head, her cheeks pinker than ever. 'I'm almost tempted to let you take me ashore, after all. Except that then I'd *have* to marry you.'

'If I thought you could be compromised so easily, then we'd be there already.' He arched an eyebrow. 'But something tells me you wouldn't let me get away with that.'

'You're right. Unlike ladies, shopkeepers are allowed to be slightly scandalous. It might actually sell more biscuits, especially if you *do* turn out to be an earl.'

'Well, in that case…'

'No!'

'Just as long as you're thinking about it.'

'I am.' She leaned back again, a smile dancing about her kiss-swollen lips. 'I *am* thinking about it, Captain.'

Chapter Seventeen

Anna pulled back the green-velvet brocade of her bedroom curtains to look out at the dawn. The park around Staunton was shrouded in a thin layer of mist, but spring was in full flush, making the whole world look vibrant and sparkling and *green*. Not just one shade of green either, but at least twenty different shades all merging seamlessly together. It made her feel alive and happy and rejuvenated.

Now that she was at liberty to sleep in, she found she didn't want to. She was eager to start the day, to see Samuel again, too. Unconsciously, she lifted a hand to her mouth, remembering the feeling of his lips against hers. Telling him about what had happened eight years ago, not to mention meeting her uncle and grandmother, had made her feel as if several weights had been lifted from her shoulders all at once. And the

boat ride afterwards had been quite…enlight-
ening. Kissing Samuel behind her parasol had
felt wicked and thrilling at the same time. She'd
told him she could get used to this kind of life
and, surprisingly, she'd actually meant it. Not
lounging around in boats all day, of course, but
a life in the countryside. It was all so unexpectedly peaceful. And surely a countess would have
a purpose in life, too. It wouldn't all be entertaining neighbours and arranging dinner parties
and picnics. She could do some good for the estate and the people who lived there. She could…

She let the curtain fall abruptly. She was
getting ahead of herself. She'd agreed to think
about marriage, but there was no hurry, especially when so much was still undecided. Samuel
had implied that he wanted an answer *before* he
knew what his future would be, but there wasn't
just his potential inheritance to consider. There
was the matter of his grandfather's health, too.
She couldn't marry him while she was keeping
such a big secret. It would be disloyal, especially
after he'd called her honest and loyal. Perhaps
she ought to write to the Baroness and ask permission to tell him?

She started towards the writing desk in
one corner and then stopped at the sound of a
light tap on the door. At such an early hour of

the morning she assumed it could only be her mother, opening her door and feeling a thrill of excitement at the sight of Samuel instead.

'I thought you might be up already.' He smiled, his gaze skimming over her nightgown in a way that made the skin beneath tingle. 'Did you sleep well?'

'Yes, thank you.' She clutched the neck of her nightgown self-consciously. It was warm enough that she hadn't felt the need for a wrap and the top ribbon must have come undone while she slept, letting the edges fall open. By contrast, Samuel was already dressed, albeit casually, in a loose-fitting shirt and trousers paired with Hessian boots. Judging by the swathe of dark stubble on his chin, he hadn't shaved yet, either. 'What about you?'

'Surprisingly well, all things considered.' He pressed one hand against the door frame. 'I had quite lucid dreams.'

'Oh?'

'You might be better not knowing,' he teased. 'But I'm here with an invitation. I met with the estate steward last night and he told me something you might be interested in. It's in the gardens so I thought we could go and see if it's true together. Meet me in the hall in ten minutes?'

'Sooner than that.' She didn't even pause to consider. 'Give me five.'

Hurriedly, she closed the door, divesting herself of her nightgown and replacing it with a plain blue muslin dress and woollen shawl. Her hair was already impossible, most of it having escaped from its braid to surround her face with a mass of tight, bouncy curls, but she was in too much of a hurry now to do anything about it.

'I'm ready.' She hurried down to the hall where Samuel was waiting, speaking in a loud whisper so as not to disturb the rest of the household.

'I'm impressed. I know sailors who take longer when we beat to quarters.'

He gave her a conspiratorial grin, opened the front door and they crept out together. There was still a chill in the air, accompanied by a faint smell of dampness, but as they walked around the east side of the house and out of the shadows, she was enveloped in a burst of morning sunshine.

'Now can you tell me where we're going?' she asked as they hurried across the lawn.

'You'll see in a few minutes. According to the steward there's a path leading through the woods.'

They found it easily, though it was less of a

path than a trail, meandering lazily back and forth beneath a canopy of silver birch and oak. The trees were mostly leafless, but the ground beneath was carpeted with old leaves and branches.

'Wait.' Samuel came to a halt as the trees started to thin again. 'Close your eyes.'

'Close my *eyes*?' She gave him a sceptical look. 'That doesn't seem like a very intelligent thing to do in a wood. What if I walk into a trunk or trip over a root?'

'I won't let you, I promise. Take my hand and I'll lead the way.'

'All right.' She did as he asked, every nerve ending quivering as his fingers closed around hers. Neither of them were wearing any gloves and the touch of skin against skin sent a thrill of excitement racing down her spine.

'It's just a few more steps. Here we are.' Samuel sounded distinctly proud of himself when they stopped walking again. 'You can open them now.'

Anna opened her eyes and gasped. They were standing on the rim of a dip in the tree-lined hillside that contained a spectacular water garden. There was a waterfall at one end, about ten feet in height, pouring into a river that ran in a perfectly straight line down the valley. To her delight there was even a bridge and some stepping stones connecting the two banks of the river, on both sides of which were a series of circular and semi-circular pools, each with a statue in the centre.

'It's beautiful.' She breathed a sigh of admiration and then laughed. 'And I was afraid that you'd miss being close to the water! Can we go down for a closer look?'

He grinned, as if he'd been hoping for such a response, and led her down a series of small wooden steps. He was still holding on to her hand, she noticed, though she made no attempt to pull hers away, either. Somehow it felt right, as if their fingers were meant to be entwined.

'It's like a secret garden,' she marvelled as they wandered slowly towards the river.

'It's supposed to be. The steward said that my cousin had it built about eighteen years ago. The river used to be wider, but he had it reshaped and channelled into these ponds. Apparently, he wanted it hidden away so he could surprise visitors.'

'He succeeded in that. What are the statues?'

'They're mostly Grecian, I believe. This one, for example, appears to be two sirens.'

'You really *must* feel at home.'

'I'm not sure sirens are a good sign. I was

fortunate enough never to meet any at sea.' His fingers tightened subtly. 'Only on shore.'

She gave him a chiding look. 'I'm not a siren.'

'*No?* You lure men into your shop with sugary treats.'

'You make them sound like horses. They're perfectly at liberty to walk past.' She stopped halfway across the bridge and looked around. 'This is stunning.'

'It is…' He kept his gaze on her as he spoke. 'But there's one more thing I want to show you.'

'More than all of this?'

'*This* is impractical. Beautiful, yes, but not even knee-deep by the look of it. No use at all for swimming.'

'I can't swim.'

'Then you're in good company.' He grinned and tugged on her hand again, leading her up the side of the waterfall and back into the trees. 'Neither can most of the men in the King's Navy.'

'Isn't that dangerous?'

'Not as long as they stay on board their ships, but it's a good idea to learn.'

'Not today, thank you.'

'I had a feeling you'd say that, but you can still plunge.'

'I can do what?' She stared at the waterfall

with trepidation. 'Surely you don't want me to jump off?'

'Not the waterfall, no. In there.' He gestured towards a small, square-shaped pool set off to one side. 'It's called a plunge pool. Very good for the circulation.'

'An outdoor bath?' She crouched down, dipping her fingers into the water and then jolting upright again. 'It's freezing!'

'That's why it's good for the circulation.'

'I am *not* jumping in there.'

'You don't have to literally jump. There's a ladder.'

'Absolutely not. A morning stroll is one thing, *plunging* is quite another.'

'Suit yourself.' He started to unbutton his coat. 'But you'll feel better if you do, trust me.'

'I feel perfectly fine now.' Her jaw dropped as his overcoat fell to the ground. 'You mean you intend to...?'

'I'm afraid so.'

'Samuel!' She spun around as he hoisted his shirt up over his head, though not before she caught a glimpse of a taut stomach and muscular chest, liberally sprinkled with dark hair. 'Is this how you wash on board ship? You just plunge into the ocean?'

'It depends where we are. The English Channel is generally too cold so we use barrels on deck, but a dip in the Caribbean can be quite pleasant.'

'What about sharks?'

'We use sails to make an enclosed pool over the side. It's a relief to have everyone smelling fresh again, believe me.'

'Oh.' She closed her eyes at the sound of more rustling. 'Please tell me you're not taking your trousers off.'

'Not just them.' She could hear the laughter in his voice. 'I can hardly go back to the house in wet clothes. People will think you pushed me into the river.'

'Better that than them thinking you undressed in front of me!'

'*Behind* you and I thought you said you weren't bothered about being compromised.'

'That doesn't mean I want to see you naked!'

'Ah, that's where we differ, then.' His voice turned decidedly wicked. 'Because I'm rather curious about seeing you.'

There was an abrupt splash, followed by a spray of water on to the back of her dress.

'Ow!' She clutched at her skirts.

'*Ow?*' That time he laughed outright. 'Did the water hurt?'

'No, but you've got me wet.'

'So I have. Perhaps you ought to let your dress dry in the sun and join me?'

'I am *not* bathing outdoors!' She lifted her chin pointedly. 'How is it?'

'Like I'm back where I belong.' There was a taunting pause. 'Surely you're not scared of a little water?'

'If you think that goading me will work then you're mistaken. I'm not afraid, just…modest.'

'Spoken like a true lady.'

'A la—!' She whirled around on the spot, putting her hands on her hips to glare at him and then blushing all the way from the top of her head to the tips of her toes. He was standing in the middle of the pool, his biceps bulging visibly as he pushed his hands through slicked-back, soaking wet hair. As he moved towards her water cascaded over his shoulders and the almost impossibly sculpted-looking muscles of his chest, making his skin seem to glisten. She couldn't see any further down, but having grown up in close quarters with a younger brother, she knew what was there.

'I…' She felt at a momentary loss for words, wishing she hadn't spun around quite so fast after all. Now she felt more than a little breathless.

'Changed your mind?' He lifted an eyebrow.

'Only if you look the other way.' Somehow she forced the words out. Having turned around simply to argue with him, it was the only way she could now think of to make him turn away since her own eyes and feet seemed incapable of moving. Not to mention the fact that a cold dip suddenly seemed like a very good, very practical idea.

He turned his back obediently and she wriggled out of her gown, hesitating briefly over her undergarments before conceding that he was right and there really *was* no point in getting them wet. If she didn't remove them, they'd only make her dress damp afterwards, which someone would be bound to notice...

'Wait.' She paused with her chemise halfway over her hips. 'What are we going to dry ourselves on afterwards?'

'A few laps around the garden ought to do the trick.' There was laughter in his voice again. 'Or you can use my shirt if you'd rather the swans didn't watch you.'

'Very funny.' She tugged off her drawers and stockings, folding them neatly on the side of the pool before dipping her toes nervously into the water, keeping her eyes fixed on his back the whole time.

'It's best to get it over with.' He half turned his

head, causing her to drop down into a crouching position. 'It'll be a shock for a moment, but you'll get used to it soon enough.'

'I don't want to catch a chill.'

'You're more likely to if you stand there dithering on the edge. Sometimes you need to stop thinking and let go, Anna.'

Somehow those words did the trick. Before she knew what she was doing she'd placed her palms down flat on the ground beside her and pushed herself over the edge, dropping quickly into the pool and spluttering with shock as ice-cold water enveloped her body.

'Feels good, doesn't it?' Samuel started to turn around again.

'Wait!' Instinctively, she lifted her hands to cover her breasts. 'Don't look!'

'Why not?' He kept turning, though he slowed his pace. 'You're under the water. I can barely see anything.'

'Barely?' Despite the cold, she dipped lower under the surface, wondering how she could still be blushing when all her extremities felt as if they were about to fall off.

'I wasn't sure that you'd do it.' He grinned, looking boyish and genuinely pleased. 'You should dip your head under, too. Now that you've come this far...'

'I don't want…'

'Just take a deep breath like this.' He puffed his cheeks out, making a deliberately comical expression as he ducked under the surface and then sprang up again, shaking his head like a dog.

'Well, I might as well now.' She covered her face with her hands as water flew in every direction. 'Since you've made me wet enough already. Oh, bother, I'd better untie my hair or it'll end up in more knots.' She reached for the ribbon at the end of her braid, pulling it away and running her fingers through the lengths so that it unravelled in a mass of ringlets. As usual, they seemed to spring sideways, rather than downwards.

'They're like spirals.' Samuel's gaze was arrested. 'May I?'

She nodded, and he reached for one of the curls, smoothing it gently between his fingers. 'You're beautiful, Anna.'

Immediately, she opened her mouth to deny it and then stopped. Something in his voice told her he meant it. He really *did* think she was beautiful. She'd never thought of herself as a person who needed compliments before, but now the words made her feel warm and tingly inside. Which was ironic considering how cold the rest of her felt and it was about to get colder…

She drew in a deep breath, bent her knees and then dipped under the surface, screwing her eyes shut as her ears filled with a whooshing sound.

'Oomph!' she exclaimed as she burst out of the water again, making a point of shaking her head at him. 'Take that!'

'Spoken like a true siren.' He laughed, unperturbed. 'Now, tell me the truth—doesn't that feel better?'

'Yes' she agreed in surprise. Now that her body was getting used to the cold, it was actually invigorating.

'I hate to say I told you so.' He bobbed closer towards her.

'Then don't. Gloating doesn't become you, Captain.' She found herself taking another deep breath as she stared back at him. They were standing far too close together, less than an arm's length apart, although considering the fact that they were both naked, proximity was really the least of her worries. Oddly enough, however, she *wasn't* worried. The whole situation felt intimate and natural, as if the water itself was trying to sweep them together. She felt a powerful urge to reach out and touch him, to find out if his chest felt as solid as it looked.

'You know, I've been thinking about our conversation yesterday.' His gaze darkened, as if he were feeling the same impulse to touch her.

'Oh?' Her heartbeat quickened at the reminder. 'Which part?'

'About love and what it feels like. I even went to the library to look it up.'

'Love?'

He nodded, grazing his fingers lightly against the sides of her shoulders. 'According to Dr Johnson there are several definitions, but essentially it means "to regard with passionate affection". That struck me as fitting.'

'I suppose so.' Her lips and throat felt very dry all of a sudden.

'Then I read a few poems to be sure. They were slightly more dramatic, but the gist was the same.' He paused, his gaze profound and yet wondering at the same time. 'Which led me to only one conclusion.'

'Oh?'

'Yes.' His hands curled gently around her upper arms, drawing her towards him. 'Then it struck me that my first proposal wasn't very romantic, so…'

'Samuel!' she shrieked, grabbing hold of his shoulders as he started to lower himself back under the water. 'What are you doing?'

'Going down on bended knee.'

'You can't do that in a pool!'

'Why not? Apart from anything else, it gives me a chance to look at you properly.'

'That's what I'm afraid of.'

'Are you?' His voice sounded guttural. 'Are you afraid of me, Anna?'

'Not you, but…' she gestured at their surroundings '…all of *this*.'

'I know.' He stood up again, turning sombre. 'I know that it's not what you or I want, but it's made me think about what I *do* want and that's you. I'm in love with you, Annabelle Claudia Teresa Fortini, and I want to be with you no matter what the future holds. But…' he winced guiltily '…I promised you time to think about it.'

'I don't need time.' She lifted her hands to his chest. 'I love you, too, and I want to be with you…' she swallowed '…no matter what the future holds.'

It must have been the cold, she thought, making her say crazy, impulsive things. To her numb ears it sounded as if she'd just accepted his proposal— a proposal she would have considered out of the question just a few days before, which meant turning her whole life upside down, leaving her shop and becoming a countess if he inherited the estate. She didn't know which was crazier, the fact that she'd just agreed or that she meant it.

'Is that a yes?' He looked taken aback, as if he thought she were toying with him.

'I...' She took a few seconds to make sure that she wasn't delirious. 'Yes. Yes, it is. I'll marry you, whoever you are—'

She didn't get any further as he caught her around the waist, dragging the whole length of her body tightly against his and crushing his lips to hers. His body was substantially warmer than the pool, she noticed, encouraging her to slide her arms around his neck and push herself even closer, kissing him back even when his tongue slid between her lips. *That* was warm, too. Warm and soft and searching, heating her up from the inside as if he were determined to explore every part of her mouth. The water between them made their bodies slick, moulding her breasts to his chest as heat stoked and scorched between them. Her legs seemed to float up from the bottom of the pool of their own accord, wrapping around his waist as if it were the most natural position in the world.

The water was seething around them now, splashing over the edge as Samuel curled his hands beneath her thighs and lifted her higher, dragging his mouth away from hers to run it over her throat and each of her breasts. She let out a low moan, excited by the combination of hot kisses and cold water, her whole body aching with a quivering, yearning sensation deep in her abdomen.

'Breakfast.' He broke away abruptly, setting her apart and lowering her gently back into the water.

'What?' For a moment, she couldn't make sense of the word. 'Are you hungry?'

'Not for that.' His gaze still burned with heat. 'But we should get back. The others will be getting up.'

'Oh!' She felt a sudden rush of blood to the head. He was right. If they weren't careful, the whole household would see them traipsing back to the house together in broad daylight and it would be hard to look anything other than guilty. Not that it necessarily mattered now they were engaged…though the very idea seemed to make her feel dizzy.

'Where's the ladder?' She looked around the edge of the pool.

'Over here.' He led her towards the rungs and then proceeded to ignore them himself, using his arms to hoist his body out of the pool with ease. Anna started to climb out, too, and then stopped self-consciously. It was one thing to be engaged, another for them to see each other completely naked. Which seemed ridiculous considering where her legs had just been, but she still didn't dare to peek upwards, no matter how great the temptation.

'Here.' He passed his jacket across to her and then turned away, seeming to sense her unease. 'I won't look, I promise.'

'Thank you.' She climbed out and then rubbed herself down quickly, wringing the moisture out of her sopping wet hair before wriggling back into her clothes. It was strange to feel shy again, but she did. She'd never behaved so outrageously in her whole life—or at least not since she'd accepted an invitation to go walking eight years ago… That thought alone gave her pause, but she didn't want to think about that, not any more. She wanted to do what her heart told her and her heart wanted Samuel.

She loved him, she trusted him and she was going to marry him, no matter what the future held.

Chapter Eighteen

Samuel waited until the sound of rustling clothes had finished and then reached out a hand, clasping hers tight as they made their way back through the water garden and up through the woods. This time he looked around at the trees as they walked. Somehow the world looked even more beautiful now than it had earlier. The birds were chirruping, the sun was shining and isolated clusters of primroses and daffodils were bursting up from the woodland floor like a yellow carpet. It was perfect.

He stole a sidelong glance towards Anna. She looked perfect, too. Bright eyed, pink-cheeked and thoroughly bedraggled, her dark hair already starting to curl into ringlets over her shoulders. Tempted as he was, he didn't dare to put his arm around her. Just the touch of her fingers reminded him of how her body had felt in the pool. He'd managed to let go of her then, though not without a considerable effort, and the after-effects were still wearing off. For the first time since they'd arrived at Staunton he felt almost light-hearted. For the first time in a long time, in fact. From the moment the steward had told him about the water gardens he'd wanted to go and see them for himself, but he'd wanted to go with Anna, to see it for the first time with *her*. Waiting until the morning had been hard, but it had paid off. He hadn't expected her to accept his proposal so soon or so suddenly. Maybe they *could* both belong there, after all?

'I'll ride to London this morning.'

'What?' Her head spun towards him. 'Why?'

'For a special licence. We're not residents of this parish so an ordinary one won't suffice.'

'But you only got here two days ago. You can't leave without seeing Lady Staunton.'

'Something tells me she's not particularly keen to see me.'

'That's not the point. Why rush?'

'Because I don't want to wait.'

'Do you think that I'll change my mind?' She threw him a suspicious look. 'Don't you trust me?'

'It's not that.'

'What then?'

'I just showed you why. You can't expect me to keep my hands off you for much longer.'

'Who said you had to?'

'I do.' He felt his body tighten at the implication. 'If I inherit, then there'll be enough gossip about the pair of us. I don't want to provide any more fodder for the rumour mill.' He edged closer, pressing a kiss into her hair. 'I shouldn't have kept you out so long this morning as it is. I might have some explaining to do to your mother.'

'Don't worry, I'll talk to her.'

'*We'll* talk to her.'

'All right, *we* will, but I'd like to be married in Bath.' Her voice wavered slightly. 'Your grandparents are there and I'd like for Henrietta to be a bridesmaid.'

'If that's what you want,' he agreed reluctantly. 'But in that case, we're going back as soon as possible.'

'Thank you.' She squeezed his hand and then released it as they emerged out of the woodland, running her palms over her gown to smooth the creases and then tying her hair back in a loose, though still unruly ponytail. She looked so adorable that he couldn't resist the temptation to pull her back into his arms as they crept through the front door and into the deserted hallway, kissing her full on the lips.

'*Samuel!* Someone will see!' She giggled, kissing him back and then darting away, throwing a mischievous smile over her shoulder as she started towards the dining room and then froze.

'What's the matter?' He nearly walked into the back of her, following her gaze into the room ahead. Her mother was sitting there, he noticed first, *without* her usual smile, although it wasn't that which alarmed him. That was the presence of another woman in the room, a woman he'd never seen before, sitting ramrod straight at the head of the table with an expression that could only be described as ferocious. He'd seen less hatred on the faces of the French sailors at Trafalgar.

'Captain Delaney, I presume.' Her voice, when she finally spoke, was clipped and positively dripping with loathing. 'I see that you're making yourself at home.'

'Lady Staunton.' Samuel made a formal bow, not that there was any point in trying to impress the woman now, he thought with a grimace. That proverbial ship had well and truly sailed. Into the sunset and over the horizon. 'I'm delighted to meet you at last.'

'Indeed?' The Countess's tone suggested she was a long way from sharing the sentiment.

'Allow me to present Miss Annabelle Fortini.' He took hold of Anna's elbow and steered her into the room. 'My—'

'It's an honour to meet you, my lady,' Anna interrupted, making a stiff curtsy before he could announce their engagement, though the Countess merely lifted her eyebrows disapprovingly.

'Have the two of you been for a morning walk?' Her mother sounded as if she were trying to ease the heavy atmosphere of tension.

'Yes, Mama.' Anna took the seat a footman held out for her, appearing not to notice the Countess's slight. 'Captain Delaney wanted to show me the water garden. It was quite beautiful. We'll have to go...'

The sound of a fist banging down onto the table made them all start.

'*My* water garden.' The muscles of Lady Staunton's throat strained with tension. 'My husband commissioned it as a wedding present for *me*.'

There were a few seconds of silence, none of them knowing quite how to respond before Mrs Fortini came to the rescue again.

'What a charming gift. I'd like to go for a walk there myself later—with your permission, of course, Countess?'

'*You* may.' Lady Staunton twisted her head

sharply to one side. 'I wish I could go myself, but I find myself so often indisposed these days.'

'I understand. I was always exhausted when I was carrying my children. Your housekeeper told us that you've been suffering from headaches, too. I hope that you're feeling better this morning?'

'A little, although my head still pains me a great deal.'

'Have you seen a physician?'

'A physician cannot heal what I suffer from. It is a malady of the soul and spirits.'

'Of course, but perhaps you ought to try to get some fresh air for the baby's sake?'

'Perhaps, though the water gardens would likely still be too painful. My husband and I used to walk there every day when we were first married.'

Samuel cleared his throat, taking a seat at the opposite end of the table. 'I was very sorry to receive word of his death. I understand it was a wasting disease. My sincere condolences, my lady.'

'I've no interest in *your* condolences.' Lady Staunton's eyes narrowed perceptibly. 'He would have been horrified by your presence here.'

'I know it's a difficult situation, but I assure you...'

'Horrified!' she repeated. 'He remembered your father as a boy and he knew all about him as an adult, too. All about his debauchery and licentiousness. It appalled him that the son of such a man could be his heir! All he ever wanted was to have a son, to be sure that the future of Staunton was in safe hands, but I...' Her voice trailed away for a few seconds and then returned again, even more vehemently. 'To think of your whole distinguished family line coming down to a man like *you*!'

'Quite.' Samuel braced his hands on the table, resisting the impulse to get up and walk out. 'I've had similar thoughts myself.'

'It's monstrous. A disgrace! You'll ruin the estate before the year is out!'

'I'm not my father, Lady Staunton.'

'No?' She looked accusingly between him and Anna. 'Your behaviour seems quite similar in some respects.'

'I assure you that my intentions towards Miss Fortini are perfectly honourable. In fact...'

'Captain Delaney is the most honourable gentleman I've ever met...' Anna interrupted again, her voice just as vehement as the Countess's '...and I resent any insinuation to the contrary.'

'And what exactly would you know about gentlemen?' The Countess's gaze flickered. 'From what I understand you're in trade.'

'Yes, I'm a shopkeeper,' Anna replied before Samuel could say anything. 'As well as a baker. I make and sell biscuits. Often to gentlemen.'

'Biscuits?' The Countess put a hand to her throat with a shiver.

'They're quite famous in Bath, actually.'

'I don't care for Bath. I spent a winter there five years ago.'

'No, I believe it's rather out of fashion now, but it's home to me.'

'Then let us hope you can return there *soon*, Miss Fortini.'

'Yes, let's.' Anna's tone was now openly belligerent. 'Believe me, nothing would make me happier.'

'Well!' The Countess's eyes narrowed to slits. 'I seem to have lost my appetite. I shall return to my rooms.'

'As you wish, my lady.' Samuel got to his feet with relief, waiting until the sound of indignant footsteps had receded before slumping back into his chair. 'That went well.'

'Dear me.' Mrs Fortini picked up the marmalade spoon with a sigh.

'"Dear me?"' Anna echoed angrily. 'Didn't you hear what she just said about Samuel?'

'Yes, that was very unfair of her.' Mrs Fortini threw him a sympathetic look. 'But we still ought to make allowances. Think of how the poor woman has suffered. She's lashing out, but it's understandable. She's lost her husband and, if her baby's a girl, then she might lose her home and position, too. Her whole future is out of her control. Just remember that.'

'Yes, Mama.' Anna still sounded aggrieved. 'But she had no right to talk about Samuel or his father like that.'

'It's all right.' Samuel smiled, touched by her indignation. 'I've heard much worse, I can assure you.'

'That's very forgiving of you, Captain, but now perhaps the two of you can explain your behaviour this morning. You must have left the house very early.' Mrs Fortini looked pointedly at Samuel, her tone faintly accusing, as if she suspected him of having debauched her daughter among the trees. 'It wasn't very discreet.'

'No, it wasn't.' Samuel exchanged a quick glance with Anna. She'd stopped him from mentioning their engagement twice already and he had no intention of being stopped a third time. To his relief, however, she smiled excitedly.

'We really *did* go to see the water garden,

Mama, but we have something else to tell you, too. Samuel and I are engaged.'

'Engaged?' Her mother's eyes widened.

'Yes. He asked me yesterday and I accepted this morning.'

'As long as you approve?' he interjected, alarmed by the sombre expression on Mrs Fortini's face.

'Of course.' She nodded, though with a hint of uncertainty. 'I would never stand in the way of any suitor my daughter chose.'

'But surely you don't have any objections, Mama?'

'None at all. If you care for each other, then I'm delighted for both of you, but…you know it will be quite a change if Samuel inherits?'

'We know that and we hope that he doesn't. But if he does…' Anna lifted her chin '…we'll deal with it together.'

'Well then, come here and let me embrace you, Samuel.'

'With pleasure.' He walked around the table, kissing her on both cheeks before going to stand behind Anna's chair. 'We've decided to marry as soon as we return to Bath. Which, given our recent reception, might be sooner rather than later.'

Her mother's expression turned startled again. 'But surely you'll stay for a few days, at least?'

'I don't think the Countess wants us here.'

'Perhaps not at the moment, but give her time. You might regret it later if you don't try.'

'A few days, then. Until the end of the week if it pleases you.'

'Thank you.' Her answering smile faltered.

'It's all right if you want to stay at Feversham for longer, Mama,' Anna hastened to reassure her. 'It might be best for your health, too.'

'I admit I would like to,' her mother conceded. 'Your Uncle Tobias invited us both to stay for as long as we wish, but you can't travel without a chaperon.'

'Yes, we can. You can send a maid with us, too, if you want, but we intend to marry as soon as possible so there won't be any scandal. You can trust me, Mama.'

'I do trust you. Both of you.' Mrs Fortini looked between them and smiled. 'And I suppose I shouldn't be surprised when the apple falls so close to the tree. I know there's no point in arguing once you've made up your mind. I wish you both joy.'

'Thank you, Mama. There's just one other thing.' Anna glanced towards Samuel for confirmation. 'I think that we ought to keep our engagement a secret from the Countess. You're right about this being a difficult time for her. No matter how offensive her comments, we don't want to make the situation any worse if we can help it.'

'Good idea,' Mrs Fortini nodded. 'In that case, I shan't make any mention of your engagement at Feversham either, not until I receive word from you in Bath.'

Chapter Nineteen

Over the next few days, Samuel had the distinct impression that the two main women in his life, neither of whom he'd met a month ago, were trying to torture him. Being so close to Anna meant that he'd had to make several solitary trips to the plunge pool just to dampen his ardour, whereas living under the same roof as Lady Staunton, infrequent as her appearances were, was like living inside a beehive filled with a swarm of particularly angry bees. Between Anna's smiles and the Countess's stings, he didn't know which was worse, only that he was counting down the hours until they could leave for Bath.

Meanwhile, his days had settled into a kind of routine. He, Anna and her mother breakfasted together before the women travelled to Feversham and he paid several discreet visits to the estate office. Contrary to his expectations the steward seemed glad, even eager, to teach him, so that he was gradually forming a clearer picture of the size and demands of the estate. It was even bigger than he'd imagined, though it helped to think of it the way Anna had suggested, as a ship in need of a captain.

He met her again in the late afternoons, when they continued their riding lessons or strolled in the park, telling each other stories about their lives. She told him all about her father and her childhood, teaching him a few more words of Italian, while he talked about his life at sea, deliberately avoiding any mention of his own family.

One day he came across a gallery in the top of the house where the family portraits were displayed along one long wall. There they all were, generations of Delaneys and their families. He found his grandfather as both a boy and a man, his uncle and cousin, too, though of his father there was no sign. He seemed to have been rubbed out of the family altogether, a dark smudge everyone preferred to forget. Overall, he supposed he couldn't particularly blame them. If his father *had* inherited the earldom, then it was highly likely that he would have gambled it all away in a year, but the exclusion still felt jarring. Wrong somehow, too, to keep on punishing a man after death. He'd have a portrait commissioned, Samuel decided, if he inherited. It shouldn't be too difficult to recreate his father considering how similar they were in appearance. He'd get one of Anna, too. She'd probably pose in her yellow shop dress just to make a point, but then why not? Maybe he'd pose next to her in his uniform. It would be a reminder of who they'd both been when they'd met, who they might still be, depending…

It was strange, but there were times when his career at sea felt so distant it was like another lifetime. Trafalgar seemed like years rather than months ago. Would he still go back to that life if he didn't inherit? The thought of spending long periods of time away from Anna made him feel preemptively heartsore. He missed her just during the days when she was at Feversham. How would he ever cope with months at sea?

A year ago, he would have laughed at the idea of feeling this way about a woman, but now there was no denying the strength of his feelings. He didn't need Johnson's dictionary to define them any more, either. Friendship, admiration and attraction had grown into love. He'd started to fall in love with her that first day in her shop and now it was too late to do anything about it. He'd come to rely on her, too, on her honesty and loyalty, as if she were an anchor holding him in place. He had the unnerving suspicion that she'd become indispensable to his very existence. Which made the days until their wedding drag even more.

'Are you glad to be leaving?' Anna asked him as they walked along the terrace on the morning of their departure. They'd finished breakfast and waved a cheerful goodbye to her mother as she'd departed with her belongings for a longer stay at Feversham.

'I'm glad that I came...' he replied, wrapping an arm tight around her shoulders and pulling her close. 'But I'm *overjoyed* to be leaving.'

'It's a pity about Lady Staunton. I thought she might thaw a little while we were here, but something tells me she'd be more than happy for us to leave without saying goodbye. I thought she'd at least have breakfast with us today.'

'Every time I've approached her she's run away as if I'm her worst enemy.'

'She ought to have given you a chance.'

'Unfortunately my father's reputation precedes me.'

'But it's not fair.' Anna shook her head. 'It can't be good for her to be so bitter and angry in her condition, either. And if the baby *does* turn out to be a girl, think how much angrier she'll be. That won't be good for either of them.'

'I know, but I don't think there's anything more I can say or do. I've tried talking to her. I've told her that she won't be homeless if I inherit, but she won't listen. She doesn't want my assurances.' Samuel shrugged his shoulders regretfully. 'I suppose we'll just have to wait and see what happens and take everything one step at a time.'

'And keep hoping for a boy.'

'That, too. It won't be long now before we find out.' He stopped walking to wrap both of his arms around her. 'You know I could stand like this all day, but the sooner we get to Bath, the sooner we can be married.'

'About that…' She looked up into his face, her own anxious. 'It doesn't have to be a big event, does it? I'll have Henrietta and a few other acquaintances, but it might look odd if you have a hundred people on your side.'

'I can't think of a quarter of that number to invite. Most of my friends are at sea or in Portsmouth waiting for billets. Frankly, I'd be happy with just the two of us…' he kissed the tip of her nose and then rubbed his own against it '…and a ten-cannon salute, of course.'

'No cannons!' She laughed. 'And I only have

the gown I wore to your grandmother's party. Will you mind?'

'You can wear a sack for all I care, but I'd be happy to buy you something new if you like. I think a captain's salary can just about stretch to a gown.'

'No. I don't care what I wear, either.' Her brow puckered. 'I suppose most people have a rough idea of which it will be when they say for richer or poorer, only in our case it could go either way. For better *or* worse.'

'We might be the only two people in England who think of an earldom as worse, but you're right. We don't know what the future will bring, just that we'll face it together. Now, I have a few things left to pack. Shall I have the carriage brought round in half an hour?'

'That sounds perfect. I thought I'd take one last walk around the water gardens since I'm going to be cooped up for the rest of the day.'

'Fancy a plunge?'

'Not this morning, thank you.' She gave him a coy look. 'Now hurry up and pack, Captain. We have a wedding to get to.'

Anna heaved a contented sigh as Samuel walked away. Despite the tension of living under the same roof as Lady Staunton, it was amazing how comfortable she felt with Samuel now. Even his smell was reassuring. Musky yet fresh-smelling with that distinctive hint of citrus. It made her wonder whether Henrietta was right and they ought to bring out a new type of biscuit. Lemon would be delicious.

She descended the terrace steps and wandered across the lawn and into the woodland. It was another gorgeous day, more like summer than spring. She'd have to dress lightly in the carriage or the heat would be stifling. It was going to be an arduous enough journey without having anyone to talk to and Samuel could hardly ride inside with her unchaperoned, no matter how appealing the idea sounded. She suspected that kissing him would pass the time quite quickly...

There was a sound of snapping twigs and she stopped at the sight of a woman walking among the trees up ahead. From a distance it looked like Clarissa, but there was something different about her, something about the way she held herself and moved. She seemed faster and more upright than usual...as if it were Clarissa and yet *not* Clarissa. A suspicion tugged at the edge of Anna's mind, unbelievable at first, but gaining in strength the longer she watched. But it couldn't be possible...could it? Surely she wouldn't be so conniving?

She stepped hastily behind one of the trees, concealing herself as Clarissa passed by and then stepped out on to the lawn. As she did so, her whole posture seemed to change, her shoulders sagging forward and her steps slowing as if she were ageing ten years before Anna's eyes.

She felt her stomach plummet to the floor, almost too shocked to be angry, waiting a few minutes to calm herself before following the other woman's steps back to the house and through the terrace doors. To her surprise, Clarissa was sitting just inside the drawing room on a low chair, sobbing into a handkerchief.

'Lady Staunton?' Anna closed the terrace door softly behind her and leaned against it for support. 'Can I help?'

'*You?*' The other woman gave a start at her sudden appearance, glaring at her through swollen, red-rimmed eyes. 'Go away!'

'I wish I could.' Anna ignored her. 'But I think that we need to talk.'

'I've no desire to—'

'You're not pregnant, are you?' Anna spoke quickly, willing the words not to be true, though she couldn't think of any other explanation that made sense.

'Of course I am!' Lady Staunton's expression

registered both shock and guilt as she gestured frantically at her stomach. 'Look!'

'It would be easy enough to fasten some padding there, I would imagine.' Anna lifted an eyebrow sceptically. 'I saw you walking in the woods just now. You were moving too fast for a pregnant woman.'

For a moment, she thought that the Countess might actually throw something at her. She looked furious enough for anything, though fortunately there were no weapons to hand. Then her whole face seemed to crumple, anger turning to anguish.

'No!' She shook her head, her narrow shoulders heaving. 'Almost twenty years of marriage and I've never once been with child. I tried everything. I've been examined by so many doctors, tried all kinds of medicines. Nothing ever worked.'

'I'm sorry.' Anna sat down on a sofa opposite, not knowing what else to say. She wasn't entirely sure what to feel, either. Indignant as she was about the Countess's deception, she couldn't help but feel sympathy for her obvious heartache. 'That must have been very hard.'

'It was the *one thing* I had to do, the one purpose in my whole life. Just give him a son, my mother told me on my wedding day, give him an heir and everything will be all right. That was the reason he married me, you know, and my parents as good as promised him that I'd be fertile…' She put her head in her hands. 'I was only seventeen and it sounded like such an easy thing to do. I assumed I'd be a mother by the end of the year. And then when it didn't happen, month after month…'

'Was he cruel to you?'

Lady Staunton twisted her face to one side. 'No. He was very loving to me at first. I told you, he built me those gardens as a gift.'

'But later?'

'He was never cruel, but he became…distant. Cold. Having a son became an obsession.'

'Because he didn't want Samuel to inherit?' Anna tried not to sound too accusing.

Lady Staunton sniffed and nodded. 'He was so afraid that he'd be like his father and gamble the estate away. He hired lawyers to try to do something about the entail, but it was no use.' She screwed her handkerchief up into a ball. 'You've no idea what it was like. We barely spoke to each other during the last few years of our marriage.'

'You're right, I don't know what it was like.' Anna placed a hand tentatively on her shoulder.

'But why on earth did you tell everyone you were pregnant? Why pretend?'

'Because this is my home!' the other woman wailed. 'I've nowhere else to go.'

'What about your family?'

'They think I'm a failure. My mother says it was a good thing my sisters were married off early or I would have damaged their prospects.' She gave a bitter laugh. 'And they've all had children. Sons!'

'That doesn't make you a failure.'

'It does to them. And if I go back now and tell them it was all a lie…'

'But you must have known they'd find out eventually.'

'Yes.' Lady Staunton's head fell forward. 'I don't know why I did it. I wasn't thinking clearly. At the funeral everyone just kept telling me that it was *such* a shame, that *if only* I'd had a son… I felt as though I were being hit in the face every time. Finally I couldn't bear it any longer. The words were out before I knew what I was saying and then everyone's behaviour changed, too. I wasn't a disappointment any more.'

'But…'

'I know, but once I'd said it I couldn't go back. And I told myself that I was doing it for my hus- band, that it was what he would have wanted and

I was making things up to him.' She paused. 'I know it was reckless.'

'Very.' Anna made a face. 'You've been keeping Samuel's inheritance unlawfully.'

'Yes.' Lady Staunton had the decency to look guilty.

'And as for the way you've been treating him…'

'I know.'

'You have to tell him the truth.'

'I *was* going to, I truly was. I told myself that I'd admit everything when you first arrived, but I didn't know how to begin. So I kept putting it off and off. Then that morning when the two of you came into breakfast looking so happy and in love after you'd been walking in *my* water gardens, I felt jealous. It's no excuse, I know, but it made me so angry.' She drew her shoulders back. 'But I'm truly sorry for the way I've behaved. I have to admit, from what I've seen of him, Captain Delaney doesn't seem like the sort of man who'd gamble everything away.'

'He's not.' Anna jutted her chin out indignantly. 'Your husband would have known that, too, if he'd given him a chance.'

'You're right. He should have met him at least. Then none of this would have happened.' Lady Staunton toyed miserably with the ends of her handkerchief. 'Can you forgive me?'

Anna took a deep breath. *Could* she forgive her? She *could* understand, but she felt as though a bucket of cold water had just been poured over her head. If only she and Samuel had left for Bath already, she could have remained in blissful ignorance, still consoling herself with the possibility that he *wouldn't* inherit. Facing an uncertain future with him was one thing. Facing an earldom, on the other hand...

'Yes.' She tried to swallow a feeling of rising panic.

'Do you think that Captain Delaney will let me stay in the dower house after this?' The Countess's tone was faintly pleading. 'I don't want to go back to my family and be treated like a failure for the rest of my life.'

'I don't know.' Anna felt as if her insides were churning. 'You'll probably need to give him some time to think about it. He'll understand why you did it eventually, but it's going to be a big shock.'

'You don't seem very pleased, either.' Lady Staunton gave her a quizzical look. 'You're going to be the next Countess. You ought to be happy.'

Anna blinked. 'You know about our engagement?'

'I assumed. It's obvious how you feel about each other.'

'Yes, but…why *should* I be happy?' Anna drew her brows together. 'You were right about what you said the other day. I'm a shopkeeper. No matter who my grandparents were, I haven't been raised for this kind of life.'

'But I have.' To her surprise, Lady Staunton actually sounded supportive. 'And I can teach you.'

'You mean like an apprentice?'

'Why not? It'll give me a chance to make amends.' The other woman reached under her skirts, fumbling around for a few moments before drawing out a small cushion. 'I don't suppose I'll be needing this any more.'

'No… Are you all right?'

'I will be.' Lady Staunton gave a loud sniff and then hiccupped. 'Do you know, this is the first time I've cried since before the funeral. It feels good.'

'Then cry as much as you want to. Howl at the sky if it makes you feel better.'

'I can't do that.'

'Why not? Because you were raised to be quiet and polite?' Anna gave her an exasperated look. 'Personally I've always thought that lady-like behaviour was overrated. Why be quiet if you want to roar? We can do it together if you like?'

'What will the servants think?'

'Maybe they'll think it's about time.'

'Oh… Will you start us off?'

'If you like.' Anna rose to her feet, sucking in a deep breath and then letting it out again in a roar.

'There.' She folded her arms. 'That's how you do it.'

Lady Staunton looked impressed, rubbing her nose vigorously with the handkerchief before standing up, tipping back her head and screaming so loudly that Anna had to steel herself not to wince. It was a wonder the windows didn't all crack at the sound.

'Very good.' She lifted an eyebrow once her ears had stopped ringing. 'Feel better?'

'*Yes.*' The other woman started to smile and then clutched Anna's hand at the sound of running footsteps in the hall. 'Oh, dear. Maybe that wasn't such a good idea, after all…'

Chapter Twenty

Samuel stood in the doorway, gaping in amazement at the sight of Anna and Lady Staunton standing side by side, holding hands. Neither of them appeared to be in any pain, as he'd assumed when he'd first heard the blood-curdling screams emanating from the drawing room, though their expressions weren't particularly reassuring, either.

'Samuel?' Anna spoke first, the look on her face turning from anxious to determined. 'Lady Staunton has something she needs to tell you.'

'Wha—?' His voice faltered as he noticed the cushion tucked under Clarissa's arm, then her noticeably flatter stomach.

'You're not pregnant.' A rush of horror slammed into him like a fist. Suddenly, he wished himself a thousand miles away, in the middle of the Atlantic Ocean preferably.

'I'm sorry.' Clarissa looked genuinely shame-faced. 'I never meant for it to go this far.'

'You're not pregnant.' He repeated the words, as if they might make more sense to him the second time.

'No.'

'You've been pretending this whole time?'

She nodded, her voice falling to a low whisper. 'I know it was wrong.'

'You *lied* to me!' He didn't intend to raise his voice, but he couldn't stop himself. Five minutes ago he'd been happily anticipating leaving Staunton. Two minutes ago he'd been running down the stairs in alarm. Now...*now* he felt several stages beyond furious. She'd lied! On top of everything else his family had done, she'd lied just to keep him *out* of the family! As if everything about him were so objectionable! Worse even than that, though, was the shock. He'd thought that he had another month to prepare for the possibility of becoming an earl, a month to spend with Anna, but now that future had been stolen away from him. His fate was sealed. He was the Earl of Staunton, his father's son, the unwanted but last surviving male heir from a jaded line of a once-illustrious family. There was no fighting that legacy any longer. He felt so disorientated that he had to clutch the door to stop the world from spinning around him. It was like sea sickness, only without the sea.

And now Anna, the one person he'd thought understood how he felt, was standing alongside the woman who'd deceived him, as if she wasn't angry at all. As if she'd sided with his family against him, too!

'Samuel?' Anna advanced towards him, her expression concerned. 'Perhaps you should sit down? You don't look well.'

'No.' He lifted a hand, preventing her from coming any closer as he narrowed his eyes at Lady Staunton instead. 'Your maids. They must have known. They must have helped you.'

'Ye-es.' He was pleased to see her face register panic. 'But only because they're loyal to me.'

'According to the law, they were *my* staff, not yours.' His voice sounded different even to him. Hard and grating and implacable. 'That kind of disobedience is grounds for dismissal.'

'Samuel!' Anna gasped. 'You wouldn't!'

'Why not?' He couldn't bring himself to look at her. 'I'm the Earl now, aren't I? That means I can dismiss whoever I want and I *want* to be rid of everyone who knew about this.'

'They only helped me because I begged them to.'

'Well, now you can tell them the consequences.'

Lady Staunton's whole body started shaking, though whether from shock or anger he couldn't tell. 'In that case, they can accompany me to the dower house.'

'I think not.' He turned on his heel, too angry to be in the same room with either of them any longer. 'You can find somewhere else to live, Countess. I want you gone from Staunton by tonight.'

'If I thought you'd meant any of that, I'd shove you in right now.'

Anna found Samuel standing by the side of the river, his back towards her as he hurled stones into the water.

'What makes you so sure that I didn't?' He didn't turn around, only pulling his arm back for another throw.

'Because you're an honourable man and Clarissa wants to stay here. It's her home.'

'Not any more. Legally it hasn't been her home since her husband died. It was my inheritance and I don't give a damn what she wants.' He flung a stone so far down the river that she could barely see the splash. 'She ought to be grateful I'm not summoning the magistrate.'

'She knows she acted badly.'

'Badly?' He spun around finally, his face blaz-

ing with anger. 'Is that all you can say? You *know* how miserable I've been waiting to find out what my future would be. I've spent five months on shore twiddling my thumbs!'

'I know, but she's been miserable, too, and she'll be even more miserable if you force her to leave.'

'I'm sure she has family she can go to.'

'A family who call her a failure.'

His expression relented slightly. 'What do you mean?'

'Because she never provided her husband with an heir. They've made her feel like a disappointment so much that she's afraid to go back to them. I think a lot of her anger has been about that, not you.'

'That doesn't make it all right.'

'No, but think how much worse they'll treat her if she goes home and admits the truth.' Anna took a step closer. 'I'm not defending what she's done, but there *are* reasons. I think she was desperate after the funeral and didn't really know what she was doing. Then she didn't know how to stop it.'

'None of which is my concern.' His jaw clenched again. 'Whose side are you on?'

'It's not a question of sides.'

'But you think I ought to just forgive and forget? I put my life on hold for *months* and she was lying the whole time!'

'I know.'

'All to stop *me* from inheriting! Because she thought I was the same as my father, just like…'

He stopped, a pained expression passing over his face.

'Samuel?' Something about that expression made her want to wrap her arms around him.

'Like all the rest of my family,' he finished saying, twisting his face to one side.

'She thought she was fulfilling her husband's wishes, but she's sorry for it now.'

'She even convinced her servants to keep secrets from me.'

'Yes.'

His shoulders slumped as the anger drained from his face suddenly. 'And sending them away won't make me feel any better, will it?'

'No. *Or* her. She's spent the last few months feeling angry and bitter and scared. Now she needs time to grieve properly.'

'All right. Tell her she can do whatever she wants.' He let out a heavy sigh. 'You know, I never really let myself believe it would actually happen. I kept telling myself that she'd have a son, that it wouldn't be long until I'd be free, but there's no escaping all this now, is there? I don't have a choice.'

'No.' She reached a hand up to his face, turning it gently back towards her. 'But you're not the man your family thought you were. You're better than them.'

He tipped his cheek into her palm, closing his eyes for a moment before opening them again with a look of determination. 'Then I'll do my duty. I'll do it properly and prove them all wrong, be the Earl my father could never have been. I'll find a way to belong at Staunton, too.'

'I know you will.'

'But I'll need my Countess by my side.' He clasped his hands around her waist. 'Come with me to Scotland, Anna. We can go to Gretna Green and be married tomorrow.'

'Scotland?' She stiffened at the suggestion. 'But why rush? We might have to delay our immediate plans, but we can still be married in Bath. Nothing about that needs to change.'

'Everything's already changed.' His grip tightened. 'We've spent too much time together. If we don't marry soon, then people will talk.'

'I don't care what people say.'

'But I do.' His tone was too vehement, his gaze too bright, in the grip of some new fervour. 'I want to do everything right from now on, start as I mean to go on. Besides, there's no reason for us to return to Bath now. Your mother's already here and I'm going to have a mountain of estate business to attend to.'

'Ye-es, but…' She bit her teeth into her bottom lip, trying to think of a reason to stall. He was right. If he was the new Earl, then Scotland was a far better idea from a practical perspective. They could be there and back in a matter of days. There was no reason for him to return to Bath except to see his grandparents, but since he didn't know about his grandfather's ill health there was no impetus for that. She'd sent a letter to his grandmother asking for permission to tell Samuel, but as yet she hadn't received any answer. All she knew was that she *had* to tell him before they were married.

'Anna?' He frowned when she didn't answer.

'It's just… I need to go back to my shop. I can't do anything until I've settled things there.'

'Why not? We can do all of that later.'

'But it's my responsibility. It matters to me. Please, Samuel, I want to be married in Bath. We can get a common licence there and…'

'You've changed your mind?' He dropped his hands from her waist abruptly.

'I never said that!'

'Then prove it. Come with me to Scotland today. We're already packed and the carriage is waiting. We can leave right now.'

'No.' She took a step backwards, annoyed by his dictatorial tone. He sounded as if he were issuing orders, as if he were turning into an arrogant aristocrat right before her eyes. 'I told you, I want to settle my affairs first.'

'You've changed your mind.' His whole face seemed to shut down as he spoke, his eyes looking paler and sharper than she'd ever seen them, like jagged shards of glass.

'That's not true, but I won't be *told* what to do. Just because you're an earl doesn't give you the right...'

'If you love me, then you'll come with me now!'

'If you love me, then you won't insist!'

'I should have known you'd take their side, too.' He gave a harsh laugh and turned away, heading towards the bridge. 'Goodbye, Anna.'

Samuel sat in a corner of the taproom at Staunton's somewhat dilapidated alehouse, his forearms resting on the table in front of him, staring broodingly into a tankard. He hadn't drunk more than a few mouthfuls, tempted though he was to drown his sorrows, but now that he'd finally calmed down after storming away from Anna, all he felt was empty.

Lady Staunton's deception had come as a

shock to say the least, but the sight of Anna at her side and defending her had made it even worse, making him feel as though the anchor he'd been holding on to had come loose. Her following him to the water gardens afterwards had given him new hope, briefly allowing him to imagine that doing his duty and becoming the consummate Earl in defiance of his family's expectations might ease the crushing sense of entrapment, but then Anna had distanced herself again. Maybe suggesting an elopement hadn't been the best idea, but he'd wanted to make everything official and to do it all properly, to start his new life with her at his side. On top of that, he'd needed to know whether the fact of his inheritance had changed her mind about marrying him and to his horror, it had. If she'd *truly* wanted to marry him, then she would have agreed to go to Gretna Green instead of making up some excuse about needing to return to Bath. He'd thought that they'd come to an understanding. He'd thought that he could trust her, too, but as it turned out, her prejudices were stronger than her feelings for him. And he'd been a damned fool, falling in love with the one woman most likely to reject him. It had been madness to think that they might belong together, that they might make a home at Staunton, either. Of course she denied going back on her word, but what else would she say?

On the other hand, a tiny part of him argued, Clarissa's deception had been a shock for Anna, too. Maybe he ought to have given her the benefit of the doubt. Maybe he shouldn't have been quite so demanding, either...

'You look like you've been in the wars.' The voice of the innkeeper came from close by. 'Trouble with love, I'll wager?'

Samuel looked up, assuming the comments were addressed to him, surprised to find them directed at a young, fair-haired man sitting at the next table instead. In the mostly deserted taproom he hadn't noticed the man's presence before, but now he had the uncanny impression of looking into a mirror. The other's position, even down to his expression of brooding melancholy, was remarkably similar to his own.

'Aye...' The man sighed. 'Dora says she can't marry me. Her father will never agree.'

'Old Turner? No, he's a funny one.' The innkeeper gave a sage nod. 'You'd best watch he doesn't catch you wi' her either or he'll have your guts.'

'Then what do I do?'

'Find yourself someone else.'

'But I don't want someone else!'

'Why won't her father agree to the match?' Samuel interjected, unable to contain his curiosity.

The man gave him a swift glance and then heaved a sigh. 'He says I'm just a farmhand and that I'll never amount to anything.'

'Then make something of yourself to show him he's wrong. If she loves you, then she'll wait.' He frowned at the words. Wasn't *waiting* exactly what he'd just refused to do for Anna?

'And how am I supposed to do that when them at the manor do nothing but put up rents and never help us with—? Ow!' He stopped as the innkeeper gave his chair a none-too-subtle kick.

'This gentleman might know them at the manor.'

'Oh.' The man's expression turned to one of alarm. 'Pardon me, sir, I didn't know I was talking to a gentleman. Too much ale.'

'I shouldn't have been eavesdropping in the first place.' Samuel picked up his tankard and stood, the similarity in their situations making him doubly curious. 'Do you mind if I join you?'

'If you want, sir.' The man exchanged a dubious look with the innkeeper.

'Thank you. Now...' Samuel took a seat again opposite '...does she love you, this woman?'

'Dora? She says she does, only she won't go

against her father. She said our last kiss was goodbye.'

'You've kissed her?' The innkeeper gave a low whistle. 'You'd better hope Turner doesn't find out.'

'I don't care if he does.'

'You will when he pummels you. He's twice your size and then some. I once saw him flatten—'

'Maybe I can help?' Samuel interrupted before the innkeeper could go into any more lurid detail.

'How?'

'Tell me what it is you need to prove yourself. Your own farm?'

The other man stared at him suspiciously for a moment and then burst out laughing. 'Aye, that ought to do it. I don't reckon there's any lying around spare, though.'

'Maybe not spare, but there must be something we can do.' Samuel nodded at the innkeeper and then gestured at their tankards. 'Two more of these and one for yourself. Then we can put our heads together and think.'

'Th-thank you, sir.' The man looked confused. 'But if you don't mind my asking, who are you?'

'Me?' Samuel took one last mouthful of ale before answering, 'I'm Captain Samuel Delaney, the new Earl of Staunton.'

Chapter Twenty-One

'Lady Staunton?' Anna found the Countess where she'd left her in the drawing room, lying on a sofa and weeping.

'Oh.' Clarissa pulled herself up with an effort. 'I'm sorry. It's just that now I've started crying, I can't seem to stop.'

'Oh, dear.' Anna came and took a seat beside her. 'It'll be all right, I promise.'

'He said I have to leave.'

'He didn't mean it.'

'He *didn't*?'

'Well, yes, he did at the time, but now he says you can go or stay as you like. He was just upset.' She gave her a meaningful look. 'It might be a good idea to stay out of sight for a few days.'

'I will.' Clarissa nodded eagerly. 'Where is he now?'

'I've no idea.' Anna leaned back against the

cushions with a sigh. 'He stormed off when I said I wouldn't go to Scotland with him. He thinks I've changed my mind about his proposal.'

'Have you?'

'No!' She was surprised by the strength of her own conviction. 'I love Samuel. I want to marry him, no matter who he is.'

'Thank you for defending me.' Clarissa looked genuinely grateful. 'I know I didn't deserve it.'

Anna pursed her lips, the words causing her a sharp pang of guilt. She'd handled the whole situation badly. She'd been trying to help and be conciliatory, but maybe she'd jumped to Clarissa's defence a little too quickly. In Samuel's eyes, it must have looked as though she'd been siding with her over him. Going after him to the water gardens had been a mistake, too. She ought to have given him a chance to get over the shock and calm down first. Perhaps then he wouldn't have been so adamant about Scotland.

'You deserved having someone to stand up for you.' Anna smiled reassuringly. 'No one should be made to feel the way you have, especially not by their families. You need a chance to work out what to do with the rest of your life.'

'What do you mean?'

'You'll want to do something, surely?'

'But there's nothing *to* do.' Clarissa sounded

confused. 'Nobody will want to marry me now, especially when I tell the truth. They'll think that I'm barren.'

'There's more to life than marriage and babies. You're free to do whatever you want.'

'But my family won't approve of my *doing* something.'

'I'm not suggesting you take to the stage...' Anna rolled her eyes '...although that would be quite exciting. As for your family, they don't get to decide, especially after the way they've treated you. It's your life, Clarissa, *you* should decide how to live it.'

It was all very well, Anna thought, pacing up and down the hallway some time later, her telling Clarissa that she was a free agent. If only she could say the same! Instead, she'd spent the past three hours twisting her hands together, anxiously awaiting some sign of her fiancé's return. She hadn't bothered with luncheon, since Clarissa had gone to lie down and the continued worry meant that she'd lost her appetite anyway.

Finally, she couldn't bear the pacing any longer, scooping up her bonnet and cloak and marching back out of the house instead. If Samuel wasn't coming back, then she'd have to go and find him, if only to make sure that he was all right. Hopefully then she could reassure him and maybe hint a little about his grandfather, as much as she could anyway. Not the exact details, but the fact that she'd been sworn to secrecy. Maybe then he'd understand that her reticence about Scotland wasn't because she'd changed her mind.

She strode determinedly across the lawns and through the woods to the water gardens, crossing the bridge and following the path he'd taken that morning. It was still early afternoon and she found herself wishing that she'd had something to drink before leaving. The sun was high in the sky and she was getting thirstier by the minute. If memory served, however, the path led to the village less than a mile away, which fortunately proved to be correct. As she approached the houses, she saw the welcome sight of a tavern on the outskirts. There were loud voices coming from inside, but surely she could get a quiet glass of water, too?

She entered the tavern by the side door, making her way along a dark, wood-lined corridor into a taproom. The voices were coming from around the corner, where a group of men were singing at the top of their lungs. From what she could gather it was a kind of sea shanty, a not particularly polite story about a young woman called Kitty...

Her jaw dropped as they embarked on the chorus and not just because of the lyrics. A *sea* shanty? They were more than a hundred miles from the sea. Why would they be singing one of those unless… She crept around the side of the bar, her heart stalling at the sight of a familiar face. *Samuel?* To her horror, he was standing in the middle, his arms draped around two other men's shoulders, swaying from side to side and making enough noise for a dozen drunk sailors.

She stiffened, grinding her teeth at the sight. The only positive was that at least he didn't look angry any more. On the contrary, he seemed completely relaxed, a broad smile on his face as if he hadn't a care in the world. And after she'd been so worried about him, not to mention the guilt! She hadn't expected the transformation to happen so quickly, but apparently it didn't take long to change from responsible sea captain into debauched aristocrat!

She took a few steps backwards without looking and collided with someone coming the other way. There was a muffled exclamation, followed by commotion as a tray of drinks fell to the floor with a clatter.

'Anna?'

She looked up as she heard Samuel call out her name, their eyes meeting briefly before another voice bellowed from the direction of the front door and a large man, flanked by two only slightly smaller, younger men, burst into the taproom, towing an extremely nervous-looking woman behind them.

'You!' The large man lunged forward at the same moment as one of Samuel's singing companions lowered his head and charged and then all hell seemed to break loose. Fists started flailing, chairs flew through the air, wood splintered and more cups clattered onto the flagstones. Anna didn't wait to see how it would end, fleeing out onto the street and back towards Staunton.

How could he? Tears blurred her vision as she ran across the fields and through the woodland. It had been barely four hours since Samuel had inherited the title and already he was drunk and brawling. So much for not wanting to follow in his father's footsteps! So much for honourable behaviour! The scene was everything she'd been afraid of and worse. He wasn't the man she'd thought he was and she'd been tricked again! Well, he'd accused her of changing her mind about his proposal and now she had—and she had no intention of staying around to discuss it with him, either. She was going to go back to Bath and her shop as quickly as possible and forget any notion of being a countess. It had been a ridiculous daydream from the start! She would be Mrs Etton instead, the person she might have been already if she'd been using her common sense. If she'd only agreed to his proposal in the first or second or even fourth place then she would never have spent any time with Samuel, never been so foolish as to trust him, never fallen in love or felt as wretched as she did now.

Samuel rolled onto his back and clapped a hand to his forehead. What the hell had happened to him? He felt as if he were back at Trafalgar with the after-effects of the smoke and noise from hundreds of guns still assaulting his senses. His eyes stung, his head ached and his throat felt as raw as if he'd just drunk a bucketful of seawater.

Reluctantly, he opened his eyes, wincing at the onslaught of daylight, and then pushed himself up to a sitting position. According to his aching head it was entirely the wrong thing to do, but at least it gave him a better opportunity to survey his surroundings. Not that that helped since he still had no idea where he was.

He clambered off the bed—what was he doing in bed?—climbed shakily to his feet and stumbled across to sit on the windowsill. Judging by the scene of activity on the street below he was in some kind of tavern. Which made sense because he vaguely remembered having entered such a place after…

After what? For some reason just thinking about *why* he'd come there made him wince again. Something had happened. Something he'd wanted to forget. Something about… He groaned, memory returning with horrible clarity. Lady Staunton had deceived him. There was no baby, no other heir, no way to hide from the fact that he was now the Earl of Staunton and…

Anna. A bolt of panic shot through the nausea. He'd argued with Anna and then stormed away from her. Worse than that, he'd seen her here afterwards while he'd been singing a less than salubrious sea shanty. He'd seen the disappointment on her face, too. It had been a long time since he'd had it directed at him, but he'd recognised the look at once. His mother had looked at him like that repeatedly over the years, usually right before she turned away.

In this case, however, it hadn't been entirely fair. As bad as drinking and carousing in the daytime must have looked, he'd barely touched his second tankard of ale and, after offering a job to his new friend, it had seemed only fitting to celebrate the occasion through song. All of which he would have explained to Anna if Turner hadn't arrived at exactly the same moment to avenge the honour of his daughter, which had led to a scuffle and then…what then? He wasn't sure, but the dizzy feeling and bump on his head were starting to give him an idea.

'Evening, sir.' The innkeeper came into the room, accompanied by a man in a sombre black suit. 'The doctor's back to see you like he promised.'

'Did he?' Samuel looked at the man in surprise. He had no memory of seeing him before.

'I'm afraid you were somewhat delirious the last time, my lord.' The doctor made a stiff bow. 'How are you feeling now?'

'Like I've had a chair smashed over my head. Or was it a table?'

'Aye.' The innkeeper rubbed a hand around the back of his neck uncomfortably. 'It was something like that. 'Course they had no idea who you were, but they're all locked up now.'

'Who?'

'Turner and his sons and anyone else who was there for good measure. They'll be brought before the magistrate tomorrow.'

Samuel groaned. 'There's no need for that. Tell the constable to let them all go.'

'But I must protest!' The doctor looked indignant. 'They caused a severe breach of the peace. Perhaps you ought to wait until your head…'

'No. I won't bring any charges…' Samuel smiled with a sudden burst of inspiration '…but only on condition that Turner agrees to the marriage.'

'I think he will now he knows who you are, sir.' The innkeeper grinned back.

'Good. Tell him I'll pay for the wedding even. Now help me up.'

'Absolutely not.' The doctor was adamant this time. 'You shouldn't be going anywhere in your condition.'

'I have to get back to Staunton.'

'Not today. You've taken a nasty blow to the head. Tomorrow, if you're not feeling sick or dizzy, but today you need to rest.'

'Try to stop me.'

'Forgive me, my lord, but I believe that your head might do that for itself.'

Samuel swung to his feet, growled an oath, then dropped down again, annoyed to find that the doctor was right. The room tilted so violently he could almost believe he was back on board his old ship again.

'Now…' the doctor's tone was infuriatingly smug '…I suggest that you drink some water and go back to sleep. I'll escort you back to Staunton tomorrow myself.'

* * *

Fortunately for Samuel, his head appeared to have completely recovered by the time he woke the next morning. *Un*fortunately, it took nearly another full hour to escape from the tavern as the innkeeper, along with Turner, his sons and the new prospective bride and groom, wanted to thank him, apologise and say farewell at the same time. By the time the doctor arrived he was raring to go, only to find that his escort believed in taking life at a sedate, some would have said glacial, pace. The result was that it was past eleven o'clock before they finally arrived at Staunton and Samuel was able to run up the front steps and into the hall, headlong into Clarissa.

'Oh!' Her eyes widened in panic when she saw him. 'Captain Dela— I mean, my lord, I was just looking for my embroidery.' She glanced towards the stairs as if she were considering making a run for it. 'I'm sorry, I'll go back to my room.'

'You don't need to apologise.' Samuel shook his head quickly. 'Or hide in your room for that matter. But while we're at it, I'm sorry, too. I overreacted before. This is your home for as long as you want it.'

'Oh, thank you, my lord.' To his horror, she

looked as if she were about to burst into more tears. 'And I just want to say—'

'Later.' He put his hands on her shoulders. 'Where's Anna?'

'Anna?' Her eyes widened again. 'Oh, yes… I'm afraid to say… The thing is…she's gone.'

'What?' His heart slammed to a halt. 'When?'

'Yesterday afternoon when she came back from the…' her cheeks darkened slightly '…the place where you were. She left straight away.'

'Did she leave a message?'

'In a manner. That is, she said…' She winced, as if she were considering the wisdom of telling him.

'What?'

Clarissa looked apologetic. 'She said that if you tried to follow her then I should tell you that a marriage between you would never have worked and that by the time you reach Bath she'll be Mrs Etton.'

'Etton?'

'Yes, but I have to say she didn't look very happy about it.'

'What time did she leave exactly?'

'It was just before three o'clock yesterday. She took the carriage.'

'Three o'clock.' Samuel glanced at his pocket-watch and calculated. It was almost noon now, which meant that a carriage travelling in daylight would have a six- or, at best, seven-hour start. A big enough lead to reach Bath ahead of him, though surely not to arrange a marriage, as well. He still had time.

'Are you going after her?' Clarissa called out as he raced back down the front steps.

'Yes!' He stopped, considered and then turned back, removing his hat and making a bow. 'Staunton is yours in the meantime, Lady Staunton. I know you'll take good care of it.'

Chapter Twenty-Two

Home. Anna pushed open the front door of Belles, set down her bag and breathed a heavy sigh of relief. She was home. There were no customers at that moment, nor any sign of Henrietta either, allowing her to look around uninterrupted. So much had happened over the past few weeks that she'd been vaguely apprehensive that things might have changed here, too, but everything was just as she remembered. The counters were gleaming, the tins neatly stacked and, judging by the empty trays on the shelves, they were nearly sold out of biscuits, too. It all looked and smelled comforting and reassuring—exactly what she needed.

'Anna!' Henrietta must have heard the bell because she came through from the kitchen after a few moments, rushing to embrace her. 'You're here!'

'Yes.' She hugged her back, feeling a rush of affection for her assistant. After Lady Staunton's bristly companionship it felt good to be greeted so warmly.

'I didn't expect to see you for another week at least.'

'I felt homesick.' Anna smiled, looking Henrietta up and down in surprise. There was something different about her, as if she'd grown in stature. She seemed older and more competent, exuding a new air of confidence, too. Maybe a few things *had* changed after all... 'You look very well.'

'Do you think so?' Henrietta smoothed a hand over her hair in her old familiar gesture. 'My brother said the same thing.'

'Managing a shop obviously suits you.'

'I've enjoyed it. Not that I didn't miss you, of course, but I was so pleased when the Baroness came and said you were going to marry Captain Delaney. I *knew* he was smitten with you. I could tell, right from the start. Is he back in Bath, too?'

'No, he has business to attend to in Staunton.' Anna shrugged her shoulders awkwardly, hurrying to change the subject as Henrietta's face fell. 'Now tell me everything that's happened here.'

'Oh... Well, mostly we've just carried on as usual, except that Nancy—you know one of

Lady Jarrow's maids—has been taking a basket around town every morning and we've made a small fortune outside the Pump Rooms. I think people want something to take away the taste of the water. And then some afternoons we've taken a basket to Pulteney Bridge, too...'

Anna listened with half an ear to the details, half pleased, half perturbed that everything had run on so smoothly in her absence. She was starting to feel discomfited altogether. As much as it all looked and smelt like home, it no longer felt quite the same. *She* didn't feel the same, as if she'd somehow become redundant in her absence. Worse than that, she wasn't sure she belonged there any more, either.

'But that's all business.' Henrietta seemed to become self-conscious suddenly. 'Isn't your mother with you, either?'

'No. She decided to stay in Feversham for a while.'

'So she and your grandmother are reconciled?'

'Yes, it all went very well. As well as we could ever have hoped for, really.' She pressed her lips together as tears stung the backs of her eyelids.

'Anna?' Henrietta peered at her anxiously. 'Are you all right?'

'No.' She gave a loud sniff and shook her

head. 'No, I don't think I am. Oh, Henrietta, I don't know what I'm going to do…'

Anna stood in the drawing room on the Circus, waiting for the Baroness to arrive. After pouring her heart out to Henrietta the night before, she'd decided to grasp the bull by the horns and report to Samuel's grandmother before she heard what had happened and came to the shop herself. At least that way *she* could be the one to announce that her engagement was over and explain why it was for the best. She could try to defend Lady Staunton, too, although she doubted the Baroness was going to be much more forgiving than her grandson.

'Anna.' Lady Jarrow swept into the drawing room finally and pressed a kiss to her cheek. 'How good to see you again, my dear, especially now that we're practically family.'

'Oh…' She steeled her resolve at the unexpected welcome. 'Yes.'

'But something tells me my congratulations are precipitous.' The Baroness fixed her with a steely eye. 'What's the matter?'

'It's just that we're not…going to be family, I mean. I came to tell you that my engagement to Samuel is over. It was all a mistake.'

'Ah. In that case you'd better sit down. Do you drink brandy?'

Anna threw a startled glance at the clock on the mantel. It was only just after nine o'clock in the morning. 'No-o.'

'Pity. I hate to drink alone and after the night I've had, I could do with something stronger than coffee.'

Anna took a closer look at the Baroness. Her features were pale and drawn and there were grey shadows beneath her eyes. 'Is something the matter, my lady?'

'I'm afraid that my husband's condition has worsened since you left. He had another bad turn last night.'

'I'm sorry.'

'It is how it is.' Lady Jarrow sat down on the sofa beside her. 'Now tell me what happened with Samuel.'

'Well…' Anna folded her hands in her lap and proceeded to give a brief, though she hoped sympathetic, account of Clarissa's behaviour and the outcome.

'So the foolish woman was pretending to be pregnant the whole time?'

'I'm afraid so, yes.'

'And Samuel took it badly?'

'Yes.'

'What about you? Did you take the change in his circumstances badly, too? Is that why you ended the engagement?'

'No.' Anna bristled, offended. 'I gave him my word that I'd marry him and I meant it, but he wanted to elope and be married in Scotland.'

'And?'

'And I couldn't do it.' She lifted her hands as if it ought to be obvious. 'Not when I was hiding the truth about the Baron's health. I know how close he is to you both.'

'He would have understood that I'd sworn you to secrecy.'

'No.' Anna shook her head. 'He told me that he valued my honesty. It would have been hypocritical of me to marry him while I was keeping such a big secret.'

'Pshaw!'

'But that's not the only reason.' Anna lifted her chin, annoyed by the other woman's dismissive tone. 'When I said that I wanted to marry him in Bath he became quite dictatorial. Just like an aristocrat.'

'Or a naval captain, perhaps? He's accustomed to giving orders.'

'They weren't *just* orders. He threatened to throw Lady Staunton out of the house and to dismiss all of the servants who'd helped her.'

'So you broke your engagement over a few foolish words?'

'No, *he* did. *He* walked away. The last I saw of him he was drunk and brawling in the local tavern.'

'I don't believe it. Samuel never drinks to excess.'

'Well, apparently he's changed now he's the *Earl* of Staunton.'

'I see.' Lady Jarrow stood up and walked across to the window. 'By the way, I received your correspondence. I wrote back and gave you permission to tell Samuel everything. You probably passed the letter on your way here.' She sighed. 'In light of what's happened I wish I'd replied sooner.'

'It doesn't make any difference now that he's shown his true colours.'

'One night of foolishness doesn't make him his father.'

'No, but it's a start. In any case, our engagement is over and I've come home. My mother is happy staying with her family for a while, but that's her life, not mine. I should never have left Bath in the first place.'

'And you intend to have nothing more to do with my grandson?' Lady Jarrow turned to face her again. 'Is that what you're telling me?'

'I think it would be for the best.'

'I see. You didn't love him, then, when you agreed to marry him?'

'I didn't say that.'

'But you can't have, to walk away so easily. I never thought of you as defeatist before.'

'It *wasn't* easy.'

'Yet you chose the easiest option of all, running away as soon as things became difficult. I'm disappointed. I thought you were the kind of woman who could face a challenge, but you've simply reverted to all your old prejudices. Personally, I don't believe that a woman in love would ever do such a thing.'

Anna leapt to her feet, stung by the words, especially the grain of truth behind them. *Was* that what she'd done? Jumped on the first excuse she could find to flee back to Bath? She didn't want to think so, but then she hadn't given herself much time to consider. She'd left Staunton as soon as she'd got back from the tavern without giving Samuel a chance to explain himself. Without even waiting to find out if he was all right. Now that she thought about it, the fight might have been dangerous. *Was* he all right?

She tossed her head at the Baroness anyway. 'That may be your opinion, but you've no right to say so.'

'I have every right. I'm his grandmother and I shall speak as I find. It seems to me that he's had a lucky escape. After everything he's been through, Samuel deserves someone who'll love him no matter what.'

'I *do* love him!'

'Good.' Lady Jarrow's accusatory manner fell away instantly. 'I thought it was about time you said so. Now sit down again, my dear, and let's start at the beginning. You accepted my grandson's proposal when you didn't know whether or not he'd inherit, is that true?'

'Yes.' Anna subsided back down onto the sofa. 'We were preparing to come back here together when we found out about Clarissa.'

'That must have been a terrible shock.'

'Yes, but Samuel's behaviour afterwards…'

'Was irresponsible, but perhaps understandable given the circumstances. He found himself trapped in a future he didn't want and doubtless afraid that you might have changed your mind about marrying him. People can behave out of character at such times.'

'Well, yes…'

'As for his threat to throw Clarissa out of Staunton—did he go through with it?'

'No.'

'And the servants who went along with the deception?'

'No.'

'Then it seems to me his behaviour consisted of a few angry words and some foolishness in the local tavern.'

'You weren't there.'

'No, I wasn't.' Lady Jarrow's voice softened. 'And I'm not trying to condone his behaviour either, but before you come to any decision, tell me, what do you know of Samuel's childhood?'

'His childhood?' Anna drew her brows together. 'Not a great deal, except that his father left his mother for another woman and was killed in a duel.'

'That's true. He and his mother came to live with Hector and me afterwards, but I'm afraid it was a difficult situation. I don't like to criticise my daughter, but she wasn't the most attentive of mothers. She felt humiliated by the scandal, you see, and Samuel looked so much like his father that she found it hard to be around him. Consequently, she spent most of her time in London. That's where she met her second husband, Lord Hammerton. They were married a year after she was widowed and went straight to his estate in Cumberland. Samuel wasn't invited to join them.'

'He said he was sent to boarding school.'

'Yes, and spent his holidays with Hector and me, though I believe he was deeply hurt by his mother's rejection. When he was sixteen he ran away from school and went to find his father's family in London.'

'Oh?' Anna leaned forward, intrigued. 'He never told me that. What happened?'

'According to Samuel, nothing. When I asked he said no one was at home so he went to a gambling club and forgot all about it. In reality, he spoke to his grandfather.'

'But why would he lie?'

'Because of what happened next. His grandfather offered him money, a sizeable amount, to go away and never darken his doorstep again. He suggested that he go to the colonies, I believe. Naturally, Samuel refused both the suggestion and the money.'

'But that's awful!' Anna's heart wrenched at the thought. 'How did you find out?'

'Because his grandfather wrote to me, expressing his outrage at my having allowed the *boy*, as he called him, to visit him. There were other comments, which I shan't deign to repeat. Suffice to say, Samuel never attempted to contact his father's family again.'

'And you've never told him you know what really happened?'

'No, he was miserable enough. I let him keep his pride, but I believe that Samuel has been made to feel second-best and rejected for most of his life. By his father, who ran away with some silly woman, by his mother, who chose a fresh start over him, and by the whole of the rest of his family who didn't want him.'

'*You* didn't reject him.'

'No. Hector and I did our best to make him feel wanted and loved, though he was quite a handful at first. There were times when I feared he might follow in his father's footsteps after all, but he had the strength of character enough to choose the opposite path. He determined to find his own place in the world and to prove his worth without help from anyone. As much as I disliked him joining the navy, it gave him something he'd never had before: a sense of self-worth and belonging. He found a place where he wasn't judged for being his father's son. When this inheritance situation arose it must have felt as though his family were trying to take that life, the one he'd striven so hard for, away from him. But then he met you and you gave him a reason to *want* to stay on shore.'

'But our engagement happened so quickly.'

Anna had to swallow the lump in her throat. 'Maybe it was a response to all of that? Maybe he was just looking for a distraction?'

'Nonsense. My grandson may be impulsive, but he always knows what he's doing. He inherited that trait from me.'

'Yes, but…'

'However, if you really can't abide the thought of being a countess, then you're quite right to say so now. And don't worry about Samuel turning out like his father, either. He has more backbone than either of his parents, I'm relieved to say, only I hate to think of him feeling rejected again, or of you ending your engagement just because you were both too much in shock to know what you were doing.' A grey eyebrow arched upwards. 'By the way, what did your mother think of all this?'

'I…' Anna looked to one side sheepishly '…I don't know. I left a note, but I didn't see her before I left.'

'Because you were in such a rush to get away?'

'Yes. I wanted to come home.'

'Because you panicked?'

'I did *not* panic.' Anna thrust her chin out. 'I never panic.'

'Goodness me—' Lady Jarrow rolled her eyes '—you really might be the most stubborn woman

I've ever met, Miss Fortini, present company ex-
cepted, of course. Once you get an idea in your
head it seems remarkably hard to dislodge it.
Now that you've run away, I wouldn't be at all
surprised if you've talked yourself into doing
something dramatic and final solely for the
purpose of justifying your decision for years to
come.' She pursed her lips speculatively. 'Travelling to Italy, perhaps?'

'No, actually.' Anna dropped her gaze at the
thought of Thomas Etton. She *had* been planning
on visiting him first thing that morning, only
somehow she hadn't been able to go through
with it…

'Then what?'

'It doesn't matter. I didn't come here to be
insulted.'

'Then why did you come here?'

'To tell you that my and Samuel's engagement was over.'

'Or perhaps you were hoping I'd talk you
around?'

Anna opened her mouth to retort and then
sighed. 'Maybe I was. I *do* love Samuel, but
maybe love isn't enough.'

'Your mother thought that it was.'

'I'm not my mother.'

'No, you're not.' Lady Jarrow's tone was

kindly. 'To be honest, your mother was a young and foolish girl with romantic notions. She was lucky your father turned out to be the man that he was. Not everyone who follows their heart is so lucky. You have a great deal more common sense, I'm pleased to say, but you do have a similar choice to make. If you follow your heart, then it will mean turning your life upside down, leaving your shop and starting all over again. It will be difficult. A lot of people will say you can't do it. Some of them will call you names. So tell me, Anna, do you love my grandson enough to stand by him whatever the future brings? Can you be Countess of Staunton?'

Chapter Twenty-Three

Samuel dismounted beneath the familiar white-and-yellow-striped awning of Belles. It was the middle of the afternoon and he was exhausted. No doubt he was covered in dust and looking a mess, too. As a gentleman, he really ought to go and wash and change his clothes before doing anything else, but then Anna didn't particularly want him to be a gentleman and, as for everyone else…he passed a startled-looking couple on their way out of the shop…well, everyone else could go hang for all he cared.

He reached for the door, then stopped and peered in through the window. In place of the usual arrangement of tins, the display inside was a model of a house complete with roof and windows and turrets, all made entirely of biscuit. He leaned forward to make sure he wasn't imagining things and bumped his forehead against the glass. If he wasn't mistaken, it was a perfect model of Staunton.

Feeling slightly dazed, he pushed on the door and went inside.

'Good afternoon, my lord.' The assistant bobbed a curtsy when she saw him, her whole face lighting up with a look of excitement. *Excitement?* 'We've been expecting you.'

'You have?' He couldn't keep the surprise out of his voice.

'Oh, yes.' She scurried around the edge of the counter, turned over the sign on the door so that it read closed, and then drew a bolt across the top. 'If you can just wait here, I'll fetch Anna.'

'She's here?' He could have kissed her for the words.

'Yes, although she was starting to worry you weren't coming. I knew that you would, but I was still afraid you might be too late.'

'Too late for what? What did Anna—?'

He caught his breath as the woman in question appeared in the doorway that led to the kitchen. She was dressed in the periwinkle gown that she'd worn to his grandmother's party, although somehow, impossibly, she looked even more beautiful than she had that evening.

'Samuel.' Her brown eyes were warm and welcoming, the very opposite of what he'd expected.

'Anna.' He took a few steps towards her as Henrietta made a discreet exit. 'I'm sorry. The other day in the tavern…it wasn't what you think.'

'I know.' She gave a quick shake of the head. 'You were in shock and I made things worse. It's understandable that you felt in need of a drink.'

'But I wasn't drunk. I'd barely touched my ale and as for the fight…well, that was a matter of honour. The couple involved are engaged to be married now.'

'Oh.' She blinked with a look of confusion.

'I've promised them some land as a wedding present, too. I suppose I should have checked there was some available first, but I'll find something. What's the point of inheriting an earldom if you can't give away a few acres?'

'I suppose so.'

'And I would have come after you sooner, but the doctor wouldn't let me.' He removed his hat, unveiling a large, purple bruise on his temple.

'Oh!' She rushed forward, lifting her fingers to his forehead. 'Someone hit you?'

'I'm told it was a chair. In the chair's defence, it wasn't meant for me, but I got in the way.' He rubbed his face against her palm, revelling in the warm caress of her fingers. 'I sent a note to Staunton, but when I got back, Clarissa said you'd already left.'

'Yes. Your grandmother says that I panicked and ran away.'

'Did you?'

'I think perhaps I did, but it wasn't what *you* think, either. There was a reason I couldn't go with you to Scotland. It's about your grandfather.'

'You mean because of his illness?'

'Yes.' Her mouth fell open. 'You *know*?'

'I've suspected for a while. My grandmother never leaves Rutland unless she has to. I knew as soon as she said she was coming to Bath that it must be serious.'

'She says he hasn't even told her.'

'He probably knows that he doesn't have to.'

'I'm sorry.'

'So am I. He's been more of a father to me than my real father ever was.' He lifted an eyebrow. 'But why did that stop us eloping to Scotland?'

'Because I promised your grandmother that I wouldn't tell you and I couldn't marry you while I was keeping secrets, especially when you said you valued my honesty.'

'So it wasn't because you'd changed your mind?'

'No.' She shook her head, threading her arms around his neck and teasing her fingers through his hair. 'It was only when I saw you drinking that I panicked. I thought...'

Her voice trailed away and he gave a wry smile. 'You thought that I was turning into my father?'

'At the time, yes, but your grandmother made me see I was just looking for an excuse to run away. Then she asked if I was brave enough to leave my old life behind like my mother did.'

He felt as if his heart had just stopped. 'And what did you say?'

'That I'd never abandon you again.'

'Anna...' He folded her into his arms, crushing his lips against hers and kissing her with several days' worth of relief.

'But we have to hurry.' She pulled away after a few moments, looking at his bruise anxiously. 'How are you feeling now?'

'Absolutely fine now that I'm here with you.'

'Good. Then we need to get ready.'

'For what?'

'Our wedding.' She paused. 'If you still want to marry me, that is?'

'If I still...?' He caught her about the waist, pulling her back towards him again. 'Anna, I love you. Of course I still want to marry you. I've spent the whole journey here worrying that you might be Mrs Etton already.'

'I could never have gone through with that. Not when I was in love with you.' She hung her head apologetically and then smiled. 'Now your grandmother's arranged everything at short notice. I don't think anyone dared to refuse her. A common licence, a supper afterwards...'

'Please tell me she hasn't invited guests, too.'

'None except me.' Henrietta poked her head into the shop again. 'Can I give you my wedding present now?'

'Another one?' Anna laughed. 'I thought the house in the window was our wedding present?'

'Oh, that was just for fun. This is your real present...' Henrietta walked towards them holding a plate piled high with diamond-shaped biscuits. 'They're a different shape and flavour to Belles so I thought they should have a different name. Maybe Countess biscuits, if you don't object?'

'I think that's the best wedding present anyone could wish for.' Samuel reached for a sample. 'Except...what about Contessa biscuits? That's Italian for countess, isn't it?'

'Perfect.' Anna clapped her hands together. 'I think my father would have approved of that, too.'

'They're savoury.' He took a bite and nodded appreciatively. 'With salt?'

'Just a hint. I thought it was fitting.'

'They're delicious.' Samuel popped the entire rest of the biscuit into his mouth. 'Can I have another? I've been riding for hours.'

'You can have them all.' Henrietta beamed and then tipped the whole plateful into one of his greatcoat pockets. 'Here, you can eat them on the way to the ceremony.'

'Wait.' Samuel held a hand out amid a flurry of activity as both women started to pull on bonnets and shawls. 'I just have to make a quick journey to the Circus first. I left some of my belongings there.'

'First?' Anna looked anxious. 'We're running out of time.'

'There's one last thing I need to do.' He bent his head, kissing her softly on the cheek. 'It won't take long, I promise.'

As wedding days went, Samuel reflected afterwards, it had certainly been eventful. After his headlong rush from Staunton back to Bath, he'd expected to have to apologise, plead and possibly beg for Anna to forgive him, but instead here he was, less than two hours since he'd reached Belles, standing in his grandparents' drawing room, a glass of champagne in one hand, his new Countess's waist in the other.

'I'm glad you wore your uniform.' His grandmother looked him up and down approvingly.

'So am I. You look very dashing.' Anna's eyes twinkled. 'If you'd told me that that was what you were hurrying back to the Circus for, then I wouldn't have protested.'

'Now you tell me.' He grinned down at her. 'I thought I ought to say goodbye to the navy properly.'

'To the new Earl and Countess of Staunton.' His grandfather lifted his glass, his hand shaking slightly though his voice was firm. 'Anna, I'm delighted to welcome you into the family. I wish you both as much happiness in marriage as I've found.'

'Pshaw,' his grandmother snorted. 'There's no need for sentiment.'

'I wish for that, too...' Anna answered, 'and we're grateful for everything you've done.'

'You mean arranging a wedding in less than a day? Yes, I rather impressed myself.' The Baroness drew herself up to her full height. 'Now I need to retire to the countryside for some peace and quiet. We'll be leaving Bath tomorrow.'

'So soon?' Samuel looked between his grandparents anxiously.

'Yes.' The Baron nodded. 'I'm missing my books. You know I enjoy nothing more than sitting in my library while this one booms in my ear.'

'I do not *boom*!'

'You'd put Wellington's cannons to shame, my dear, but I wouldn't change you for the world.' He winked at Samuel and then fixed him with a sombre look. 'I'd like to go home, my boy, you understand?'

'I do, Grandfather, but if you need me...'

'Then I won't hesitate to summon you, but you'll be heading north again soon, too, I imagine. Your place is there now.'

'In a few days, once a few things are settled at the shop. Anna's gifting it to her apprentice.' He gave a proud tug on her waist.

'Gifting?' The Baroness looked scandalised.

'Not exactly,' Anna corrected him. 'The building will still belong to my mother, but Henrietta will be free to live there and run the business for as long as she chooses. Sebastian never had any interest in the shop and it would be a shame to close Belles just because I'm leaving. I'm positive my mother will approve and you know that Nancy has asked if she can move in and continue working there? Apparently she enjoys baking.'

'Yes, I heard you wished to steal one of my maids.' Lady Jarrow's lips twitched. 'Naturally I've agreed.'

'We'll come and wave you off in the morning, of course.' Samuel leaned in to kiss his grandmother on the cheek.

'No, my boy.' His grandfather patted him on the shoulder when they went to shake hands. 'Let's say goodbye now. I couldn't possibly be happier than I am at this moment. I was always proud of you as a boy and I'm even prouder of you as a man. Now take care of your wife, you understand? Or you'll have your grandmother to deal with.'

'Then you leave me no choice.' Samuel smiled through the lump in his throat and turned towards Anna. 'We'll take care of each other.'

Chapter Twenty-Four

They declined the offer of a carriage, wending their way back to Swainswick Crescent hand in hand, Henrietta having not very convincingly remembered that she was staying with her brother and sister-in-law that evening.

'What do you think people would say if they knew the Earl and Countess of Staunton were spending their wedding night above a biscuit shop?' Anna asked, peering shyly over her shoulder as she unlocked the front door. 'It's not very grand.'

'But it's where we met.' Samuel came to stand close behind her, placing his hands on either side of her waist. 'That seems fitting for our first night together.'

'About that…' She pushed the door open, removing one of his hands and using it to lead him inside. 'I'm not sure whether…'

'It's all right.' He lifted her fingers to his mouth, kissing the backs of her knuckles reassuringly. 'I don't have any expectations tonight. I'll be happy just to hold you in my arms if you don't feel ready for more.'

'I'm ready.' She smiled at the obvious relief in his face. 'But you've had a hit on the head and you must be exhausted after such a long day. Maybe you should—'

'I'm ready, too.' He cut her off, closing the shop door and drawing the bolt firmly behind them. 'It'll take more than a bump on the head to keep my hands off you.'

'As long as you're certain.' She hesitated. 'Only the truth is that I'm not entirely sure what I'm ready for. I would have asked my mother, but she's not here, and as much as I like your grandmother...'

'She's not the kind of person you can talk to about *that*. Thank goodness you didn't try.' He advanced towards her, smiling in a way that set butterflies fluttering in her stomach. 'Remember what we did in the plunge pool?'

'Yes.' She felt her cheeks turn pink at the memory.

'Well, it's like that, only warmer, drier and usually more horizontal.'

'Oh... I see. Would you like some tea first?'

'No.' His lips quirked. 'No tea.'

'Wine?'

'Nothing.' He reached for the tasselled ends of her shawl, slowly peeling it from around her shoulders and dropping it onto the shop counter. 'I want you, Anna. Nothing else.'

'Oh...' She swallowed at the touch of cold air on her skin. It was a relief since the room seemed to have become ten times hotter all of a sudden. His hands surrounded her waist again, his gaze dark and hungry-looking, holding her own so intently that the fluttering sensation in her stomach felt more like flapping now, as if the butterflies had somehow transformed into birds. She took a faltering breath, her thoughts spinning as he lowered his lips against hers, softly and searchingly at first, then kissing her so deeply that she felt as if all the blood in her body had rushed straight to her head. She curled her arms around his neck, though she didn't realise they were moving until her back touched the counter.

'Samuel?' She tipped her head back, breaking the kiss to catch her breath. 'Should we go upstairs?'

'Probably,' he murmured against her neck, covering her skin with hot, open-mouthed kisses. 'While I still can walk.'

'Why wouldn't you—?' She opened her eyes

wide as the lower half of his body pressed against her. 'Oh.'

'Oh,' he repeated, a smile in his voice as he slid his hands over her hips and bunched his fingers in the folds of her skirts. 'I've wanted to do this from the first moment I saw you.'

'Not the *first*,' she protested.

'The very first. I was standing just outside that window and you were scowling from behind the counter.'

'I was trying to scare you away.'

'I know. You have a very attractive scowl.'

He pressed a kiss into the hollow at the base of her throat. It felt so tender that she heard a moan escape her lips even before she'd opened them. Mercifully, the flapping in her abdomen had stopped, only it seemed to have been replaced by a throbbing sensation instead, making her legs so unsteady that she doubted she could make it up the stairs now, either. And he certainly couldn't carry her in his...*condition*. Which left only one alternative...

She braced her hands on the edge of the counter behind, pulling herself up to perch on the edge.

'Anna?' Samuel's gaze looked arrested.

'You said like the plunge pool.' She frowned. 'Or does it *have* to be horizontal?'

'No…' There was a raw edge to his voice as if he were struggling with the question himself. 'But this is your first time. It might be better if we…' He didn't finish the sentence as she leaned forward, pressing her breasts against his chest and skimming her lips along the curve of his ear with a small shushing sound. For a moment his whole body seemed to tense at the contact, but then he reached up, cupping her face in his hands and kissing her even more deeply than before. 'I want you.'

Moving by instinct, she wriggled forward until there was no space left between them, wrapping her legs around his waist while his fingers unfastened the hooks at the back of her gown, tugging it down over her shoulders. His mouth fell to her breasts, and she pushed her hands beneath his shirt, feeling the muscles of his shoulders flex as she smoothed her fingers greedily over the hard contours of his body.

'Anna.' His voice sounded guttural, making her heart clench with anticipation as he unfastened the front of his breeches and then slid a hand between her legs, touching her so intimately that she sucked in a breath of surprise. 'I don't want to hurt you.'

'You're not,' she gasped as hard flesh pressed against the entrance to her body. 'I want you, too.'

Determinedly, she clutched hold of his shoulders, moving her hips forward so that she slid on to him herself, biting her lip to hold back a cry at the new sense of intrusion. Samuel groaned, too, a low exclamation followed by a muffled oath as if she were the one hurting him.

'What's the matter?' She started to move back in alarm, but he grabbed at her waist, holding her where she was.

'Nothing's wrong.' He closed his eyes. 'You just feel too good.'

'How can it be *too* good?' She slid farther along his length, feeling a hot burst of pain followed by a tingle of pleasure.

'Wait.' He made a sound at the back of his throat, something between a laugh and a growl as he tightened his hold on her. 'You'll find out if you're not careful.'

'Maybe I want to find out.' She tried moving again, writhing her hips despite the arm clamped around her waist. Somehow the movement caused a fresh spasm of pleasure.

'Anna…' He sounded as if he were speaking through clenched teeth, pushing himself even deeper.

'Mmm…?' The spasm felt so good that she couldn't stop herself from moving again, bucking against him as she pursued the feeling. He didn't protest this time, bracing one hand on the counter as he moved with and against her, faster and deeper while the spasms seemed to build in intensity, one upon another, sending vibrations of feeling out along every nerve and through every limb. At last they all seemed to join together at once, mingling into one extended burst of feeling that wrenched a cry from her lips and left her feeling dazed and satiated. She let her head fall backwards, her body turning limp as Samuel thrust one last time and then shuddered inside her.

'Anna?' He pressed his face into her neck, gasping for breath.

'Yes?'

'Are you all right?'

'Yes.' She laughed at the question. 'I'm *very* all right.'

'Good.' He sounded relieved, letting out his own ragged laugh. 'So much for horizontal.'

'Horizontal is definitely more comfortable,' Anna sighed, tucking her head into the curve between Samuel's neck and shoulder after their second lovemaking, this time in bed. 'Although there's something to be said for shop counters, too.'

'I'll never look at one in the same way again,'

Samuel murmured, stroking a hand over her hip and drawing one of her legs up over his body.

'Me neither. It's probably a good thing I'm leaving or I'd never be able to sell biscuits again without blushing.'

'No regrets?'

'None, except…'

'What?' His hand stilled instantly.

'Part of me wishes my mother could have been at our wedding, after all. And then there's Sebastian. I wish I even knew where he was.'

'It's not unusual for ships to be out of contact with the Admiralty for this long, but I'll write and ask if there's been any word.' He raised a hand to her hair, looping his finger around a stray curl that hung over her forehead. 'He—and your mother, too—can come to Staunton and celebrate with us as soon as he gets shore leave.'

'Thank you.' She nuzzled closer. 'You know, I always hoped that if I married then it would be a love match like my parents, but I never thought I'd be so lucky.'

'Certainly not with an earl.'

'*Definitely* not with an earl, but nobody's perfect.'

'How flattering.' He tugged gently on the curl. 'Are you sure you don't mind leaving Belles? It's going to be a big change.'

'Yes, but at least I have a manager I can rely on. Henrietta's enthusiastic and she seems to genuinely love baking. I think she'll make a bigger success of the place than I ever did.'

'She ought to. You're paying her twice as much as my steward with free lodgings to boot.'

'Do you object?'

'Not a bit. I'll have to raise my steward's wages to match. I'm just glad you're not closing the doors altogether. Belles is a Bath institution, after all, and you're the original Belle.'

'The Countess who smells of the shop.' She smoothed a hand over his chest. 'Of course, that's only an insult if you don't like the smell of biscuits.'

'And who in their right mind doesn't? Personally speaking, I adore it. I'm going to need a supply of Contessas just for the journey north.'

'Are we going to share a carriage this time?'

'What do you think?' He raised his eyebrows. 'I'm a newly married man. It would be remiss of me *not* to seize the opportunity of being in a closed carriage with my wife for two days. There are all sorts of things we can do to entertain ourselves.'

'All sorts?'

'Well, one sort really, with several variations.'

'Mmm.' She smiled lazily. 'In that case, when are we leaving?'

'Just give the order. Are you ready to start a new life with me, Countess?'

'If you're ready to leave the sea behind, then yes, Captain Delaney, I believe that I am.'

'Well, then…' he murmured, pressing a kiss onto the top of her head. 'Clear the decks and anchor aweigh.'

Epilogue

Six months later

Henrietta bolted upright with a gasp, startled awake by the sound of a thud from downstairs. As she listened, there was another, and another, all in quick succession, muffled but unmistakable. She judged, by the pitch blackness outside her small window in one of the attic bedrooms above Belles, that it was still the middle of the night, which meant that whatever, or whoever, it was shouldn't be there.

She tossed her blankets aside and flung her legs over the side of the bed, palms sweating and heart pounding like a drum, which was both terrifying and inconvenient since it made it impossible for her to listen for anything else. Slowly, she crept out into the hallway, pausing at the top of the stairs as she considered whether or not to wake Nancy, the Baroness's former kitchen-maid-turned-shop-assistant. Much as she wanted some moral support, however, she decided against it. There were no sounds coming from below now, making her wonder if she'd dreamt the thuds, after all. She'd been *so* certain, but what if...?

Just to be sure, she descended the wooden staircase to the parlour, feeling her way as her eyes grew accustomed to the dark, taking care not to creak any floorboards, but that room was so still and silent and looking so much like normal that she began to relax and feel foolish. It was typical of her wayward imagination to run away with her. Thank goodness she hadn't woken Nancy or she'd have to explain herself and...

A shiver raced down her spine at the sound of another distinct thud from below. Instinctively she reached for the nearest weapons, a pair of tongs and a metal shovel poking out of the coal bucket, before carrying on downstairs. Each step seemed to go on for ever, giving her sufficient time to terrify herself about what she might find. Thieves? Cutthroats? Probably not highwaymen since she wasn't on horseback *or* in a stagecoach, though the image of a masked man still popped into her mind with startling clarity.

For the first time in months she wished she had a husband there to protect her. Once upon a time she'd thought of marriage as the answer to all of her problems, but after several upsetting episodes she'd come to realise that commitment wasn't what most men had in mind when they looked at her. Now she was older and wiser, she understood the world a bit better and a husband was the last thing she wanted.

She was married to Belles now—and if there were thieves below stairs then she'd deal with them herself!

She braced herself, tightening her fingers around her makeshift weaponry as her foot touched the bottom step. The shop itself was completely swathed in darkness, which meant that the thuds had to be coming from the kitchen. Which struck her as odd since there wasn't much there to steal except for a few sacks of flour and sugar and assorted baking utensils, but perhaps the thieves were hungry? She pressed her ear against the door to listen, stifling a yelp of alarm at the sound of footsteps inside. They seemed to be coming closer, too, as if whoever it was had heard her approach. If she didn't act quickly, then the door would open and she'd be caught.

Unless she caught them first.

Without pausing to reconsider, she grabbed

hold of the handle, gave it a quick twist and then shoved as hard as she could, knocking the wooden door against something large and heavy. There was a thwack, followed by a volley of expletives and then another thud, as if she'd just knocked someone off their feet. Seizing the advantage, she pushed again and jumped inside, swinging the shovel up over her head and thrusting the tongs out in front of her.

'Get out!' She tried to sound as threatening as possible, relieved to find that the *thieves* were in fact just one *thief,* sprawled on the flagstones behind the door.

'What the blazes…?' The man stared up at her with one hand clamped over his face. In the shadowy light of the still-glowing hearth, it made him look like the masked highwayman she'd envisaged. All she could make out were dark eyes, black hair and what looked like a red trickle streaming between his fingers.

'Oh!' She started forward and then stopped. Just because he was injured didn't mean she should help him. If anything, it served him right!

'You might give a man some warning when you're about to open the door.' He pulled his hand away, revealing a handsome, albeit bloodstained and somewhat swarthy, countenance. 'I think you just broke my nose.'

'Good! That'll teach you to break into people's property in the middle of the night! Now get out or I'll scream for the night-watchman.'

'Wait!' He reached into his jacket pocket and pulled out a white handkerchief, waving it in the air like a flag of surrender before using it to wipe the blood off his face. 'I didn't break in. I have a key and I was trying *not* to make noise, if you must know, only things seem to have moved around since I was last here. Where's Anna?'

'You know Anna?' Henrietta blinked in surprise, lowering the coal shovel a few inches.

'All my life.' He looked her up and down speculatively. 'By the way, would you mind putting those tongs down? I'm afraid to ask what you intended to do with them, but they're making me want to cross my legs.'

'Oh.' A hot flush rushed through her body at the implication. The look of bemused interest on his face made her feel hotter still, as well as acutely conscious of the fact that her only clothing consisted of a plain cotton nightgown that stopped halfway down her calves. Thank goodness for the dark. 'No! Not until you tell me how you know Anna.'

'Well…' He jumped to his feet so abruptly that she took an instinctive step backwards. 'I believe that we first met in the cradle. She used to sing me lullabies, as I recall. Allow me to introduce myself. Sebastian Fortini, at your service.'

'Anna's little brother?' Now that he mentioned it, she could see the resemblance. His dark hair was wavy and dishevelled rather than curly, but he had the same square-shaped jaw and soulful, deep-set brown eyes. Judging by the crinkles around them, she had the impression that he laughed a lot. They held a mirthful glint now that made her want to smile, too.

'The one and only.' He winked good-naturedly and made an elaborate bow, flourishing the now bloodstained handkerchief out in front of him. 'As for you, I assume that you're a figment of my imagination caused by the blow to my head.'

'Oh, dear.' She put the tongs and shovel down by the fireplace. 'Sorry about that. I really thought you were a burglar.'

'Perfectly understandable.'

'My name's Henrietta Gardiner.'

'Delighted to meet you, even under the circumstances.' His sudden grin was dazzling. 'So, Miss Gardiner, has my sister employed you to guard the shop against night-time marauders?'

'Not exactly. I'm the new manager.'

'Manager?' His gaze sharpened. 'Why is Anna employing a manager?'

'Because she's…' She hesitated, looking at

him askance. 'Wait, didn't you get any of her letters?'

'No. My ship's been stuck out in the Pacific for the past year. I haven't heard anything from home in the whole time. What's happened? Is she all right? Has something happened to our mother?'

'Oh, no, everything's all right.' Henrietta hastened to reassure him. 'They're both perfectly well, only...' She sucked on her bottom lip, wondering where to begin. 'I think I'd better put the kettle on. Are you hungry? There are some leftover biscuits somewhere.'

'You mean Belles?' He sat down at the table with a nostalgic expression. 'I can't remember the last time I had one of those. I hope Anna hasn't been messing around with the recipe.'

'You might be surprised by what Anna has done.' Henrietta stifled a smile. 'Welcome home, Mr Fortini, we have a lot to talk about.'

* * * * *

MILLS & BOON

Coming next month

STOLEN BY THE VIKING
Michelle Willingham

'I am Breanne Ó Callahan,' she answered. 'My foster father is King Feann MacPherson of Killcobar.'

'I know who he is.' He turned at that moment, and his gaze fixed upon her. 'I recognised you the moment I saw you. And you are worth more than a slave.'

'How could you possibly know me?' she demanded. 'I would have remembered you.' Heat flared in her cheeks when she realised what she'd said. But it was too late to take back the words. Breanne tightened her grip upon the drying cloth, and in that heated moment, she grew aware of his interest. He studied her face, his gaze drifting downward to linger upon her body. There was no denying that he wanted her.

But worse was her own response. She was caught up in his blue eyes and the dark hair that framed a strong, lean face. There was a slight scar on his chin, but it did nothing to diminish his looks. The *Lochlannach* warrior was tall and imposing, his physical strength evident. Only the slight limp revealed any weakness.

'What do you want from me? A ransom?'

He reached out and cupped the back of her neck. It was an act of possession, but instead of feeling furious, his sudden dominance made her flesh warm to the touch. His blue eyes stared into hers as if he desired her, and she was startled by the unbidden response. Though she tried to meet his gaze with resentment, her imagination conjured up the vision of his mouth descending upon hers in a kiss. This warrior would not be gentle…no, he would claim what he wanted from her. Heat roared through her, and she thought of his hands moving down to pull her hips against his.

That might be what he wanted from her, after all. She was well aware of how female slaves were used as concubines. The thought shamed her, but another part of her was intrigued by this man. She could not deny the forbidden attraction, and she had the strange sensation that his touch would not be unwelcome.

As if to make his point, Alarr stroked the nape of her neck before releasing her. 'You will remain with me at all times, obeying everything I ask. If you do this, then I will remove your bindings.'

'When?' she demanded.

'When you have earned my trust. Not before.'

Continue reading
STOLEN BY THE VIKING
Michelle Willingham

Available next month
www.millsandboon.co.uk